The major went inside, and there was
Susanna Hopkins at the ticket window.
He had no doubt it was her: medium
height, blonde hair. He couldn't discern
her figure because of her overcoat, but
she looked surprisingly tidy, considering
her days on the train from Pennsylvania.

Interested, he watched her. The station master pointed to
the fare chart. Joe watched as she took another look into
her wallet. The station master shrugged his shoulders, then
gestured for her to move aside. She sat on the bench by the
potbellied stove.

He saw her face when she turned around and it was a sweet
face, heart-shaped. Her blonde hair had a dark blaze by her
temple. Gold-rimmed spectacles were perched on her nose,
but they could not hide the bleakness in her eyes. He knew
he was looking at a fearful woman.

Joseph Randolph's heart went out to the woman who sat,
terrified, on a bench in the dirty stage depot. *She may be
divorced, but what drives a woman to this?* he wondered,
even as he loosened the muffler about his neck, removed
his hat and started to unbutton his greatcoat. Whatever her
marital woes, Mrs. Susanna Hopkins looked as though she
needed good news.

* * *

Her Hesitant Heart
Harlequin® Historical #1135—May 2013

Her Hesitant HEART

CARLA KELLY

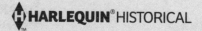

HARLEQUIN® HISTORICAL

Recycling programs
for this product may
not exist in your area.

ISBN-13: 978-0-373-29735-1

HER HESITANT HEART

Copyright © 2013 by Carla Kelly

Printed in U.S.A.

www.Harlequin.com

To Captain Andrew and Elizabeth Burt, Ninth Infantry.

CARLA KELLY

has been writing award-winning novels for years—stories set in the British Isles, Spain and army garrisons during the Indian Wars. Her specialty in the Regency genre is writing about ordinary people, not just lords and ladies. Carla has worked as a university professor, a ranger in the National Park Service, and recently as a staff writer and columnist for a small daily newspaper in Valley City, North Dakota. Her husband is director of theater at Valley City State University. She has five interesting children, a fondness for cowboy songs and too many box elder beetles in the fall.

Prologue

December 31, 1875

Dearest Tommy,

I am somewhere in Nebraska. I am told by other travelers on the Overland Express that when the sun comes up we will see Chimney Rock, that prominent landmark to settlers and gold seekers years ago.

Be diligent in your studies. It is my fondest wish that you will do well in your schooling and be a blessing to all who know you.

I think of you constantly and would give the earth to see you. I wish you well with all my heart.

Love,

Mama

On a separate sheet she wrote,

Frederick,

If you have commandeered this letter like all the others, rest assured that I will continue to write to Thomas, even when I arrive at Fort Laramie. Should some spark of sympathy enter your heart, send his letters to me, care of Captain Daniel Reese, Company D, Second Cavalry, Fort Laramie, Wyoming Territory.

Please, Frederick!

Susanna

Susanna Hopkins sealed the letter, and tried to make herself comfortable. Her back ached from sitting upright since she had boarded the Pennsylvania Central some days ago. Her coach ticket had been a gift from her uncle. He had not mentioned a Pullman berth and she had been too shy to ask.

Susanna knew her relatives were relieved to send her to a place so distant that it wasn't even a state yet. She knew her aunt was overjoyed to have her gone from the house in Shippensburg, where she had fled from Carlisle for refuge more than a year ago. Now her aunt could invite her friends into her home again, without the presence of an embarrassing niece.

Susanna waited for the steward to turn out the lamps. Apparently the Union Pacific felt that if its less well-heeled clients could not afford a sleeper car, they should sit in the dark, contemplating the sin of poverty.

The trip had been pleasant enough, except for her hunger. Quick stops at cook shacks along the route were designed for aggressive men who snatched pie and coffee before the train whistle blew. The last stop had found her with only a piece of corn bread. Just as well. She had no idea how much the Cheyenne-Deadwood stage would cost, once she reached Cheyenne, and she needed to save her money.

Susanna regarded her reflection in the glass. Her eyes were only the barest outline, but she removed her spectacles and fingered the bone under her left eye, seeking out the ridge where the occipital bone had almost reconnected, leaving her with a little droop.

"You're lucky to have an eye, Mrs. Hopkins," her physician had told her, prescribing a mild correction to the lens.

With the lights out, she would be able to rest her eyes. It was treatment the doctor would have ordered, and apparently the Union Pacific agreed.

Susanna turned her attention to the full moon. As her eyes accustomed themselves to the dark, she saw large, dark shapes in the near distance. She touched her cheek. *I could have dodged his hand,* she told herself for the hundredth time. It was the sight of Tommy, rushing to grab his father's upraised hand, that had surprised her. *Tommy, you should have stayed in bed!* The blow had driven her face against the mantelpiece.

She closed her eyes against the memory of her son's efforts to help her, and then his cries of protest as his father carried him upstairs. It had been her last glimpse of her son. Some instinct had warned her that to remain this time would be to die.

"Pardon me, ma'am."

"Y-yes?"

"If you have two cents, I'll take that letter to the mail car," the porter whispered.

She handed two pennies and her letter to the porter. He came back later with a blanket and pillow.

"I cannot afford those."

"No one's using them" was all he said.

She nodded, still surprised at unexpected kindness.

"Ma'am…"

"Yes?"

"Happy New Year."

Chapter One

Emily Reese, not the brightest lady, had been unable to furnish Major Joseph Randolph, Fort Laramie's post surgeon, with a working description of Susanna Hopkins, her older cousin. "I think she is thirty-two," Emily had said. "Old, anyway."

Joe smiled at that. "I doubt traveling females will be thrilled if I ask if they are thirty-two," he had told her. "Give me a better description, Emily. She's *your* cousin."

He knew her well enough to call her Emily. Almost five years ago he had delivered her son, Stanley, in an army ambulance between garrisons. Emily Reese had been neither his best patient nor his worst one.

Emily obliged with a better description. "She is of medium height, average figure, and her hair is blond."

She became serious quickly. "I appreciate this, Major," she told him. "If you can take her in the ambulance, so much the better. She does not have much money." She thought a moment, then whispered, "Susanna is divorced."

"That is *not* my business," Joe said.

"You're a surgeon," she countered. "Anything I tell you is confidential."

He sighed, wondering how Emily Reese's husband managed to keep from drinking himself to death. Some men must prefer stupid wives. Come to think of it, Captain Daniel Reese wasn't the brightest company commander in the army. "Emily, I'm not a priest. I keep *medical* matters confidential."

She couldn't seem to stop. "She abandoned her son. I can't imagine that, but she is a relative, and my parents had to help her."

"I'm certain she had her reasons," Joe replied. *Good God, what kind of relative would blab such a scandal?* he asked himself. *They sound as horrible as mine.* "I hope you won't reveal this to anyone else," he said, not sure how much force to apply to a scold. "You know what gossips army people are."

"Should I make up a story?"

"Say nothing. All anyone wants is a teacher."

"I know! I will say she is a war widow!"

Joe sighed. "Emily, don't. Can't you imagine how distressed the veterans would feel about such a lie? We saw our friends die from Bull Run to Appomattox Court House! Please, please don't."

Joe hadn't minded the diversion of looking for a lady on the train. General court-martial duty in Cheyenne right before Christmas was never pleasant, unless those presiding thought to catch the eastbound Overland Express for home. He probably wouldn't have been involved in this unshirkable army duty, except that one of the defendants was a major, and there must be majors and above weighing him in the balance.

Joe had no plans. His former home was a plantation west of Richmond and his two widowed sisters residing there had long ago turned his portrait to the wall, and returned his letters, except the one containing a bank draft for taxes on the place. *No wonder I am a cynic,* Joe told himself on more than one occasion.

Unexpectedly, the court-martial had dragged on much longer than anticipated, and the officer board watched its holiday plans turn to gall and wormwood. The defendants—officers who should have been cashiered years ago—had argued long and eloquently to avoid removal from the army.

The matter had ground on, each officer on the board growing surly as the likelihood of Christmas at home vanished. To no one's surprise, revenge came as both defendants were cashiered.

Major Walters, a single fellow like himself, was in no hurry to return to dreary Fort Fetterman. The officers' mess at Fort Russell, near Cheyenne, was better and Joe had time to meet the westbound train in Cheyenne that afternoon.

But there was no Susanna Hopkins. He rode the three miles back to Russell, arriving in time to watch Walters dress in his better uniform for the evening's New Year's festivities.

Immune to parties, Joe walked to the post hospital. It wasn't his hospital, but he knew the surgeon well. Sitting close to the heating stove, they toasted the season and swapped gory stories from the late war until the hospital steward came on duty in the morning.

As a consequence, Joe was late to the depot; the train had already departed. Joe directed the ambulance driver to the Cheyenne-Deadwood Stage depot, a noisome place with sawdust on the floor to absorb tobacco juice and spittle.

The major went inside, and there was Susanna Hopkins at the ticket window. He had no doubt it was her: medium height, blond hair. He couldn't discern her figure because of her overcoat, but she looked surprisingly tidy, considering her days on the train from Pennsylvania.

Interested, he watched her. The stationmaster pointed to the fare chart. Joe watched as she took another look into her wallet. The stationmaster shrugged his shoulders, then gestured for her to move aside. She sat on the bench by the potbellied stove.

Joe saw her face when she turned around, and it was a sweet face, heart-shaped. Her blond hair had a dark blaze by her temple. Gold-rimmed spectacles perched on her nose, but they could not hide the bleakness in her eyes. He knew he was looking at a fearful woman.

Joseph Randolph's heart went out to the woman who sat, terrified, on a bench in the dirty stage depot. *She may be divorced, but what drives a woman to this?* he wondered, even as he loosened the muffler about his neck, removed his hat and started to unbutton his greatcoat. Whatever her marital woes, Mrs. Susanna Hopkins looked like she needed good news.

Susanna felt tears behind her eyelids. She raised her spectacles and pressed her fingers hard against the bridge of her nose to stop the tears. Crying in front of strangers would only lower her further into that class of pitiful women without purpose or goal. *I am not there yet,* she reminded herself.

She had passed a Western Union office on her short walk from the depot to the stage station. Perhaps she could wire Emily at Fort Laramie and explain her plight. Maybe she could leave her luggage at Western Union. Surely some establishment needed a temporary dishwasher, or even a cook.

If not that, perhaps she could find a church, and pour out her troubles to a minister. Her optimism faded. If she had to tell her whole story to a minister before he would help her, she would fail. Her own minister in Carlisle had counseled her to return to the man who had abused her. When she refused, he had shown her the door without another word.

"Mrs. Susanna Hopkins?"

Startled, she looked up at a tall man in uniform. His greatcoat was unbuttoned, and she saw gold braid and green trim on his collar. She glanced at his face and then looked away,

shy, even though her brief glance took in a kind face. "Do…
do I know you?" she stammered.

"No, ma'am, you don't, but I have been sent by Mrs. Emily
Reese. She said you were medium height and blonde, and
I've been looking."

She took a deep breath. "You're from Fort Laramie?"

"Yes, ma'am." He gestured to the bench. "May I sit?"

"Of course, uh, Captain…" She paused, not sure of his
rank.

"Major, ma'am, Major Joseph Randolph, with the Army
Medical Corps."

They shook hands. Before she could stop herself, Susanna
blurted out, "I'm three dollars short of the fare for the Cheyenne-Deadwood Stage."

"It happens," he told her, unperturbed.

He was a big, comfortable-looking man, his hair dark but
graying. Fine lines had etched themselves around his eyes and
mouth, probably from the sun and wind. Susanna thought his
eyes were brown, but she gave him only a glance.

"When Emily heard I was to be in Fort Russell, she thought
I could spare you a trip on the Shy-Dead."

"How kind of you!" She stopped, embarrassed.

She could tell her exclamation startled him. "It's easy,
Mrs. Hopkins, if you don't mind keeping company with men
in an ambulance."

"An ambulance?" she asked doubtfully. "Someone is ill?"

"We travel that way in the winter, when we can."

He had a distinct Southern drawl, stringing out his words
in a leisurely way, and saying "ah" instead of "I," and "own"
instead of "on." She hadn't thought to hear a Southern accent
from a man in a blue uniform.

"I was planning to meet the train, but New Year's inter-
fered," he said.

She had to smile at that artless declaration. "Too much good cheer?"

He smiled back. "Medicinal spirits! Fort Russell's post surgeon and I refought Chattanooga and Franklin, and before I know it, I was late. We're leaving tomorrow morning, ma'am. There's room for you."

"I'm obliged," she said. "I'll be ready." She stood up, as though to dismiss him, unsure of herself.

He stood, too. "I can't just leave you here until tomorrow morning," he told her. "I'll take you to a hotel."

She shook her head. "I'll be fine." She looked around at men sitting on benches, a cowboy collapsed and drunk in the corner, and an old fellow muttering to himself by the water bucket.

"A modest hotel," he insisted.

She could tell he wasn't going to leave her there. "Quite modest, Major Randolph," she replied.

"Cheyenne has only modest hotels," he informed her. "There is a pathetic restaurant close by, and we'll stop there, too."

"That isn't necess—"

"I'm hungry, Mrs. Hopkins," he said. "So is my driver. Be my guest?" He peered at her kindly. "Don't argue."

"Very well," she said quietly.

"Excellent," he said, as he buttoned his greatcoat and put on his hat. "You'll find it a relief from those cook shacks along the UP route."

"I never got close enough to the counter," she said, then stopped, embarrassed.

"In two *days?*" the major exclaimed. "Mrs. Hopkins, you are probably hungry enough to chew off my left leg."

She had the good sense to capitulate. "I *am* famished, but not quite that hungry!"

He picked up both of her bags. "This all your luggage?" he asked.

"I left a portmanteau at the depot."

"Then we'll get it."

He helped her into the boxy-looking wagon with the straight canvas sides. The vehicle was unlike any other she had ever ridden in, with leather seats along each side, and a small heating stove. "This is for wounded people?" she asked, after he got in and seated himself opposite her.

He nodded. "You can take out the seats and stack four litters in here. Wives and children in the garrison generally travel this way."

The major fell silent then and she was content not to make conversation with someone she barely knew. At the depot, the private retrieved her portmanteau and stowed it beside her other luggage in the rear of the ambulance. She was soon seated in the café with the major, the private having found a table in the adjoining bar.

She ordered soup and crackers. The major overruled her and chose a complete dinner for her. "You're my guest," he reminded her, "and my guests eat more than that, Mrs. Hopkins."

She was too hungry to argue. "Thank you."

"You're welcome. How would it look if you starved while in my company? The Medical Corps would rip off my oak leaf clusters and kick me down to hospital steward."

He left her at the Range Hotel, but not without making sure the clerk put her in a room between two families. "This town's just a rung up from Dante's inferno. Never hurts to be careful," he told her.

She gave him the same startled look that had puzzled him in the stage station, but he understood now—Susanna Hopkins was unused to kindness.

He would gladly have paid for her room, and she must have known that. Before he could say anything to the desk clerk, she took out the money she must have reserved for the stage, and laid it on the counter. She hesitated for a moment.

She kept her voice low. "Major, do I pay something for my transportation?"

"No, ma'am, that's courtesy of the U.S. Army."

"How kind," she said, and returned to the desk clerk. Joe was struck again at her wonder, as though good fortune had not been her friend, or even a nodding acquaintance recently.

He reflected on that all the way back to Fort Russell. He had learned from childhood that women were to be protected and cherished. Hard service in the war had showed him the other side of that coin, when he saw too many thin, tight-lipped women, unfamiliar with kindness. Susanna Hopkins had that same wary look, and he wondered why.

Chapter Two

Susanna waited in the lobby the following morning. Breakfast had been amazingly cheap: a bowl of porridge and coffee for a dime.

The major arrived before the sun rose, wide-awake this time. "You're a prompt one, Mrs. Hopkins," he told her.

A glance from the major sent the desk clerk hurrying to carry her luggage to the ambulance. Susanna let the major help her into the vehicle, which was already warm. Bundled in overcoats, two other officers nodded to her.

There was space next to one of the men, but someone had left a book there. The only other seat was a rocking chair—close to the little stove—that had been anchored to the wagon floor and covered with a blanket.

"That's for you," the major said.

"But…"

"For you," he repeated. "Let us come to a right understanding. We take good care of the ladies in the army."

The other men nodded. "They're scarce," said one about Major Randolph's age.

Susanna seated herself on the rocking chair, grateful for the warmth.

"Let me introduce you, Mrs. Hopkins," Major Randolph

said. "Major Walters, who understands the scarcity of ladies, is from Fort Fetterman."

The officer tipped his hat to her. The surgeon indicated the other man. "Captain Dunklin is from Fort Laramie. This is Mrs. Hopkins, gentlemen."

"For God's sake, close the door," Captain Dunklin demanded.

Major Randolph closed the door behind him and latched it. He picked up his book and took his seat, and she heard the driver chirrup to the mules.

Susanna pulled the blanket close around her. She glanced at Major Randolph, who was staring at her with a frown. She looked at him, then realized he was staring at the blanket. She stared at it, too, wondering.

"Mrs. Hopkins?"

She looked at Major Walters. "Your blanket is too close to that stove," he whispered.

She looked. The blanket was not close to the stove, but she pulled it to her anyway. "Better?"

"Perfect."

She glanced again at Major Randolph, who sat back with a relieved expression on his face. *I don't understand what just happened,* she thought. *I should say something.* "Captain, uh...excuse me...."

"Dunklin," he offered, as if relieved to break the charged silence.

"Captain Dunklin, you have children who will be attending school?" She glanced at Major Randolph, who stared straight ahead, as if seeing something no one else saw. In another moment, he settled back with a sigh.

"I have one son, aged nine. High time he went to school."

She couldn't hide her surprise. "My cousin wrote that there is a school already."

"Yes, one run by the private."

Susanna heard the disdain in his voice.

"The army requires that children of enlisted men must be educated, but officers' children are merely invited," Major Randolph explained.

"Not required?"

"No, ma'am," he said. "Strange to you?"

"A little. Surely an officer's child could learn *something* from a private."

"We try not to mingle," Dunklin said. "Joe, you'd understand if you had children."

Susanna could tell from the post surgeon's expression that he understood no such thing. *I should think any school would be better than no school,* she thought. Captain Dunklin was already reminding her of Frederick, because he seemed so *certain* that he was right. "Probably the private does his best," she said, defending her profession.

"He does," the surgeon said. "Private Benedict has eleven pupils now, all ages." He must have noticed her expression of interest. "I head the post administrative council, and one of my responsibilities is the school."

"Is there a schoolhouse?"

"No. They meet in a room in the commissary storehouse."

"Between the salt pork and the hardtack," Dunklin interjected. He laughed, but no one joined him.

From the look the post surgeon exchanged with Major Walters, Susanna suspected Dunklin was not a universal favorite.

The silence felt heavy again, but Dunklin filled it. "Where are you from, Mrs. Hopkins? Your cousin mentioned Pennsylvania."

"Shippensburg, originally," she said, afraid again. Major Randolph glanced at her. It was the smallest glance, but some sixth sense, honed to sharpness by years of fear, told her he knew more.

"My wife is from Carlisle!" Dunklin exclaimed. "She won't waste a moment in making your acquaintance."

Please, no, Susanna thought in a panic. "I…I didn't get out much in society," she stammered.

Dunklin nodded, his expression serious. "Your cousin told us of your loss. Too many ladies are war widows."

Her heart plummeted into her stomach. She wondered what story her cousin had started, in an attempt to make her more palatable to the people of Fort Laramie. Suddenly the twenty miles between Shippensburg and Carlisle seemed no longer than a block.

"Mrs. Hopkins?" Major Walters asked, concerned.

"I shouldn't have brought it up," Dunklin said.

"No, it's just…" She stopped. *Do I explain myself to these men?* she thought in desperation. *Do I say nothing?* She sat there in misery, trapped. "Don't worry, Captain Dunklin," she said, becoming an unwilling party to a lie. "I am resigned to my lot."

Dunklin nodded. He placed a board on his knees, took out a deck of cards and was soon deep in solitaire.

Major Randolph regarded her, and she realized with a shock that he knew she lied. What had Emily done? *I must explain to him at the first opportunity,* Susanna told herself. Drat Captain Dunklin for having a wife from Carlisle.

They stopped midmorning, which felt like an answer to prayer. For the past hour she had been wondering how she could delicately phrase the suggestion that they stop for personal purposes. And if they did stop, what then? A glance through the canvas flap revealed no shielding trees or even shrubs.

Without a word, the men left the ambulance. A shift of weight told her that the driver had followed them. Major Randolph was the last man out. Without a word, he lifted the seat where Captain Dunklin had been sitting, nodded to her and left. Speechless with embarrassment, she stood up and looked down at a hole and the snowy ground beneath. "That's clever," she murmured.

She peeked out the canvas flap to make sure no one stood nearby. There they were, standing off the road, their backs to her. By the time they returned to the ambulance, the seat was down again, and she had returned to her chair.

"We're stopping tonight at Lodgepole Creek stage station," Major Randolph informed her as they started again. "I have a little errand of mercy, a small patient."

They stopped at a roadhouse for luncheon, which turned out to be a bowl of greasy stew and a roll amazing in its magnitude and excellence.

"This joint is famous for the rolls, but you don't get one unless you suffer the penance of the stew," Major Randolph joked.

Susanna ate quickly and excused herself, wishing for solitude, even if solitude meant cold. She was scarcely out the door when she heard someone behind her. She turned around, dreading to see the post surgeon, but it was Major Walters.

"It's too warm in there," she said.

The major extended his arm, so she had no choice but to tuck her arm in his. "Let's walk."

She let him lead her away from the roadhouse toward a line of trees, stopping by a frozen stream.

"Does it ever warm up?" she asked.

"With a vengeance," he assured her. "One day it's like this, then everything starts to drip and thaw."

They stared down at the stream, where Susanna thought she could see the shadows of fish. She pointed to them. Major Walters nodded. "Everything's just waiting for better days."

So am I, she thought.

Major Walters seemed in no hurry to turn back. Hesitant,

she said, "Major, I have to ask…. Why did Major Randolph seem so intent on that blanket and the stove? It wasn't close."

"No, but that doesn't matter to Joe," the major said, starting back now. "As you might have noticed from his accent, Joe is from Virginia."

She nodded.

"He was part of the Medical Corps before the war, and stayed in when others went to the Confederacy. Good surgeon, from all accounts." Walters sighed. "A pity he couldn't save the one person he loved."

The major stopped, even though the other officers had left the roadhouse and were looking in their direction.

"He met Melissa Rhoades in Washington—her father was a congressman from Ohio—and they married after the war. He continued in federal service." They started walking again. "On the regiment's march to Fort McKavett in Texas, Melissa's skirt brushed too close to a cooking fire."

"God," Susanna whispered.

Major Walters lowered his voice. "She suffered agonies for nearly a day, and there wasn't a thing he could do to help her." The major gave her a wry smile. "That's why he gets concerned when any woman is close to a fire."

Susanna nodded. "He hasn't remarried?"

"No. Perhaps ten years hasn't been enough to erase that sight from his mind." Walters shook his head. "I shouldn't dredge up sad memories of the war for you, Mrs. Hopkins. My apologies."

Aghast that her cousin's lie was sinking her deeper into falsehood, Susanna held her breath, then let it out slowly. To her shame and confusion, her kind escort took her silence as agreement.

Major Randolph stood by the ambulance, looking at her with a frown. *He knows I am a liar,* she thought miserably.

She looked at the roadhouse, and back down the snowy track that led to Cheyenne. There was nowhere to run.

Joe stared at his book for much of the afternoon as the ambulance trundled forward, reading and then rereading each page until it made no sense. What he really wanted to do was reassure Mrs. Hopkins.

He hadn't mistaken the fright in her pretty eyes. She seemed to sense that he knew more than the others. He had to assure her that her secret was safe with him.

He watched the clouds over the bluffs, threatening snow but going nowhere, much like his own life. He dutifully returned to his book, but his mind was on Susanna Hopkins.

She was pretty—maybe some seven or eight years younger than he was. What intrigued him the most were her eyes, large and brown behind her spectacles. He wanted to look closer out of professional interest, because one eye appeared slightly sunken, as though the occipital bone was damaged.

He knew he needed to put her mind at ease. His opportunity came when they stopped at Lodgepole Creek stage station. He reached for his medical saddlebag as the other men left the ambulance.

"Mrs. Hopkins, come along with me. I delivered a premature baby four weeks ago, on our way to Cheyenne."

Before he allowed her time to consider the matter, he closed the door after the others, and the private in the wagon box clucked to the horses. She sat there in silence. It made him sad to think how hard she worked to keep her composure.

"We're only going a short way. Jonathan is the mixed-blood son of the man who runs the stage station, and Betty is Cheyenne."

A month ago, he had been yanked away from supper at the stage station when the owner recognized him as a surgeon. A few hurried words, a grab for his medical bags and they were

on horseback to the cabin. He owed the successful outcome
more to Betty's persistence than any skill of his.

When the ambulance stopped, Joe helped Mrs. Hopkins
out. The door to the cabin was already open, with the young
father motioning to him, all smiles. Inside, Joe sighed with
relief to see the baby in a padded apple crate, warm as it rested
by the open oven door. Mrs. Hopkins went to the woodstove
to watch the infant. She held out one finger and the baby
latched on to it.

"Since he was so small, I told them to keep him warm,"
Joe said. "He appears to be thriving. What did you name
him, Betty?"

Her husband put his hand on Betty's shoulder. "We were
waiting for you to come back. What's *your* name?"

"Joseph," he said, touched.

"Joseph, then," Jonathan said. "What about a middle name?
Does this kind lady have a favorite name?"

"Thomas," Mrs. Hopkins said.

The Cheyenne woman nodded and handed the baby to
Mrs. Hopkins, who took him in her arms. Joe watched in
appreciation as she put the baby to her shoulder with practiced ease. She moved until the infant's head was cradled in
that comfortable space in the hollow of her shoulder that all
mothers seemed to know about.

Mrs. Hopkins rubbed her cheek against the baby's dark
hair, then handed him over when Joe nodded. He ran practiced hands over the small body, then held him up to listen
to the steady rhythm of his heart.

Joe's prescription was simple. "Keep Joey warm by the
oven for a little longer, maybe until it warms up or until
he gains another pound or two." He nodded to the parents.
"You're doing fine."

The father put his son back in the apple crate. Joe ushered

Mrs. Hopkins out the door. He looked at the ambulance and then at the stage station in the near distance.

"Private, go ahead. We'll walk."

He didn't dare look at Mrs. Hopkins, but he could feel her tension. There was that feeling she was weighing her options and finding none.

"It's not far."

He started walking, hoping she would come along, but knowing she had no choice. After walking a few feet, he heard her footsteps and he let out the breath he had been holding, and wondered why it mattered to him.

He eased casually into what he had to say. "Mrs. Hopkins, who is Thomas?"

He heard the tears in her voice.

"My son."

Chapter Three

Somehow, Susanna hadn't expected that question. Better to forge ahead, even if her teaching career at Fort Laramie ended in the next five minutes.

"Major Randolph, I think my cousin told you that I am divorced. I have a son, name of Tommy, who is in the custody of my former husband. There was nothing I could do. And when Captain Dunklin assumed that…"

"Wait." The major took her arm, and she needed all her resolve not to draw back from him in fright. "Just sit down on this stump a minute."

He increased the pressure on her arm, then he stopped suddenly and released her. Susanna remained upright, unsure.

"I'm not going to force you to sit if you don't want to," Major Randolph said.

She heard the apology in his voice, which also baffled her. No one in recent memory had apologized to her. She wasn't even sure she liked it.

"I couldn't help noticing that look you gave me when I agreed with Captain Dunklin that I was a widow," she said. "It was a lie and you know it. Please believe me. I did not start that lie."

"I know you didn't. *I* heard the beginning of that pernicious fable, and I thought it was a foolish idea. The fault lies with your cousin."

Susanna sat down. "Why would Emily do that? All I ever said in my letter to Colonel Bradley is that I was Mrs. Susanna Hopkins, and available to teach."

The cold from the stump defeated her and she stood up. She looked toward the roadhouse, wanting the warmth, but not wanting more questions from Captain Dunklin.

"If we walk slowly, we won't freeze," the major joked. "Why would she do that?" he repeated. "Let me tell you something about army society. It is close-knit, snobbish and feeds on gossip. There is an unhealthy tendency to hold grudges."

"That sounds as bad as Unity Methodist Church back home," Susanna murmured.

The major threw back his head and laughed. "It's this way—the army unit is a regiment, which travels together when it can, but generally finds itself spread over a large geographic area. Many a promising career has withered and died on a two-company post. I could include my own career, I suppose, but I like what I do."

She didn't know how it happened, but the major had tucked her arm through his as they strolled along.

"I was a state regimental surgeon during the late war, on loan from the regulars," he said. "The Medical Department has placed me in the Department of the Platte. There are three companies of the Second Cavalry at Fort Laramie, plus more companies of the Ninth Infantry."

"You are everyone's surgeon?"

"I am. The number of surgeons varies. One surgeon, the estimable Captain Hartsuff, is on detached duty at Fort Fetterman, and the contract surgeon—he's a civilian—is hoping for furlough as soon as I return to Fort Laramie. He'll be lucky to get it. Contract surgeons have less seniority than earthworms."

Susanna smiled at that.

"I tend to anyone's needs—from the garrison, to teamsters, to sporting ladies at the nearest cathouse, to any Indian brave enough to try white man's medicine."

He peered at her, and she saw nothing but kindness in his expression.

"But this surgeon is digressing," he said. "Fort Laramie—a run-down old post—is full of social climbers, backbiters and talebearers. That's what happens when people live in close quarters and know each other's virtues and defects."

She couldn't help her sigh.

"Yes, it's daunting. They are a censorious bunch." He glanced at her again. "If you just do your job, you should brush through this awkwardness with Captain Dunklin."

"I'm an expert at keeping my head down," she assured her escort. "But the captain worries me."

"Dunklin is a tedious bore," the post surgeon told her. "Let me engage him in conversation so you can escape to your room, which I doubt will be anything fancier than a blanket serving as a sort of amateur wall. A warning—we all snore."

Major Randolph was as good as his word. She took a bowl of stew from the kitchen to her blanketed-off corner of the sleeping room, while Major Randolph, an efficient decoy, chatted with Captain Dunklin.

Her tiny corner was frigid, the small window opaque with ice, the logs rimed with frost. Huddled on the bed, she drank her soup, which cooled off quickly.

She debated about removing her clothes, then decided against anything beyond her shoes and dress. She drew herself into a ball, her arms wrapped around her knees, wishing for warmth.

There was a gap in the blanket wall and she looked into the main room at Major Randolph's profile. He was reading now, looking up occasionally to add his mite to the conversation between the other officers. He had an elegant mustache, which he tugged on as he read. She could see no obvious military bearing there; he looked like a man built more for comfort than warfare. He looked like someone she could talk to.

They observed rank even in bed on the men's side of the curtain: two majors in one bed, and Captain Dunklin in the smaller bed. The two privates who took turns driving the ambulance rolled in their blankets and lay down in front of the cookstove, which looked to Joe like the warmest place in the roadhouse. He hoped Dunklin was cold, sleeping by himself.

John Walters was soon asleep beside him. Joe closed his eyes and did what he always did before sleep came. Starting with South Mountain in 1862, when he had been a new surgeon, he performed a mental inventory of his hardest cases. If he was tired, he never got much beyond South Mountain, because it had been the worst, for reasons that continued to plague him.

The cases that stood out were the ones where he still questioned his decisions. For years, he had wondered if he was the only surgeon who did that. Just last year, he had asked Al Hartsuff if he ever rethought his Civil War cases. Al nodded, drank a little deeper and replied, "All the livelong day, Joe."

On a bad night, he rethought the whole war. On the worst nights, he relived the death of his wife, as her skirts caught fire on a windy evening by a campfire, and she blazed like a torch. No amount of rethinking ever changed that outcome. Her screams had echoed in his head for years.

He didn't get that far tonight; he had Susanna Hopkins to thank. After all his companions started snoring, she must have felt secure enough to cry, knowing she would not be heard.

He was on the side of the bed closest to her flimsy partition. First he heard deep gulps, as though she tried to subdue her tears. As he listened, he heard muffled weeping.

All he knew of Susanna Hopkins was that she was divorced and her son taken from her. He knew she was a lady looking for a second chance. He listened to her, wondering how to best alleviate her suffering. Medically, he had no reason to throw back his covers, pick up his greatcoat and tiptoe around the partition, but he did it anyway.

"You're probably cold," he whispered as he lowered the overcoat on her bed. She had gathered herself into a tight little ball—whether from fear or cold, he had no idea.

"Go to sleep," he whispered. "I'm of the opinion that most things generally turn out for the best."

Joe tiptoed back to his side of the partition and lay down again. He was warm enough, because Walters radiated body heat. Joe closed his eyes, listening. Soon he heard a small sigh from the other side of the blanket, which told him she was warmer now. He remembered that Melissa used to sigh like that, when she was tucked close to him and content.

For a change, the memory of Melissa soothed him to sleep. *I miss you, M'liss,* he thought.

Two more days and they arrived at Fort Laramie, not a minute too soon for Dr. Randolph. Ignoring the startled expression from Major Walters, Joe had kept up a running commentary with Captain Dunklin any time the man had so much as looked in Susanna Hopkins's direction to make a comment.

Joe knew Major Walters was puzzled. He said as much during a break, when they stood next to each other and created circles of steaming yellow snow.

"Joe, I like conversation as well as the next man, but with *Dunklin?*" Walters commented.

Joe finished his business and buttoned up. He spoke cautiously, not wanting to expose the real reason. "Dunklin is a busybody."

"The whole Ninth Infantry knows that," Walters replied, amused.

"I think Mrs. Hopkins would rather keep her late husband to herself," Joe said, cringing inside as he continued the lie begun so stupidly by Emily Reese.

"I think you deserve a medal," Walters teased.

Joe's heart warmed to watch Susanna Hopkins, who quickly discerned what he was doing and why. She still sat too close to the ambulance's stove for his total comfort, but she kept her nose in her book, giving Dunklin no reason to speak to her.

Joe's head well and truly ached by the time the ambulance stopped at the fork where Major Walters's escort from Fort Fetterman waited, walking their remounts to keep them warm. Joe helped Mrs. Hopkins from the vehicle.

The three of them walked toward the patrol and Major Walters took Mrs. Hopkins by the hand. Joe noticed her slight hesitation, followed by a deep, careful breath, and he wondered how hard it was for her, in this world of men. He was beginning to understand her wariness.

"Mrs. Hopkins, so pleased to have made your acquaintance," Walters said.

He turned to Joe. "Do you figure you'll take part in the spring campaign, probably being planned in Washington as we speak?"

"It's unlikely," Joe replied, as his face grew hot. "You'll recall who heads the Department of the Platte. General Crook has no use for me."

"Maybe someday he'll change his mind."

"When pigs fly," Joe said, wishing now for the conversation to end, as much as he liked Walters.

Walters mounted the horse waiting for him, and the patrol

loped away to the north and west. Mrs. Hopkins seemed in no more hurry to return to the ambulance than Joe was. He wondered if she would ask him what the major had meant.

What she said surprised him. "You have a headache."

"I do, indeed," he told her, touched at her discernment.

"All in the service of distracting Captain Dunklin," she said. "That's not written anywhere in Hippocrates's oath."

Her concern touched him, she who had bigger problems than he did. Perhaps she wouldn't mind a tease, since she seemed brave enough to voice her own.

"I'm certain Hippocrates intended it," he told her. "The gist was perhaps lost in translation."

To his pleasure, she smiled at his feeble wit. "Would it help if I feigned sleep this afternoon? That way, he won't try to talk to me, and your headache will abate."

She did precisely that as the ambulance bumped and rolled toward Fort Laramie, feigning sleep so expertly he wondered if she really did doze off. If she wasn't actually asleep, then she knew precisely how to pretend.

He thought suddenly of his late wife, who had never feigned sleep because he never gave her reason to. He recalled Melissa's pleasure at waiting up for him in the tent on that fatal march to Texas. Not for Melissa the hope that he would think she slept, and not trouble her with marital demands. She'd waited up for him, and showed him how quiet she could be as they made love in a tent. He couldn't help smiling at a memory that used to sadden him.

They spent the last night out from Fort Laramie at James Hunton's ranch, a more commodious place with actual rooms for travelers. Joe gratefully turned the entertainment of Captain Dunklin over to James, a gregarious fellow who had close ties to Fort Laramie. After dinner, neither man even noticed when Joe and Mrs. Hopkins quietly left.

"Is your headache gone?" she asked, speaking to him first, which made him hope she was beginning to trust him. It was a small thing, but Joe Randolph noticed small things.

"Yes, thank you."

He only glanced at her, but it pleased him to see her smile. *I can't be certain—God knows she hasn't said—but why would any man dare beat a woman like this?* he asked himself. He could imagine no other way for her occipital bone to have a dimple in it. He knew it was not something he could ever bring up. He glanced again, and she looked as though she wanted to say something.

"Yes?"

"What is this spring campaign Major Walters mentioned?"

They had reached the edge of the ranch yard. Mrs. Hopkins turned around and he offered her his arm again. This time, she took it.

"I will give you a short course in the dubious business of treaty making, Mrs. Hopkins. If it is so boring that your eyes roll back in your head and you feel faint, let me know."

"I am made of stern stuff," she assured him.

"According to the Treaty of 1868, the Sioux and Cheyenne have been assigned reservations on the Missouri River, but also given a large tract of western land over which to roam, in search of buffalo."

"That sounds fair enough."

"Treaties always *sound* fair," he said. "Included in that land, never actually surveyed, is the Black Hills. It's sacred to the Sioux, and wouldn't you know, someone has discovered gold there."

"Oh, dear," she murmured. "Prospectors want it, and the Indians are not happy."

"They are not. President Grant offered to buy it, but Lo the Indian is not interested."

She stopped. "Ah! I have heard that before. 'Lo! The poor

Indian, whose untutored mind, sees God in clouds or hears him in the wind.'" She grinned at him. "Alexander Pope, who probably never saw an Indian. I ask you, shouldn't poets write about what they *know?*"

"They should, but don't. 'Lo' is our nickname for hostiles." Joe stopped, certain that her feet must be cold, but unwilling to continue this conversation inside, where Captain Dunklin would interrupt. "The plan now is to insist that Lo, Mrs. Lo and the Lo kiddies who traipse about in the unceded area— we call them Northern Roamers—be forced onto the reservations. Then Uncle Sam will turn that land and the Black Hills into one large For Sale sign."

"If they won't?"

"They have until the end of January, but I ask you, how easy is it to move a village in this cold? Very few Roamers have come to the reservations." He sighed. "That is precisely what General Sherman wants—he's general of the army. By February, I am certain a campaign will begin, to round up the Northern Roamers. You will see troops on the move this summer. Sherman is hoping for a fight."

"All I want to do is teach school," she said. "That sounds so self-centered, but it is the truth."

"You're not asking much."

"I never do," she replied quietly.

"Maybe you should," he said on impulse.

She just shook her head and started for the roadhouse. It was his turn to stop at the door, thinking of another day of talking to Captain Dunklin, and feeling appalled by the idea.

Mrs. Hopkins must have been a mind reader. "Captain Dunklin reminds me of a pompous hypochondriac who taught in a school where I once worked. To shut him up, I would look at him with great concern, tell him I was worried about, oh, whatever I could think of, and suggest he see a doctor."

"But *I* am the doctor!" Joe declared in humorous protest. "How can that work?"

"Who better to tell him that he should really rest his throat, because you're concerned about that raspy, irritating sound he makes when he wants to get someone's attention? You know the one I mean! You'll have to be more diplomatic, but you understand."

"I believe I do. We are now official conspirators."

Her smile this time was genuine and made her eyes light up. Even if their precariously cobbled plan didn't work, the major knew he would cherish the look in her eyes, a combination of gratitude and mischief that stripped away years from whatever burden she bore, at least for the moment.

He considered it a fair trade.

Susanna slept no better than usual, coming awake with that instant of terror, wondering how lightly she would have to tiptoe that day, before her conscious, rational mind reminded her that she was nowhere near Frederick Hopkins.

She followed her morning ritual, thinking of Tom first, hopeful that Frederick's housekeeper had gotten him off to school with a minimum of fuss. Tommy had become adept at calling no attention to himself, so he wouldn't upset his father. It was no way to live, but that was his life now.

"Tommy, I miss you," she whispered.

When she came into the kitchen, she witnessed Dr. Randolph's creativity. Captain Dunklin was dressed and wearing his overcoat, even though the kitchen was warm. Around his neck the surgeon must have wound a gauze bandage. She smelled camphor.

Susanna almost didn't have the courage to look Major Randolph in the eye, not from fear, but from the conviction that she would burst into laughter, if she did.

The doctor made it easy. With a frown, he motioned her into the room.

"Don't worry. Captain Dunklin isn't contagious."

"What could be wrong?" she asked, knowing she could play-act as well as anyone.

"I mentioned to the captain that he has a raspy way of clearing his throat that concerns me." The major touched Captain Dunklin's shoulder. "I wrapped his throat."

"Major, I…" Captain Dunklin began, but the major shook his head.

"Don't trouble yourself. I'm happy to help. When we get back, I'll give you a diet regimen that should solve the problem. I gave him a stiff dose of cough syrup." He sighed. "He'll probably doze, but at least he won't strain his vocal cords."

"Captain, you may have my place by the stove, so you can be warm."

Captain Dunklin looked at her with so much gratitude that Susanna felt a twinge of guilt. It passed quickly. "Thank you," he whispered.

"That's enough, Captain," Joe admonished. "I would be a poor doctor if I advised you to eat anything more than gruel for breakfast. Would you like me to help you?"

"I do feel weak," the captain whispered.

Susanna turned away and stared at a calendar until she regained her composure. "Let me feed him," she whispered, when she turned around. "Women's work, you know."

It amused her that the doctor couldn't meet her gaze. She took over the task of feeding a patient who had nothing wrong with him besides pomposity. When Dunklin looked at her with gratitude and tried to speak, she only shook her head and put her finger to her lips.

Swaddled in another blanket and seated in her chair by the ambulance's stove, Dunklin promptly fell asleep, thanks to that dose of cough syrup. Susanna took his former place next to Major Randolph, who said nothing until they were under way.

"How will you treat him at Fort Laramie?" she asked, still not trusting herself to look at her partner in medical crime.

"I'll prescribe bed rest and a low diet for five days," he whispered. "His much-put-upon lieutenant will thank me, if he dares."

They continued the journey in peace and quiet. Afternoon shadows began to gather as the ambulance stopped, and Major Randolph opened the door to look out. He opened the door wider. "The bridge is almost done."

As she looked out the door, interested, the major left the ambulance to speak with a corporal wearing a carpenter's apron. The cold defeated her, so she closed the door, only to have the post surgeon open it and gesture to her. Captain Dunklin muttered something, but did not wake.

"We'll walk, but the driver will take Captain Dunklin across."

She looked down dubiously at the frozen water under the few planks that spanned the bridge.

"You're looking at the only iron bridge between Chicago and San Francisco. It will be the only bridge across the Platte, so it opens up the Black Hills from Cheyenne. Say goodbye to the buffalo and Indians. Here comes the gold rush."

She took his gloved hand and crossed the river. When they were safely across, the corporal waved to the driver and he crossed.

"Of course, I can also say goodbye to drownings from the ferry," the post surgeon said. "I hate those. Up you get. Next stop is Fort Laramie and your cousin."

"I wish I could see more," she grumbled, as the ambulance trundled along.

"Nothing simpler," the major said. "You pull on that cord

and I'll pull this one. Makes it frigid in here but maybe we ought to revive the captain."

"We're coming in behind the shops and warehouses," the major said. He pointed to the hill. "There's my hospital, still standing. A good sign, when you leave a contract surgeon in charge."

They came over the brow of the hill and Fort Laramie sprawled below. In the light of late afternoon, more forgiving than the glare of midday, the fort was a shabby jumble of wooden, adobe and brick buildings.

"Why is everything painted *red?*" she asked.

"Apparently some earlier commander noted in a memo to Washington that the old girl was looking shabby. Next thing you know, there was a gigantic shipment of what we call quartermaster red. For reasons known to God alone, we also have a monstrous supply of raisins. Welcome to the U.S. Army."

Chapter Four

"It's so shabby," Susanna said. "This is it?"

Joe laughed, which made Captain Dunklin flutter open his eyes. "As forts go, Fort Laramie is old. Forts out here are built for expediency, not permanence. When Lo is on reservations and the frontier shifts, this old dame will disappear." He pointed to a row of houses. "We'll let out Captain Dunklin first."

The ambulance slowed, then stopped in front of an adobe double house. Captain Dunklin croaked out his thanks as the post surgeon helped him from the ambulance.

Susanna watched with interest as doors opened along Officers Row. On the other side of the largest building on the row, she thought she saw her cousin standing on a porch. She squinted, impatient with her bad eye.

The post surgeon shook his head when he rejoined her. "Captain Dunklin thinks he's on his deathbed. Mrs. Dunklin is sobbing. Who knew he was so susceptible to diseases of the imagination?"

The ambulance continued down the row, passing the largest building.

"That is Old Bedlam, built almost thirty years ago."

"Old Bedlam?"

"It's been used as a headquarters, officers' apartments, but most often as quarters for bachelor officers, hence the name."

She wondered what the building with its elegant porch and balcony would look like, painted sensible white. To her Eastern eyes, Old Bedlam was grandiose and totally out of place, even painted red. "Do you live there?"

"No. Rank hath its privilege. I am two doors down from your cousin, in quarters with six rooms, as befits a major. I know. It hardly seems fair I should have so much space—two rooms more than Captain Reese—but I use one room as my clinic for women and children. Ah. There is Emily Reese."

He helped Susanna from the ambulance. The Reeses lived in one half of a duplex, with what looked like a half floor above. Susanna stood beside him, gazing up at her cousin, whom she had not seen since Emily's wedding five years ago.

Emily Reese was as pretty as Susanna remembered, with the family blond hair. Uncertain, Susanna stood where she was, expecting her cousin to come down the few steps to welcome her. As she waited, she felt dread settle around her.

Major Randolph seemed to sense her discomfort. He took her by the elbow and steered her toward the porch. Susanna saw the door on the other half of the duplex open and a lady with red hair step onto the porch, smiling more of a welcome than Emily. Susanna smiled at the other lady, who gave a small wave, then stepped back inside her own quarters, closing the door quietly. *Someone is glad to see me,* Susanna thought. *Too bad it is not my cousin.*

"Mrs. Reese, here is your cousin," the major said. "You should invite her in."

It was gently said, and seemed to rouse Emily to do more than stand there. She came no closer, but took Susanna's hand when she and the major climbed the steps.

"So good to see you," Emily murmured.

I wish you meant that, Susanna told herself. "It's good

to see you, Emily," she said, wanting to shake off her well-honed feeling of dread, but not sure how. "I appreciate this opportunity you have given me."

She wondered how long her cousin would have kept them on the porch, if Major Randolph hadn't taken matters into his own hands and opened the door. "Emily, you'll catch your death out here," he chided, as though she needed reminding.

Once inside her own house, Emily Reese took charge. She indicated that the ambulance driver should take Susanna's luggage upstairs.

The major took Susanna's hand. "I'll leave you two now. Good night."

Susanna was left with her cousin. *Take a deep breath and begin,* she told herself, smiling her company smile at her cousin.

"It's good to see you, Emily," she said. "I hope…" *Actually, I wish you would look me in the eye,* she thought in alarm. *What now?* "It's been a long time, hasn't it?"

"Five years," her cousin said, making no move to take the overcoat that Susanna had removed.

Embarrassed, Susanna cleared her throat. "Emily, where should I hang this?"

Emily opened a narrow door under the stairs. "Next to the mop. I'm sorry we haven't more pegs in the hallway, but the captain's overcoat and hat take up room."

Susanna nodded, amused to hear her cousin-in-law, Daniel Reese, referred to as "the captain." She wondered if Emily was equal to a little tease about relegating relatives to the broom closet, and decided she was not.

When Emily just stood there, Susanna prodded a little more. "Where did you have the private take my belongings?"

"Upstairs. Let me show you where you'll be staying." Emily smiled her own company smile. "Come along. It isn't much."

Emily was right; it wasn't much, just a space behind an army blanket at the end of the little hall. *At least I have a place to stay,* Susanna reminded herself as she and her cousin stood on the small landing. One bedroom door was open, and she looked in, charmed to see her little cousin, Stanley, stacking blocks, his back to the door.

She glanced at Emily, pleased to see some expression on her face now, as she admired her son.

"Stanley is four now," Emily whispered.

"I'm certain we will get along famously," Susanna assured her, thinking of her own son at that age—inquisitive, and beginning to exert a certain amount of household influence.

As Stanley stacked another block, the wobbling tower came down. The little boy put his hands to his head in sudden irritation and declared, "That's a damned nuisance!"

Emily gasped and closed the door. "Cousin, this is the hardest place to raise children!"

"I imagine there are plenty of soldiers who don't think much of letting the language fly," she said, putting a real cap on her urge to laugh. "Must be a trial."

"It's not the soldiers," Emily snapped, the portrait of righteous indignation. "It's the no-account Irish living next door!" She lowered her voice slightly. "You'd be horrified what we hear through the wall."

Susanna stared at her. "Here on Officers Row?"

It was obviously a subject that Emily had thought long about, considering that she never thought much of anything. "That's what happens when the army promotes a bog Irishman from sergeant to captain of cavalry. So what if he earned a Medal of Honor in the late war? They're hopeless!"

"I have a lot to learn," Susanna murmured, hoping that the unfortunates on the other side of the wall were deaf. She thought of the pretty redhead who had given her a welcoming wave, and decided to form her own opinion.

Emily pulled back the army blanket strung on a sagging rod, revealing an army cot and bureau obviously intended for someone with few possessions. *That would be me,* Susanna thought.

"You should be comfortable enough here. I had a private from the captain's company hammer up some nails to hang your dresses."

"I am certain it will do," Susanna replied. "I am grateful. Major Randolph said something about captains being alloted four rooms, not including the kitchen."

She quickly realized this was another unfortunate topic, because Emily sighed again. "I think it's…it's unconscious for a widower to have six rooms!"

Do you mean unconscionable, Cousin Malaprop? Susanna thought, remembering Emily Reese's bedroom back home. "I suppose that's the army way. Now I'll unpack…."

Emily was just warming to the subject. "There are captains here with five rooms."

"Why not Dan?"

"We came here at the same time as another captain and his wife who have no children, but this is what we have." Emily frowned. "He was even in Dan's graduating class!"

"Why did you get this smaller place?" Susanna asked, interested.

"Because Dan was academically lower in his class," her cousin said. "Is that fair?"

I suppose that's what happens when you marry someone no brighter than yourself, Susanna thought, amused. "What happens if someone comes to the fort who outranks the man who outranks…your husband?"

"We all move up or down, depending," Emily said, "and the Major Randolphs just roll merrily along in their excess space." She sniffed. "I didn't know about this when I married the captain."

No, you were mostly interested in how grand he looked in uniform, Susanna thought, remembering the wedding five years ago, where Tommy had been ring bearer. That was before Frederick started drinking each night. "There is a lot we don't know, before a wedding," Susanna murmured.

"Maybe it's just as well," her cousin said, with another noisy sigh.

No, it isn't, Susanna almost said. *If I had known...*

No matter that it had been ten years since Melissa's fiery death, Joe Randolph never opened the door to his quarters without the tiny hope that this time she would be there to take his coat, kiss his cheek and ask how his day had gone. As a man of science, he knew it was foolish, but that little hope never left him.

He had been gone nearly a month this time on court-martial duty, but he had learned that whether left empty three weeks, two months or two days, houses without women in them soon felt abandoned. He still missed Melissa's rose talc.

"I'm not busy enough, M'liss," he said out loud to her picture, when he looked up from unpacking. There she was, smiling at him as much as she could, considering how long she had to hold that pose for the photographer in San Antonio.

On that journey to Texas, he had pillowed her head on his arm as they whispered plans for the future. Their last night had its own sweetness, as they made plans for the baby she was carrying. He was no ignorant physician; he had picked up on signs and symptoms before M'liss overcame her natural reticence and spilled those particular beans. He smiled now, remembering how she had thumped him when he had said, "I kind of suspected. I *did* graduate first in my class at medical school."

She had kissed him, rendering the thump moot, and snuggled close in a way that made him feel like Lord Protector.

Too bad he couldn't protect her that next morning, when she stood too close to a campfire and went up like a torch.

Even four years of war had not prepared him for that horror. There wasn't even a bucket of water close. Burned, blind, swollen beyond recognition, Melissa Randolph had suffered agonies until nightfall, when, jaw clenched, he'd administered a whacking dose of morphine that killed her immediately. The steward standing by never said a word to anyone.

There she was in the frame, forever twenty-four. Joe admired her for a long moment. "M'liss, what would you have me do?" he asked her picture. "I am thirty-eight and I am lonely." He looked down at his wedding ring. He had never taken it off his finger since she'd put it there.

He took it off now. Her wedding ring had gone with her into Texas soil, mainly because he would have had to amputate her swollen finger to release it, and he could not. She had earlier removed a ruby ring he had given her. When he could think rationally again, he'd put the ring on a chain, and he wore it around his neck.

Joe lifted the delicate chain over his head now, unfastened the clasp and slid his wedding ring onto it. After another long moment he put the necklace and rings in his top drawer, under his socks.

His bedroom seemed too small after he closed the drawer, so he put on his overcoat again and went outside. He looked up Officers Row and saw lights winking in windows of houses with families. He stood there until he had formulated a good enough excuse to visit the Reeses again, and walked two houses down.

He chuckled to think of Emily Reese forced to live next door to the far kinder O'Learys. He would suggest to Mrs. Hopkins that she might find their Irish company enjoyable. Katie O'Leary had more brains than both of the Reeses, and Mrs. Hopkins would appreciate her.

Pipe in hand, Dan Reese opened the door to Joe's knock. "Come in, Major," he said, then called over his shoulder, "Mrs. Reese, is someone sick?"

What a blockhead, Joe thought, not for the first time. "Captain, I just wanted a moment with your cousin."

The captain gestured him inside. "Is Mrs. Hopkins sick?"

"Not that I know of," Joe replied, wishing he could laugh. "I'm current president of the administrative council and Mrs. Hopkins needs to make a visit to our commanding officer tomorrow. She has some credentials to show him."

"Of course." He looked over his shoulder again. "Susanna?"

It wasn't a fluke. He saw relief in Susanna Hopkins's eyes when she came out of the parlor, cousin Stanley riding on her hip, reaching for her spectacles. Captain Reese wandered back into the parlor, obviously the possessor of a shorter attention span than his son.

Susanna set down Stanley and cleaned her spectacles on her apron. Spectacles off, she looked at him, and he was struck with her mild beauty. He probably shouldn't have—it smacked of the grossest impertinence—but Joe touched that dimpled spot under her left eye. She stepped back, startled.

"Beg pardon, ma'am. I am curious—can you see out of that eye?"

He supposed she could have ordered him from the house, but she didn't. She put her glasses back on. "I have a corrective lens in that side. The other lens is plain glass."

He had his suspicions, but he wanted to ask how she had come by such an injury. Yet he knew he should beg her pardon. She held up her hand, maybe knowing what he intended.

"Don't apologize. I know your interest is medical."

He nodded, wondering if she was right.

"I'm a blockhead," he said simply. "Will you come with me tomorrow morning after guard mount to see Major Townsend?

He needs to see your certification. Since I am president of the administrative council, you are my responsibility." *Good Lord, you sound like a jailer,* he thought, disgusted.

Susanna Hopkins didn't see it that way, apparently. "Certainly! The sooner I offer my credentials, the sooner I can get out of…"

She blushed, which he found charming.

"This house?" he asked in a whisper. "Tell you what, Mrs. Hopkins, after we visit the colonel, I'll introduce you to your next-door neighbor. She's clever, witty and…"

"Not what my cousin has already said?" Susanna finished. "I thought as much. I would like that. But tell me, what is guard mount?"

He was on sure ground now. "It's our one daily affair, when the night guard goes off duty and the day sentries come on. In the summer, when there is no danger of trumpeters' lips freezing on their mouthpieces, the band plays and the companies and troops go through the manual of arms." He bowed. "Mrs. Hopkins, I will meet you on this porch at nine of the clock."

"You don't march?"

"Doctors don't have to, thank God. And now I'd better go see if the hospital is still standing."

It was a feeble witticism, but she nodded as though he had said something profound, and held the door open for him. Joe wasn't going to look back at the Reese quarters as he started toward the hospital, but he turned around and there she was, watching him.

It was a small thing, but it gratified him as he walked to the hospital on its knoll behind the cavalry barrack. Not since Melissa had another female paid him any attention—at least, not that he was aware of.

The hospital was still standing. According to Theodore Brown, his steward, the contract surgeon had done no harm, all a man could hope for. Ted's notes and files were impeccable as always, and much easier to read than Joe's own scrawl. There was nothing to do but take an unnecessary ward walk, and return to his empty quarters.

Most of the quarters on Officers Row were dark now. He glanced at the Reeses' duplex again, even though he knew it was silly to think that Mrs. Hopkins would still be standing there. To his surprise, she was.

I will be her friend, he thought as he went into his quarters. He knew someone as pleasant as Susanna Hopkins would make friends soon enough. From habit, he pressed the extra pillow next to him, and was soon asleep.

Chapter Five

"Can't you sleep, cousin?" Emily asked Susanna, coming downstairs after closing the door to her own room. She came to the window to stand beside her. "Is there something unusual outside?" she asked. "Indians? Coyotes? Should we raise an alarm?"

Susanna sighed inwardly, certain that her cousin had never been inclined to stand at a window and think. She had just watched Major Randolph return from the hospital.

Touch me, Emily, she thought. *Just put your hand on my shoulder. We used to be close, and now we are not.* She tried to think of the last time anyone had touched her, until she realized that it was an hour ago, when Major Randolph had touched her eye out of professional curiosity. His fingers had been gentle.

Her cousin made no move. There had been a time when they had shared secrets, and a bed when they went to visit their mutual grandmamma, a tough old boot from Gettysburg who had spent that battle frying doughnuts for whichever army happened to control the town on any particular day and tramped near her kitchen.

One of them had to speak, and Susanna knew she was the one with both gratitude and grievance. "Emily, I appreciate your arranging this teaching position," she said, before the silence between them reached an awkward stage.

Emily turned startled eyes on her. "I had nothing to do with it," she exclaimed. "Mama knows a lady in town who is a sister of the colonel of the regiment. Mama inquired about any teaching positions out here, and word eventually got to the colonel. Mama contacted me." There was no ignoring her tiny sigh, until Emily put on her company face again. "I told her we didn't have room, but you know my mama."

"I appreciate your sacrifice," Susanna said. She knew her aunt's expertise in twisting Emily's arm, even through the U.S. mail. "This is a fresh start for me."

She should have left it there, but she couldn't, not with her anxiety about Captain Dunklin and his wife from Carlisle. "Why did you tell people I am a widow?"

Emily's company face vanished as her eyes grew smaller. "Do you think I want *anyone* to know that you abandoned your child, and your husband divorced you for neglect?" she whispered.

Susanna gasped. "Emily, what have you heard? If I hadn't left the house, Frederick would have beaten me to death!" She closed her eyes, remembering the pain and terror, and Tommy's mouth open in a scream on the other side of the window as he watched her stagger down the walkway. "I didn't abandon him! I had to save myself!"

"The newspaper Papa sent me said abandonment," Emily told her, sounding virtuous, superior and hurt at the same time. "Such a scandal! I had to say what I did, or you never would have been hired. You should thank me for thinking of it."

"What the papers printed was a lie. My former husband— when he sobered up—hired a good lawyer and paid all the other lawyers in a fifty-mile radius not to take my case," Susanna said, trying not to raise her voice. "You never had to say *anything*. I am just Mrs. Susanna Hopkins. All they want is a teacher."

Emily looked at her with sad eyes. "What did you do to make him so angry?"

"I didn't *do* anything," Susanna replied, wanting to end this inquisition, because her cousin's mind was already made up. Pennsylvania may have been miles away, but nothing had changed. "About five years ago, Frederick's business began to fail and he started drinking to excess. After that, nothing I did was right. Nothing."

She stopped, thinking of those afternoons she had come to dread, waiting for Frederick to return home. She'd always tried to gauge his attitude as he walked up the front steps. Was he going to be sober and withdrawn, ready to sulk in his study? Or would he be drunk and looking everywhere for something to touch off a beating or more humiliating behavior, once Tommy was asleep? She never knew which it would be.

For all his simplicity, Susanna knew Emily's husband was a kind man and her cousin would never suffer such treatment. Emily hadn't the imagination to think ill of Frederick, who could put on a company face as good as her own.

"I'm certain you meant well," she told her cousin. "Captain Dunklin informed me that his wife is from Carlisle, too. Suppose she writes someone back home and mentions Susanna Hopkins?"

"Carlisle is so far away," Emily said, locating it somewhere next to Versailles. "I'm sorry if I did the wrong thing, but you don't know these women, Susanna! They're so superior. If they knew you were a notorious divorcee, no one would receive me, and Captain Reese's career would suffer. I had to tell that little lie!"

"*Notorious* divorcee?" Susanna said, stunned. "Emily, I

am nothing of the sort! I have been wronged in the worst way, whether you believe it or not."

They stared at each other, her cousin with a wounded expression, and Susanna wondering how Emily had become the victim.

"When did you start wearing spectacles?" Emily asked, obviously wanting to change the subject.

"After Frederick pushed my face into the mantelpiece and fractured the bone under my eye," Susanna said, not so willing to let Emily off the hook. "I don't see too well out of that eye." Susanna touched Emily's arm. "We'll hope that Captain Dunklin's wife has no curiosity about doings in Pennsylvania."

"I won't give it another thought."

I don't doubt that for a minute, Susanna thought as she said good-night. After she closed the army blanket around her quasi room, Susanna sat still, her mind in turmoil. As she contemplated the gray blanket that constituted a wall, she felt a chill more than cold seeping into her bones.

She undressed in the cold space, then did what she always did, closed her eyes and thought of her son. Usually she got no farther than that, but this time she added Major Randolph to her mental inventory. It was not a prayer, because she had given up pestering God.

A bugle woke her in the morning, followed at an interval by a different melody. After the second call, she smiled at a massive groan from the Reeses' bedroom, which suggested to her that Emily's lord and master was not an early riser by inclination.

Captain Reese eventually clumped downstairs, swearing fluently, which told her the true source of his son's salty language, rather than the family through the wall. Susanna heard Captain—O'Leary, was it?—go down his own set of stairs on the other side of the wall, and decided there wasn't much privacy in army housing.

As Susanna lay there, she heard Mrs. O'Leary, in her bedroom through the wall, reciting the rosary. Her low murmur sent Susanna back to sleep.

When she woke again, Stanley had pulled back her blanket and was staring at her. She remembered the times when Tommy had done the same thing: same solemn stare, same lurking twinkle in his eyes. With a laugh, Susanna pulled him down beside her. Stanley shrieked, then giggled as she snuggled with him.

"Did your mama send you to wake me up?"

"Damn right," he said, the twinkle in his eyes daring her.

Time to nip this in the bud, Susanna thought.

"Do you know what I used to do to your cousin Tommy when he said things that he knew would shock me?"

Stanley shook his head. "Mama usually shakes her fist at the wall."

Susanna sat up, her arms around Stanley, who had settled in comfortably. "*I* reach for a bar of pine tar soap, shave off a handful and make Tommy chew it."

Stanley's eyes grew wide. "You would *do* that to a small child?" he squeaked, which made her cover her mouth and turn her head slightly, to keep her amusement private.

"Yes! Tommy never cusses anymore. I would advise you not to, either," she said, looking him right in the eye.

Stanley considered the matter. "Would you make my father chew soap, too?"

"I'll leave that to your mother. But as for you..." Susanna reached around him into her carpetbag and found a bar of soap.

Stanley flinched but did not leave her lap. With that dignity of children that always touched her, he eyed the soap and said, "I'll tell Mama that you will be down to breakfast directly. Major Randolph is waiting, too."

Oh, he is, she thought, flattered. "I'll hurry. Stanley, no more cussing. Promise?"

He nodded. She put the soap back in her carpetbag and hugged him, then set him on his feet. "Stanley, I knew you would see the good in doing right."

He nodded in that philosophical way of four-year-olds and went down the stairs at a sedate pace that lasted for only a few steps. Susanna dressed quickly, wishing that everything she owned wasn't wrinkled. She had no washbasin, so she went into her cousin's room and washed her face, hoping Emily wouldn't mind.

Major Randolph sat in the dining room, frowning at a bowl of oatmeal. "My mother always told me it was good for me."

"It is, Major," Susanna said, standing in the doorway.

"Very well. I'll eat it if you'll join me," he said, indicating another bowl of oatmeal.

She sat down beside the major and picked up her spoon. "Race you," she said.

He smiled and started to eat. Emily came into the room and sat down, too, a stunned look in her eyes.

Susanna put down her spoon. "Emily?"

"Stanley told me he will never swear again. What did you *do?*"

"I threatened him with pine tar soap, then appealed to the better angels of his nature, to quote our late president," Susanna told her.

Emily's eyes were wide with puzzlement. "Our late president?"

"Abraham Lincoln. Stanley knows his limits now. I am fond of little boys."

Susanna glanced at the post surgeon, who was smiling at her. She returned her attention to her oatmeal, pleased.

When Emily returned to the lean-to kitchen, Major Randolph whispered, "After sick call this morning, I went to Captain Dunklin's quarters, prescribed a moderate diet and praised him for bearing up under the strain of what I am calling erobitis."

"Erobitis?" she repeated. "I am afraid to ask. I know that 'itis' means inflammation of, or disease of."

"I expected a teacher to know that. Just spell 'erob' backward and you have it."

"Where is this *erob* located on the body?" she asked when she could speak.

"Somewhere between the spleen and the bile duct, I should think, right next to the coils of umbrage," he said serenely. "More coffee?"

"If I drank coffee right now, I would snort it out my nose," she joked.

"Bravo, Mrs. Hopkins," the doctor replied with a grin. "I have never heard anything resembling wit come out of Captain Reese's quarters."

"Hush," she whispered. "You will get us both in trouble."

Before the major could say anything, the bugler blew another call.

"Guard mount," Major Randolph said. "To the porch."

He gestured toward the front door as Stanley ran in from the kitchen. The major scooped up the little boy and carried him outside. He set Stanley on the porch railing and held him there, then pointed toward the end of the parade ground. "The bugler stands in front of the adjutant's office, or post headquarters."

"And the bugle calls?"

"Rubbing the sleep from his eyes before any of us—unless I have some calamity to deal with in hospital—the bugler starts with reveille first call, which is followed by reveille, and then assembly, when all the men line up in front of their barracks to be counted." Major Randolph touched Stanley's head. "What comes next, lad?"

"Breakfast call," the child said promptly. "My favorite."

"That is followed by surgeon's call," the major continued, "my favorite, Stanley. The infirm, lame and malingering stagger to the hospital, or I am summoned to the barracks. I just came from surgeon's call, so the call that followed was guard mount."

Susanna looked at the other porches down Officers Row, where other women and children watched.

"Usually the band performs for guard mount. They won't play outdoors until at least the end of February. The night watch will pass—here they come now—and be replaced by the day watch, which means the guard for a twenty-four-hour period is mounted. Right now, the new guard is being inspected by the sergeant major—see? Over there in front of the old guardhouse."

She looked. "I gather the sergeant major is someone to be obeyed."

"I never cross him, even though I far outrank him," Major Randolph joked. "Now he is giving the new guard their assignments. Here comes the officer of the day, Lieutenant Bevins of Company D. That means I am on high alert today, because his wife is about to present him with a child. He will be unbearable if I do not stop by his quarters a few times today."

"You know these people well."

"There are few secrets in garrison, and I am privy to most of the sordid details," he told her.

Let's hope my fake widowhood remains a secret, Susanna thought, returning her attention to the parade ground. "What is Lieutenant Bevins doing? He's the one with the bright red sash?"

"Indeed he is. He's inspecting the guard now, and will

probably lead them through a short version of the manual of arms. Before frostbite sets in, he will give them the new password and the guard will take positions inside the guard-house. Done for another morning. What comes next, Stanley, my man?"

"Fatigue call," the little boy piped up, making the same sounds as the bugler, his fist to his mouth. He looked at Susanna for approval, and she kissed the top of his head.

"That means work detail," the post surgeon explained, as he helped Stanley down from his perch. "They'll work at various duties until the bugler blows recall, and then it'll be mess call, Stanley's other favorite call. There are other calls. You'll learn them, because this is how we tell time at a fort. Now let us visit Major Townsend."

"But it was Colonel Bradley who wrote to me about the teaching position. Is he not here?"

"He's back East and Major Ed Townsend is commanding officer until he returns in a few weeks. Your credentials, madam?"

Susanna retrieved her credentials. Major Randolph waited in the parlor for her.

"Are you ready to sign a contract?"

She was, but Susanna only nodded, not trusting herself with words, because she wanted that contract so much. *This will be a fresh start,* she told herself as they walked along the row.

Major Randolph interpreted her silence correctly. "All the major wants is a schoolteacher," the surgeon said. "He has a garrison to run, and more important concerns than your cousin's lie."

"I don't relish pretending I am someone I am not, but Emily has already baked my cake for me, hasn't she?" Susanna asked.

"Yes, sad to say," he agreed. He stopped. "Should we say

something to the major about Emily's lie? It makes me uneasy, but would talking about something that might never happen make it worse?"

"I don't know," she said. "Let's...let's not."

They went to the adjutant's office, a small building located between two double houses. A corporal seated at a high desk stood and saluted, then knocked on an interior door and went inside.

"Major Townsend is second in command of the Ninth Infantry," Major Randolph explained. "Because there are more companies of the Ninth Infantry here than of the Second Cavalry, Major Townsend also commands this garrison. That's the army way."

When the corporal came out, he ushered them into Townsend's office. Her former husband would have described Townsend as someone built like a fireplug, and so he was, Susanna decided. His hair was white and his smile genuine. He gestured to a chair in front of his desk and she sat. With what she thought was real impertinence, Major Randolph perched on the edge of the desk.

"We are friends of long acquaintance, Mrs. Hopkins," Townsend said, correctly interpreting her expression. "It took only a brief stay in Joe Randolph's aid station during the siege of Atlanta to form a friendship."

Townsend nodded to his corporal, who brought another chair into the small space, so Major Randolph could sit.

Susanna took out her teaching certificates. "You're a busy man. I won't take up much of your time."

"That makes you more efficient than most of my company officers," he said, taking the papers from her. "Let us see here. Hmm, a second grade certificate, and you attended Oberlin College for three years." He put down the paper and looked at her over his glasses. "This already makes you more intelligent than most of my officers. All they did was go to West Point and accumulate demerits."

Susanna laughed. "Major Townsend, I doubt that!"

"I exaggerate only slightly," he admitted. "Most served with distinction in our late war. You will teach a four-month school, ending in mid-May, for which the officers with school-children have contracted to pay you forty dollars a month?"

"That is my understanding," she replied. "My certificate is valid only in Pennsylvania, but the closest examination site here is Denver."

"No matter. Pennsylvania's loss is our gain."

"Thank you, Major Townsend," she said. "I believe there is a contract…"

"…which I have right here." The major took a paper from his corporal. "Women and children in garrison come and go, but right now, you have ten students ranging in age from seven to fifteen. Each classroom day will begin following guard mount. Mess call will be observed, and then you will resume teaching until an hour before stable call."

The major correctly interpreted her perplexed expression. "Let's make that from nine-thirty to noon, and then one to three o'clock. Four and a half hours to educate a collection of children not used to school." He leaned back in his chair. "My children are being educated in the East, with my dear wife. Army life often means separation. Your being here means officers' children will be able to stay with their families. I doubt the children will be grateful, but I am. Sign, Mrs. Hopkins."

She signed. He took the contract from her and stood up, ending their brief interview. "Joe can show you our idea for a classroom. Good day."

She nodded to Major Townsend and was almost through the door when he stopped her.

"Mrs. Hopkins, I am sorry for your loss," he said simply. "It always seems that war is hardest on those who don't wage it."

Red-faced, Susanna nodded and let Major Randolph usher her out. "I hate deception," she whispered, when they were outside in the cold again. "Maybe I should have said something. You know him well. Should I?"

The surgeon remained silent for a long moment, then shook his head slowly. "I think the moment for that passed when Emily told her lie," he whispered back. "I confess I am not certain what to do. What do you think, Mrs. Hopkins?"

I think this will not end well, she told herself.

Chapter Six

She let him take her arm on the icy steps outside. The cold air felt good on her face; too bad it could not calm her conscience.

"I think this the best place for school," the major was saying as they continued around the parade ground until they stood in front of Old Bedlam, with its bizarre red paint. "The front room used to be headquarters, during the late war," he said, careful with her on the steps. "It'll be a good classroom. As you will see, we've been accumulating desks."

He opened the door and it swung on creaky hinges. He went to the window and pulled back the draperies, which made her cough.

"God, what a firetrap," the surgeon said mildly. "What do you think?"

When the dust settled, Susanna walked around the room, admiring the mismatched but suitable desks. She looked at a connecting door.

"Bachelor officer's quarters," he said. "Some overworked second lieutenant with no family lives there. We call them orphans. This building is referred to as the orphanage."

He walked to a small desk with delicately turned legs, the best desk in the room. "This will be yours. Well?"

"This will do," she said, feeling her spirits rise as she began to see a classroom in the dust, mouse nests and cobwebs. "I'd like to start school on Monday. Is there time for a miracle?"

"That's barely a challenge for the U.S. Army," Major Randolph said. "I probably have half a dozen stools in the hospital for the desks, and we can find more. The officer of the day is always looking for work projects for his guardhouse jailbirds, who can clean this room."

He must have interpreted her dubious look correctly. "Mrs. Hopkins, you are in no danger! When I finish organizing this little work party, I'll introduce you to Nick Martin. There is no prisoner who will do *anything* other than what he is told, once Nick fixes the stink eye on them."

She looked in the post surgeon's eyes. "You're going to keep me safe, aren't you?" she asked.

"To quote your cousin, the profane Stanley, 'Damn straight,'" he told her. "I doubt we'll ever have another teacher with three years' matriculation at Oberlin College. You're valuable."

With a nod, Major Randolph left her in the dusty room. She watched his jaunty stride to the adjutant's office, and then across the parade ground to the guardhouse, a man on a mission. The room was cold, but she took off her coat any way, and her bonnet. Standing on the stool, she unhooked the draperies from the metal rods and sent them to the floor in a cloud of dust. "'You're valuable,'" she repeated out loud. "Major Randolph says so."

By the time the corporal of the guard quick-marched a half dozen soldiers dressed in coats with a large *P* on the back into her classroom, three privates from the quartermaster department clattered up with brooms, buckets, mops and scrub brushes. The corporal found a keg somewhere and sat on it, as she handed each prisoner a broom and issued her own orders for the removal of the draperies.

No one had anything to say—Susanna didn't know what

was proper with prisoners—so they worked in silence until the bugler blew what must have been recall from fatigue, because the men put down their brooms and mops. The corporal stood up and spoke for the first time.

"We'll be back here in one hour, ma'am," he told her, as his prisoners lined up and marched out.

"Amazing," she said, looking around at the bare room, which smelled strongly of pine soap now. She knew it was time for luncheon; the bugle said so.

Her stomach growled, but she sat on the stool, reluctant to return to her cousin's quarters because she felt no welcome there. Probably Major Randolph had returned to his hospital.

Funny she should think of him. A moment later, she heard a man clear his throat and then tap on the open door. "Meditating? Nurturing second thoughts? Hungry?" the major asked, standing there.

"Two out of three," she replied. "I quit second thoughts somewhere around Chicago."

"Excellent!" He turned around. "She'll be pleased to see you, Katie."

As Susanna watched, the surgeon ushered in the woman who'd been on the porch yesterday. She was in an advanced stage of pregnancy, and possessed of lively green eyes and red hair.

Susanna stood up and gestured to the stool. "Please have a seat."

The lady glanced at the surgeon. "Should I sit before I actually admit who I am?" she asked him, humor evident in her lovely brogue.

"I suspect she knows who you are," Randolph replied. "Let me introduce Katie O'Leary, your neighbor through the wall."

Susanna offered her hand, and Katie shook it before sitting down. She handed Susanna a sandwich wrapped in waxed paper. "It's only bread and butter with a lump of government beef that I mangled with my food grinder to make it less intimidating. That is, if you're hungry."

"I am. Did you bring a sandwich for yourself, Mrs. O'Leary?"

Katie nodded and pulled a second sandwich out of a cloth bag. "I have carrots for later." She frowned. "Major, I didn't prepare a morsel for you."

Randolph held up his hand. "No worries. I think there is some kind of mystery chowder lurking in my quarters. I wanted you two to meet. I'll be back later."

He turned to leave. "Major..." Susanna began.

He looked back, with a kind expression. "Mrs. Hopkins, make no bones about this—I respond better to Joe."

"I couldn't possibly," Susanna said automatically.

"Try it sometime," he told her. "Until then, yes, what can I do for you?"

"I doubt this fireplace draws well."

"I'll have the quartermaster clerk send over our nearest approximation to a chimney sweep."

"And that would be..."

He shrugged. "I have no idea, but I doctored two of the clerk's children through a fearful round of diarrhea, and he will help me, by God. Good day, ladies."

With another nod in their direction, he left. Susanna looked at Katie O'Leary. "What do you make of that?" she asked.

"It is simply Major Randolph," Katie replied. She put her hand to her mouth as though trying to stop a laugh. "I don't know that I've seen him quite this animated before."

"I couldn't possibly call him Joe."

Katie shrugged, and eyed her sandwich. "I never knew Major Randolph not to mean what he says."

"But you call him Major Randolph!" Susanna exclaimed.

"I do," the woman replied simply. "He never suggested I call him Joe." She laughed. "Let's eat."

Katie unwrapped her sandwich and took a bite, rolling her eyes. "My husband, Jim, loves Fort Laramie," she said. "There's nowhere nearby he must run to, to satisfy my midnight food cravings."

"I take it you have other children," Susanna said, enjoying the pleasant lilt to her companion's voice. She took a bite of the sandwich and decided the government beef had been helped along magnificently by sweet relish. "Nice sandwich, Mrs. O'Leary."

"It's Katie," the other woman said. "Surely we can stand on less ceremony than you choose with Major Randolph. I suppose your cousin has other names for me."

Susanna felt her face grow warm. Before she could comment, Katie touched her arm.

"No fears! Jim is certain she calls us the trolls through the wall. We have one son, Rooney." She patted her belly. "And another soon."

"Your son…"

"…is home with my servant," Katie finished. "Your cousin envies me because servants are hard to keep. Mary Martha is a corporal's wife who helps me during the day." She winked. "She's Irish, too. I have it on good authority that she prefers me to your cousin."

"Will you have any children in my school?"

Katie nodded. "Rooney is six, and he will go. I've taught him his letters and he can count to twenty-five." She ate the last of her sandwich and pulled out a sack of carrots. "Yes, I can read and write, and no, we don't swear through the walls to trouble little Stanley."

"Emily has always enjoyed an exalted opinion of her own gentility," Susanna said. "Stanley and I have had a few plain words about his bad habit, which you and I know can be blamed on his father!"

"That expression 'swear like a trooper' had to come from

somewhere," Katie joked. "What should I do? You may have my afternoon."

That's a charming way to put it, Susanna decided. *No one except Katie O'Leary and Major Randolph have given me anything lately.*

They decided Katie would sweep the floor while Susanna washed the windows. The corporal of the guard returned with two prisoners who wiped down the desks, then left. Susanna perched on a ladder to reach the top of the tall windows, balancing a bucket of ammonia and water on the crosspiece.

"If you make it too clean, some lieutenant will claim it for his own quarters and eject you and your pupils," Katie told her as she scrubbed.

"Over my dead body!" Susanna looked around, satisfied at the work of one day.

She sat on top of the ladder, already seeing her pupils studiously applying themselves at their desks. Katie had finished her sweeping and was sitting on the stool again, her hand against the small of her back.

"I've kept you here too long," Susanna said as she climbed down. "Tell me about the families whose children I will be teaching."

"I can sum up the families in two words," Katie said, as she stood up. "High sticklers. They will expect far too much of you."

"Daunting," Susanna murmured.

"The children of the garrison are charming enough, but their mothers… They're another matter." She lowered her voice. "Remain above reproach and you will have smooth sailing." She touched Susanna's sleeve shyly. "I know you will do well."

Until someone finds out I am not who they think I am, Susanna thought as she closed the door behind them. *Joe, please be right. Let nothing come of Emily's lie.*

* * *

Joe Randolph glanced at his watch and pocketed it again, pleased with his timing. The ladies stood on the broad porch at Old Bedlam. He had come from the quartermaster store-house, followed by a dubious private with a long-handled brush.

"I hope you did not mop any floors," he told Susanna as he joined them on the porch. "You see here Fort Laramie's answer to a chimney sweep. Go to, lad. Be brave. Come, ladies."

Katie O'Leary took his arm, but Mrs. Hopkins hung back. "It seems so early to return to quarters," she murmured.

It's that difficult there? he thought. "It's almost time for recall from fatigue," he told her. "I'll squire Katie home, and take you to meet your fellow educationist for the enlisted men's children."

"I'd like that," she said, and sat down to wait for him.

Home for Katie was only two doors from Old Bedlam, but he would always be a Virginian, and prone to good manners. "What do you think?" he asked Katie, when he knew the two of them were out of earshot.

"She's sweet, but there is such sadness in her," Katie said, as she opened her front door. "I remember how I used to worry about my Jim before every battle, but he always came home. I'd hate to be a widow, and on my own."

He returned some answer, writhing inside to continue perpetuating a lie to such a kindly woman. He toyed briefly with telling her the truth, but only tipped his hat and thanked her for her time, so generously given.

Mrs. Hopkins was shivering on the porch when he returned to Old Bedlam. "You'd be warmer in Emily's house," he said.

"I know, but I'd rather meet the teacher," she said quickly, then glanced over her shoulder. "The chimney sweep must have found a bird's nest. He swears better than Stanley."

So you want to change the subject? he asked himself. They

walked across the parade ground to a storehouse by the bakery, where children were coming out. Susanna watched them, and he noted the interest on her intelligent face.

"Where does Fort Laramie find teachers for enlisted men's children?" she asked.

"From the ranks. It's fifty cents a day extra duty pay," he told her. "Sometimes it's a malingerer wanting to get out of more arduous fatigue detail. I've even seen prisoners, clinking about a classroom in chains. Seriously." He gestured to the open door. "Sometimes we get lucky, as we did with Private Benedict."

He watched her expression as she stepped into the commissary warehouse, where barrels of victuals lined the walls. The room smelled of raisins and apricots, pungent dried herring, and vinegar. Her smile grew as she saw the blackboard pretty much where Captain Dunklin had so snidely described it, leaning on top of bags of wheat.

"Not fancy," he said, feeling apologetic.

"No, but I like raisins."

"You won't after a winter of nothing but raisins," he assured her.

Seated at a packing crate desk, Private Benedict looked up as they approached. He was on his feet at attention then, snapping off a smart salute, which Major Randolph returned.

"Private, let me introduce Mrs. Hopkins, teacher for the officers' children."

She extended her hand with no reticence, to Joe's pleasure.

"I'm delighted to meet a fellow teacher," she told Private Benedict.

"Where's your classroom, Mrs. Hopkins?"

"A place not nearly as pleasant-smelling as yours," she said. "It's that first floor room in Old Bedlam, complete with a chimney probably full of bats or birds, and maybe a ghost or two, if I can believe the corporal of the guard."

They laughed together, comrades already. With a friend in Katie O'Leary and a colleague—however improbable—in Private Benedict, Mrs. Hopkins would rub along at Fort Laramie, Joe thought. Now if he could convince her to give him some spare time at the hospital…

The private offered Mrs. Hopkins his chair, and in no time they were deep in conversation. Joe perched himself on an apple barrel, content to watch her. He knew she must be tired after a day's hard labor in an old building, but she had found a friend in Private Benedict.

He had admired blondes before, but Melissa's brunette glory had always stirred him, especially the sight of her wavy dark hair spread on his pillow. He folded his arms and decided that Mrs. Hopkins's blond hair, coupled with her brown eyes, could prove endlessly fascinating. He liked the trimness of her figure. Mrs. Hopkins was also tidy and impeccable of posture. She had a full, deep laugh, not ladylike, but so infectious.

They were both looking at him now, as though waiting for a reply to a question he had not heard, so busy was he in admiring Mrs. Hopkins. "Beg pardon?" he inquired.

Private Benedict asked again, "Sir, may I walk Mrs. Hopkins back to her quarters? I'd hate to keep you from work."

Hell, no, he thought. He took a few deep breaths, surprised at his resistance to a kind offer. "Actually, I had hoped to quick march Mrs. Hopkins to my hospital and introduce her to the redoubtable Nick Martin." Joe paused, hoping Susanna Hopkins would see his interest. He was not a man to encroach; blame his Virginian upbringing. "Mrs. Hopkins, it's your choice."

Please choose me, he pleaded silently, yearning for her approval like a schoolboy.

He realized he was holding his breath until Mrs. Hopkins replied. "Private, I trust we will have plenty of occasions to discuss both your pupils and mine."

Private Benedict sketched a charming bow to her. "We will."

"Good day, Private. We'll speak again soon. Major, shall we go?"

When he was a boy, living on his father's plantation, Joe Randolph had had a one-eyed dog. Brutus belied his name, being most tame and possessed of a self-effacing nature, at least until the post rider happened by.

Brutus became a different dog then, considering it his duty to give chase. The post rider always managed to escape Brutus's retribution, until one day when the energized dog latched on to the horse's tail.

The horse stopped, looked around at this source of discomfort, and did nothing. Joe remembered watching, eyes wide, as Brutus sank to the road and also did nothing. Once he had caught the post rider's horse, he had no idea what to do with it.

Joseph Randolph, grown now but possibly no wiser, had no idea what to do with Mrs. Hopkins. He had never supposed she would abandon a conversation with a fellow educationist. But here she was, probably with nothing on her mind beyond avoiding her cousin's house for another hour. That thought channeled him toward his best efforts to relieve at least some of her anxiety. He couldn't call it a smooth recovery, but Mrs. Hopkins probably knew better than to expect miracles from men.

"Yes, I promised you Nick Martin and I suppose you are wondering why," he said, as they left the warehouse.

"True. I can control a classroom," she assured him. She ducked her head against the wind that roared down the parade ground, and staggered with the force of it.

He steadied her automatically. "Some ladies in the regiment sew lead shot into their hems, to keep the wind from, well, doing what it does to skirts," he told her.

"I'll remember that."

As they walked toward the hospital, the bugler in front of the guardhouse played recall from fatigue, or tried to play it, considering that the wind grabbed the notes and hurtled them toward Omaha as soon as he blew them.

"Soldiers have been known to commit suicide from too much wind," he commented, then could have smacked himself. *Do I not remember a single bit of idle chatter?* he asked himself.

"One can scarcely blame them," Mrs. Hopkins said. "Now, sir, Nick Martin."

"Let us call him a deterrent," Joe said as they struggled toward the hospital. "Some of your scholars have been running wild for years. They will not take kindly to a classroom. Sit Nick in the back row and you will have a most efficient monitor."

"Has he nothing better to do?"

"Probably not. None of us know much about him," he said, raising his voice to be heard above the wind.

"He's not a soldier?"

"I don't really know. No garrison has declared him missing." Joe chuckled. "Of course, there are company captains who would wish some of their worst miscreants to go missing."

She gave him a long look. "You are being inscrutable, Major Randolph."

"It's all I can be. Nick showed up one hot August, rail-thin and full of lice. The adjutant brought him to me, and I cleaned him up." He took a chance and put his arm around her as the wind strengthened. "He informed me that he was Saint Paul. Nick, not the adjutant."

Joe smiled as her jaw dropped. "I would never lie to you, Mrs. Hopkins. I have no idea what his real name is."

"Then why…"

"…is he Nick Martin? Jim O'Leary named him after the worst malcontent in his regiment during the Civil War." Joe shrugged. "It seemed as good a name as any. Nick answers to it when he feels like it, or to Saint Paul."

"He's harmless?"

"Completely," Joe assured her.

Mrs. Hopkins hurried along beside him, holding her dress down with both hands. In a few more minutes, they were in his hospital.

Joe looked around with pleasure. The building was only two years old, and had replaced a disgraceful structure that may have caused more illness than it ever cured. He probably sounded like his long-dead mother when he ushered her inside, apologizing for the odor of ether and carbolic.

"Hospitals are supposed to smell this way," Mrs. Hopkins said, cutting through his commentary, a practical woman.

He laughed, which brought Nick Martin into the hall. Joe knew Nick generally lurked there, waiting for him to return so he could help him off with his overcoat, but he had surprised Mrs. Hopkins, who stepped back.

Trying to look at Nick Martin through her eyes—or the Apostle Paul, depending on his moods—Joe could understand her fright. Nick seemed to think long hair was a requirement, and he was taller than most mortals.

The only way to find out whether Nick was an apostle was to ask, but that seemed a little crass. "Nick, this is Mrs. Susanna Hopkins," Joe said, when she had recovered.

"The Lord bless and keep you, Mrs. Hopkins. I know He has preserved me on my many missionary journeys," Nick said.

"Saint Paul, he has certainly saved you from shipwrecks," Mrs. Hopkins replied. She held out her hand and Nick shook it.

"I hear that Major Randolph plans for you to sit in my classroom and keep order," she told the tall man.

"As long as it doesn't interfere with those missionary journeys," Nick told her. He nodded to Joe. "I must return to my duties. The church at Corinth is particularly fractious." He left them in the hallway.

"My goodness," Susanna said. "What duties does Saint Paul perform in your hospital? I mean, when he's not helping Corinthians. Does he write letters? One would think Paul was good at that."

You are a wit, Joe thought appreciatively. "He just sits there in the ward. No one seems to mind, or perhaps they're too cowed to object. At any rate, I have an orderly hospital."

He watched her lively face, wondering what she was really making of his madman.

"I hope his missionary duties are few this school term," she said, as he opened the door to his office. "If he can't read or write, I can probably teach him. That will make Romans through Hebrews easier to compose someday, don't you think?"

Joe laughed out loud. "Generations of earnest Christians will applaud you! The rest of us, not so much."

The door opened immediately and Nick brought in two cups of coffee. "Thank you, Saint Paul," she told him. The door closed again.

Joe took a sip, satisfied. "Nick makes the best coffee." He leaned back in his swivel chair. "I don't know what creates people like Nick Martin. I think he was a teamster who suffered hard usage of one sort or other, and found a better world in madness." He thought of her own ill usage. "I imagine it is a safe place."

"Where does he live?"

"Here. I have a storeroom with space for a cot in the alcove. He eats with my hospital steward. You may have noticed the small house beside the hospital." *He eats better than I do,* Joe wanted to add, but he was not a man to play a sympathy card.

"You're a kind man."

"I couldn't send him to an asylum."

Mrs. Hopkins sipped her coffee, breathing deeply of the government issue beans that Nick turned into something wonderful. Joe cleared his throat, and she looked at him, her expression sweet in a way that charmed him.

"If you should find the time, I could use your help here, reading to my patients, or writing letters for them. Young men so far from home find comfort in ladies." *Heaven knows I do,* he thought.

"Show me your ward," she said.

She surprised him. He had asked other garrison ladies to do what he was asking her, but his efforts usually involved much cajoling. No one had asked to see the ward.

"Come along," he said, opening the door quickly, before she changed her mind. "It's only a twelve-bed ward."

"And when women and children are ill?" Mrs. Hopkins asked, going with no hesitation through the door he held open.

"I treat them in their homes." He gestured into the room, which had six metal cots on either side. "I also have an examination room in my quarters, where ambulatory civilians come."

"And here?" she asked, looking around with interest.

"There is another examination room, but no operating bay. Anything needful in that realm I also do in the exam room. Mrs. Hopkins, meet my hospital steward, Sergeant Theodore Brown. He's a better post surgeon than I am, or Captain Hartsuff."

Brown looked up from a chart he was examining. "You, sir, will have people believing that, except I do not think Mrs. Hopkins is gullible."

"Nor do I," Joe replied, after a glance at her.

She held out her hand to his steward, who took it, and even favored her with a courtly little bow, which impressed Joe.

After exchanging a pleasantry or two with his number-one man, she walked the length of the room, obviously unfazed by the broken jaw in bed six, the result of a horse barn misunderstanding, or the burn victim from the bake house, who looked with real terror on the steward.

To Joe's further surprise, Mrs. Hopkins sat down beside the latter patient and took his unburned hand with no hesitation. She looked back at Joe. "There is a hospital in Shippensburg," she told him. "I did this a lot last year, while my eye healed."

She turned her attention to the private in the bed, speaking low to him while the hospital steward sat down with his tweezers and bowl on the man's other side. Joe nodded to Sergeant Brown and wheeled over a hospital screen.

"Do you need me, Sergeant?" he asked.

"No, sir." His steward glanced at Mrs. Hopkins, no more nonplussed than he was, which appeared to be not at all. "I'll send her back to your office when we're done."

Well, well, Joe thought, as he looked at charts. *People continually surprise me.* He worked his way out of the ward and back into his office for another half hour of paperwork until the sun sank lower, the retreat gun sounded and his steward finished.

"Here she is, sir," Brown said when he ushered in Mrs. Hopkins. "Our patient decided to be brave for the lady. You'll come back?"

"I will. I can read to them."

With a salute less casual than normal, the steward left.

"Mrs. Hopkins, you amaze me," Joe said frankly.

She surprised him again. "Most people just want to have someone touch them kindly."

He thought about that during their quiet walk to Officers Row. When she slowed down as they approached the Reeveses' quarters, he slowed down, too. He couldn't overlook her small sigh as she went up the steps, and the unconscious way she squared her shoulders.

"Good night, Mrs. Hopkins. I kept you away too long and worked you too hard today."

"I didn't mind," she told him, her voice soft.

He walked to his own quarters. There were notes tacked to the little board he had nailed next to his front door. He removed them, reading them after he'd carried the lamp to his kitchen. He didn't bother to heat the stew, because he didn't care. He spread the messages in front of him and mentally planned tomorrow.

He held the note from Sergeant Rattigan in his hand for a long time. "It's Maeve," was all it said, but he needed nothing more. *Another baby begun?* he asked himself. *That makes number seven since I've been here. Wouldn't we all be pleased if one of them lived to term? I'm coming, Maeve, for whatever good I will do.*

Chapter Seven

Susanna tried to trick herself into believing that the evening stretching before her would be easier this night. Maybe it was. Her cousin-in-law tried a little harder to be company, instead of hiding behind a months-old newspaper.

She carried on a decent patter about her day and mentioned Nick Martin, which made the captain pull a face and mutter something about "sending him to the federal insane asylum." She exhausted all topics soon, almost wishing for Emily to hurry downstairs and save her from her cousin-in-law. Major Randolph saved her, as he had been saving her since Cheyenne, even though he wasn't present this time.

"Cousin, I know this is none of my business…." she began, then watched with something close to unholy glee as his interest picked up. What had Major Randolph told her about the U.S. Army containing more gossips per square foot than any other organization he knew of?

Appeal to his masculine pride, Susanna, she advised herself. "I know so little about the army, and you know so much," she began. "Someone told me that Major Randolph wouldn't be going on the midwinter campaign because of some general or other. Why not?"

She could tell by the way Dan's eyes lit up that she had hit on a topic guaranteed to please. "It's a bit of a scandal," he began, not even trying to feign some reluctance at proceeding. Major Randolph was right about gossip, but this was at his expense, and she felt a momentary pang.

"It happened during the Battle of South Mountain in 1862," Reese began, tucking away his old newspaper. "More properly, it was during a skirmish at Boonsboro Gap, in a forward aid station when a Union soldier and a rebel soldier were brought in." He clucked his tongue. "Major Randolph took one look at the Union man and knew he didn't have a chance—head half blown off, or something. He turned his attention to saving the Confederate, when Crook—he was a colonel then, in an Ohio division—came into the aid station, took a look and went bat-shit crazy."

No wonder Stanley has such a colorful vocabulary, Susanna thought. "Surely the major tried to explain…"

"And Crook didn't hear one damn word of it." Reese leaned closer, as though the room was full of Rebel sympathizers. "Some say Crook tried to yank the major out of that tent, but Joe Randolph held him off with a scalpel and backed Crook into a corner." He shrugged. "That's when the Union soldier died."

"Surely it was obvious…" Susanna tried again.

"Nothing's obvious in the heat of battle. When the Union secured South Mountain, Crook pulled enough strings to have Randolph sent to Florida among the saw grass and alligators. Maybe he hoped Joe would die of malaria."

"That's so unfair. Had he no friends?"

"Precious few. Joe is from Virginia, remember? Well, General George Thomas—he was also a Virginian—did manage to retrieve him from Florida. Joe served with Pap Thomas and the Army of the Cumberland until the war ended."

"Thank goodness for General Thomas."

"Too bad he isn't still alive. Joe was supposed to serve

with General Thomas in the Department of the Pacific, but the general died on his way to San Francisco in 1870. The Medical Department reassigned Joe here to the Department of the Platte, which Crook heads now. Talk about bad luck. Crook's going to lead this winter expedition, so Joe will get left behind with hemorrhoids and the clap."

"It must be humiliating to be passed over like that," she said.

"I've wondered why Joe doesn't just leave the army. He could practice anywhere."

"Maybe he just doesn't care," Susanna said.

Let this be a cautionary tale, she told herself, as she went to the upstairs window in the hall that overlooked the parade ground. *You mustn't quit caring.*

She finally retired to her blanket-partitioned bedroom, wondering how a well-educated man could tolerate such scorn heaped on him. She was drifting to sleep when she realized that for the first time in more than a year, her son wasn't square in the middle of her thoughts. *I am not alone in misfortune,* she thought.

Nick Martin was waiting for her on the porch of Old Bedlam the next morning. Wrapped in an army blanket, he was covered in a light skiff of snow.

"Nick, tell me you haven't been here all night!"

He stood up and shook himself like a Saint Bernard emerging from a snowbank. "No. The major was all night at Sergeant Rattigan's house, and I went there first." He shook his head. "Maeve Rattigan needs a miracle, and so I have informed my superior."

"The Lord God Almighty?" Susanna asked.

"The very one," he replied. "Major Randolph says she tries and tries to have babies and they never make it."

Poor woman, Susanna thought. "Is Major Randolph as tired as you?"

"More. When someone dies, no matter how small, he just paces and paces in his office." Nick folded his blanket. "What can I do for you, my child?"

"Let's see what's inside, and then I'll tell you."

She looked around in surprise at the dirty space that was rapidly becoming a classroom. Without the heavy drapes, sunlight poured in and warmed the place, even without a fire lit in the newly swept fireplace. The desks were clean and someone had polished them. There was even a blackboard now, and a pile of books by the door.

"Looks like the miracle happened right here, Nick," she said.

The windows were dusty again, probably from the work of the chimney sweep, so she sent Nick up the ladder to wash them once more. She admired a handsome bookcase near her desk. "Where did this…"

Nick looked down from his lofty height. She almost expected him to raise his hand in a blessing. "I *have* seen one like that in the major's quarters," he said, then turned his attention to the window. "The Lord provides."

"My goodness, I wonder when he found the time," she murmured.

"Ye of little faith," Nick scolded, but gently.

She started sweeping, but stopped when Katie O'Leary arrived with a globe.

"Hi, Nick," Katie said cheerfully. "I am continually amazed what lurks in dark corners at old forts." She set the globe on top of the providential bookcase. "Not you, Nick! It happens that the quartermaster clerk is from County Mayo, where Jim was born, so he found me a globe." She laughed. "Life in the army depends on who you know, even though the other officers' wives think I don't know anyone!"

"You're giving my pupils the world, Katie," she teased.

"Mrs. Hopkins—may I call you Susanna?—you are a hopeless romantic!"

"Of course you may call me Susanna, and I am an educator, *not* a romantic."

"I don't know about that." Katie took off her overcoat. "What will you have me do?"

Just keep reminding me how truly lucky I am to be at Fort Laramie, Susanna thought. She noticed the note on the books. "'Since I head the advisory committee this year, I am also over the post library. Use what suits you. J,'" she read out loud, then looked at Katie. "Major Randolph takes a serious interest in his post duties."

"You can think that," Katie said, all complaisance. "I think he is interested in you."

Susanna felt her face flame. "Surely not," she murmured. "Now I will change the subject. Watch me! You, madam, may dust the books while I sweep and mop."

Katie sat on one of the stools, took a cloth Susanna handed her, and started through the pile, sneezing at the dust. Susanna stopped sweeping and leaned on the broom. "My cousin-in-law told me such a story about Major Randolph last night. Does General Crook truly mean to snub him by keeping him here during that winter campaign?"

"I'm certain he does," Katie replied. "It's what the general has been doing for years." She put down the dust cloth. "For my part, I am glad enough. I'd rather Major Randolph delivered this next O'Leary, and he can't do that in the Powder River country." She sighed. "The general has been plaguing Major Randolph's life since he took over the Department of the Platte."

"It's so unfair," Susanna said, attacking the dusty floor with more vigor. "Does Major Randolph just not *care* anymore?"

Katie was silent for a long moment, returning her attention to the old books. "Do you know what happened to his wife? It was so terrible I hate to think about it."

Susanna nodded. She started sweeping slowly.

"I think if he could have crawled into the coffin with her, he would have," Katie told her, after a glance at Nick on his ladder. She crossed herself quickly, and then was silent again. The whoosh of the broom was the only sound in the room. "I noticed something yesterday. He's not wearing his wedding ring. I don't know when he stopped doing that, but I noticed yesterday." She gave Susanna a shy look. "You don't wear yours. I suppose it's difficult."

I pawned mine, Susanna thought. *The engagement ring got me to Chicago, and the wedding ring got me almost here.* "Rings need to be tucked away, eventually," she said, resisting a strong urge to tell the truth to Katie O'Leary.

The work was done by noon, or mess call, which Susanna recognized. Even though she assured him she was capable, Nick threw the mop water outside the front porch for her and returned the mop and pail to the hall closet. "Do you go back to the hospital steward's house for noon?" she asked gently, when he just stood there, a puzzled look on his face.

"I do, I do, indeed." He executed a courtly bow that made Susanna smile. "Thank you for reminding me. God will bless you."

"You're kind to him," Katie said as they both stood on the porch of Old Bedlam and watched him walk away. "He's a lost soul, and hardly anyone treats him kindly. Sometimes children are mean."

"I know what that feels like," she said simply. Katie could take that however she chose; it didn't matter to Susanna.

As she looked across the parade ground, Susanna watched Major Randolph walk by the new guardhouse construction, his head down, his hands behind his back. She pointed him out to Katie, who was buttoning the only three buttons on her coat that closed over her pregnant belly.

"I don't think things went well at Sergeant Rattigan's house," Susanna whispered, even though he was too far away to hear her.

"The Rattigans? Oh, no!" Katie said in genuine distress. "You haven't met her yet, but Maeve Rattigan gets in the family way every few months, and just as regularly loses her baby." She looked down at her own swollen body, evidence of fertility that the sergeant's wife couldn't match. "I'd go to her, but I fear I would only make her more sad."

"Perhaps I could go," Susanna offered.

Major Randolph was closer now. She thought he was headed to his quarters, but he veered toward Old Bedlam. He looked up and squared his shoulders in a gesture that went right to Susanna's heart.

"It must be so hard to do what he does," she whispered. "I couldn't."

They waited for him on the porch of Old Bedlam. The parade ground was busy now with soldiers heading to the mess halls behind their particular barracks, but the post surgeon hardly seemed aware of them. *You have no one to go home to and talk out the misery you see every day,* Susanna thought. *What a shame.*

He didn't have to say anything when he got to the porch, because Katie was in tears. Without a word, he took out a handkerchief, wiped her eyes, then put the handkerchief over her nose. "Blow, sweetheart," he told her.

He looked at Susanna. "I had a note tacked to my door last night, and I've been in the Rattigans' quarters since then. I wish I knew how to help her, but…" He shook his head.

"Is there anything I can do?" Susanna asked.

"Are you finished here?"

She nodded.

"You wouldn't mind visiting a sergeant's wife over on Suds Row? Emily would probably be aghast."

"I'm going to overlook that question," she said, more crisply than she intended, but at least it brought a momentary smile to his face. "What would you have me do?"

He thought a moment. "I'll get a book from my quarters. I'll introduce you, but would you stay there this afternoon and read to her? She might listen, she might just doze. She'll know someone cares, and that's all I care about."

He left the porch with a quicker step than he'd arrived, and hurried to his quarters. "What's Mrs. Rattigan like?" Susanna asked Katie.

"Quiet. Calm. She worships the ground Sergeant Rattigan treads on." Katie shook her head. "All they want is a baby. It seems so simple."

The post surgeon was in no hurry to return to Old Bedlam, apparently. When Katie started rubbing her arms to warm them, Susanna told her to go home. Katie left with no argument, walking carefully down the icy steps. Before she reached her quarters, her husband joined her. Susanna sighed to see them continue arm in arm, her head close to his shoulder.

When she began to wonder if the post surgeon had forgotten her, he hurried from his quarters and up Officers Row again, a book and package in his hand.

The package was a cheese sandwich. "I eat a lot of these. This one's for you."

She smiled her thanks and sat down to eat it. He pulled a half-eaten sandwich from inside his overcoat and peeled back the waxed paper. "It wasn't so appealing last night," he told her as he chewed and swallowed. "I knew it could wait."

"You should eat better," she admonished, wishing for water to wash down the dry bread. The man was no cook.

"I should do a lot of things better." He said it mildly

enough, but she heard the regret in his voice. "Poor Mrs. Rattigan. She just can't carry a child to term, and I have no idea why." He sighed. "She looks at me so patiently, and I feel more inadequate than a first-year medical student. Give me a festering wound any day."

He waited until she finished. "Tonight, after supper, if you wish, I'll take you around to meet your pupils."

She nodded. "I'd like that."

He held out a book. "Up you get, Mrs. Hopkins. Here's your text for this afternoon."

She took it. "I have heard this is quite good."

"I bought it in Cheyenne. Mark Twain always makes me smile. I doubt it will have the same effect on a lady who is sad, but we shall see."

The bugler blew fatigue call as they crossed the parade ground and walked by the construction.

"It's the new guardhouse," he commented, taking her arm and walking her around a pile of lumber. He pointed to a footbridge over the frozen Laramie River. "Can you swim? I'm joking. Over there is Suds Row, called so because of the laundresses. Noncommissioned officers and their families live here, too. This is where Private Benedict's pupils come from, and this is Sergeant Rattigan's quarters." He opened a neat little gate.

"I don't know if I can help," she said, hanging back.

He pushed against the small of her back and moved her forward. "You can. She needs female company."

"Do you bully everyone like this?" Susanna demanded.

"Yes. I always get my way," he replied, a smile lurking around his lips.

He knocked and walked in. "I'm glad you're sitting up, Maeve," he said to a blanketed figure in an armchair, her feet propped on an ottoman. "Meet Mrs. Hopkins. She'll be teaching the officers' children starting Monday, and I've asked her to keep you company until your man returns. Mrs. Hopkins, this is Maeve Rattigan, just about my favorite person, because she makes me soda bread and peppermint tea."

Susanna held out her hand. Maeve's hand was cold, so Susanna did not release it, but put her other hand around it and sat on the edge of the sofa.

"I had…we had…a bad night," Maeve said, not withdrawing her hand. She glanced at the post surgeon. "Did he tell you?"

"He did, and I'm so sorry," Susanna replied simply. "May we ask the major to bring us peppermint tea?"

"Aye," she said. "He doesn't mind a little step and fetch."

Her brogue was so charming that Susanna had to smile. "Do you know, I have only been here a few days, and I am rather smitten with the Irish accents I have heard. Thank you, Major. How prompt you are! Just set the cups on that little table. I need to take off my coat."

She released Maeve's hand and let Major Randolph help her with her coat. He hung it on a peg and returned to the lean-to kitchen. The house appeared to have two more rooms, and that was all. She looked around appreciatively. Everything was spotless.

She took Maeve's hand again, pleased to feel more warmth. Major Randolph returned with something wrapped in a blanket. He lifted the blanket covering Maeve's legs and pulled out a similar package. "Iron pigs," he told Susanna. "I'll leave the cool one in the oven and you can exchange it for this hot one, when it cools. Keep your feet warm, Maeve."

He patted the blanket back in place and smiled at his patient. "Lean forward, my dear Maeve," he told her, pulling out a thinner pad. "I'll put this one back in the oven, too." He returned to the kitchen, coming back with another blanket, which he put in place when Maeve winced and leaned forward again. "I'm not sure of the science behind a warm blanket on the back, but it feels good," he told them. "You can trade it off, Mrs. Hopkins."

He straightened up, took a professional look at Maeve Rattigan, then kissed her cheek. "Don't tell the sergeant," he said with a wink. Nodding to them both, he let himself out quietly.

Maeve shook her head. "I honestly think he feels worse about this...." She stopped and dissolved in tears, as though she had been holding them back until there were only women in the house.

Susanna gulped, then hesitated no longer than the major had. Quickly, she plucked a chair from the dining table and sat as close to Maeve Rattigan as she could. She leaned forward to hold her in her arms as the sergeant's wife sobbed every tear in the universe. Tears came to Susanna's eyes and she cried, too, both of them denied motherhood, one by cruelty and the other by biology.

They cried until there were no more tears. Her arms were still tight around Maeve Rattigan, and Susanna knew the warmth was gone from the blanket at the woman's back. "Lean forward," she said. "I'll make it warm again."

She did, returning with the oven-warmed blanket. She slipped it in place, and Maeve leaned back gratefully. Her eyes were raw and swollen with weeping, but her face was calm now.

"May I read to you?" Susanna asked. "Major Randolph has a brand-new book here." She opened it. "I do like Mark Twain. Do you?"

No answer. Maeve just looked at her with the same expression in her eyes as when she had looked at Major Randolph, as though there was something she could actually do that would end the pain. Susanna touched her hand. "It's called *Sketches New and Old.* Let's see now. Ah. 'My Watch.' Maeve, dear, would you mind if I take off my shoes and put my feet by that pig, too?"

Maeve smiled and shifted slightly so there was room. "It's still warm. 'My Watch,' you say?"

Susanna made herself comfortable. She cleared her throat and began. "'My beautiful new watch had run eighteen months without losing or gaining, and without breaking any part of its machinery or stopping. I had come to believe it infallible in its judgments....'"

She looked at Maeve, already asleep, and closed the book. "You dear lady," she whispered.

Chapter Eight

When Maeve woke up an hour later, Susanna made her comfortable, with no embarrassment. When she finished, Susanna sat beside her and took her hands.

"Johnny helps me, but it pains him," Maeve said simply. "Major Randolph, too, I think."

Susanna nodded. She opened the book to "My Watch," and continued reading through the afternoon. Maeve dozed, then woke for the story, which was starting to make her smile, then dozed again. She laughed out loud with "…I brained him on the spot, and had him buried at my own expense," and gave a satisfied sigh when Susanna closed the book.

"I can leave it here so you can finish it on your own," she said, looking at the clock.

There was no overlooking the color that bloomed suddenly in Maeve's pale cheeks. "I can't read," she said softly.

I think I have my work cut out for me at Fort Laramie, Susanna thought, gratified. "Would you like to learn?"

"Aye," came Maeve's equally quiet reply. "Will you have time?"

"I can teach you at night." *And keep myself out of Emmy's unwelcome parlor,* she added to herself. "Private Benedict told me about night classes for the enlisted men."

"Johnny doesn't want me there."

Susanna sat back, her finger still in the book. "Might there be other ladies who would like to learn in a separate class?"

"There might be." Maeve turned her head toward the door, her face alert. "Here comes my Johnny."

Susanna didn't hear anything, but she wasn't married to Johnny Rattigan, and from the soft look on Maeve's face, in love with him. "I should leave," she said.

"Not yet, please. Meet him."

The door opened to reveal a handsome man with worry on his face. His eyes brightened to see Maeve, but the worry was still there. Major Randolph was right behind him. The two tall men seemed to fill the sitting room, the modest allotment of a sergeant in the U.S. Army. They brought with them a rush of cold air, and the winter Susanna had forgotten about for a few hours with Maeve Rattigan, struggling with sorrow, and Mark Twain, who had made them both laugh.

The sergeant knelt by his wife's chair. Susanna felt the tears start in her eyes when Maeve pulled him tenderly toward her and kissed his head. Susanna glanced at the major, who was looking at her. She had already decided the post surgeon wasn't a man well versed in hiding his emotions. He seemed to be telling her, *Look, some marriages are lovely.*

Major Randolph introduced her to the sergeant, who was feeling the warming pad behind his wife's back now. He took out the pad and went to the kitchen. He had obviously done this small thing for his wife many times, which made Susanna swallow and wonder why she had ever thought for the smallest moment that hers were the worst troubles in the universe.

At his wife's whispered words, the sergeant put the newly warmed pad on her abdomen this time. Susanna knew he must be a man used to command, but his voice was calm and quiet. "I greatly appreciate your kindness," he told her, his accent as charming as Maeve's.

"Glad to help," she said. Were all sergeants so handsome? "If you're busy tomorrow, I will happily return." She touched Maeve's blanketed foot with her hand. "We have more stories to read."

"I *am* busy tomorrow," he said. "The army doesn't stop for family difficulties."

"Then are we agreed?" Susanna asked. She looked at the sergeant, feeling decisive for the first time in months. "What time do you have breakfast here?"

"Around six, I suppose, eh, Maeve?"

"If the post surgeon can locate us some eggs, I'll make an omelet. I know he has cheese and it's not very good, but…"

"That's army issue," the major interrupted. "Likely found in the dark corner of a warehouse sometime after Appomattox, reboxed and christened Aged Cheddar. I have eggs."

"Major, they're so dear," Maeve said in protest.

"Not as dear as you, Mrs. Rattigan," he told her cheerfully. "Come, Mrs. Hopkins. I want you to meet some of your Monday-morning pupils. Good day to you both." The post surgeon put the back of his hand against Maeve's cheek. "If you feel so much as a twinge, send the sergeant on the double. He knows where I live."

The Rattigans looked at each other and smiled, but only an idiot could not have seen the sorrow, too. They knew only too well where Major Randolph lived.

Outside, Susanna took a welcome lungful of winter, then shivered against the January cold. She stopped in surprise on the Rattigans' postage-stamp porch when the post surgeon pulled her muffler tighter around her neck.

"Mrs. Hopkins, if you won't button that top button on your coat, you'll have to do better with your muffler."

She was silent as he arranged her muffler to suit himself, not fooled at all.

"How do they bear it?" she asked, when he offered his arm and she took it with no hesitation. The walk was icy.

"I don't know. There aren't two people in this whole garrison who love each other as much as Maeve and John Rattigan, and she cannot give him what they both want so much. When they make love, it only leads to sorrow. I'm sorry for my plain speaking."

"It only leads to blood in a bucket. I can speak as plain as you," she finished. "How tragic." She stopped before the footbridge. Children returning from Private Benedict's school were running across the icy planks. "Did you take me here today to remind me that it's time I quit feeling sorry for myself?"

"No, but if that's a byproduct…" He took her arm again when the children were across the bridge. "I took you because the last thing Maeve needed to see was another sergeant's wife towing her own children over, to sit and commiserate, which I swear the Irish do better than anyone. You watch— she'll be fine in a few days. But right now, a reminder of children isn't good. What did you learn today?"

"That I like to prop my feet up on a warm pig, too, and maybe I could teach some ladies to read. Can you really find eggs?"

"Bam, can you change a subject," he joked. "I have a small pig in the hospital which I will gladly loan you for cold nights, and yes, I have an egg source, officially listed in my supplies as medicinal. As for teaching ladies to read, bravo."

He was quiet then as they strolled along. She could tell how tired he was. "When did you last sleep, Major?" she asked.

"Two days ago, I think."

"I can meet my students tomorrow afternoon," she offered.

"Tomorrow there will be some other crisis," he told her, pointing to the adobe house on the end of Officers Row. "Let's begin here."

"There really isn't any point in arguing with you, is there?"

"None whatever."

It was dark by the time they finished the visits. It amused her to see eagerness on some faces and discontent on others, who probably saw her as a spoilsport ruining their idyllic existence.

"*I* would be upset if Mrs. Hopkins showed up, ready to confine me to a classroom, when there is a fort full of swearing men, tales of scalps being lifted, and the promise of riding with Papa on campaign," she told him as they neared the last house.

"There will be Nick Martin in the back row with his gallows smile," the major said. "A daunting prospect." He stopped then. "Speaking of daunting prospects, here we are at Chez Dunklin. I saved the worst for last."

Susanna felt her heart thump harder. "I hope Mrs. Dunklin takes no interest in Shippensburg gossip."

"We'll know soon."

The Dunklin quarters were overheated like all the others, but with heavy, dark furniture. Obviously not for the Dunklins were packing crate settees, which Susanna found charming, or light folding chairs, easy to move to the next garrison. The Dunklins seemed to be doing their best to bring Pennsylvania to the West.

To her relief, Captain Dunklin dominated the conversation in his own parlor, as he had attempted in the ambulance from Cheyenne. He complained of headache, which Major Randolph assured him was the principal symptom of erobitis.

"It will run its course by tomorrow afternoon," the post surgeon said with a straight face. "Here is your scholar. Bobby Dunklin, Mrs. Hopkins has so much to teach you."

Bobby scowled. Susanna decided to seat Nick Martin directly behind him, starting Monday. She glanced at Mrs.

Dunklin, aware that Bobby must have inherited his scowl from her. Goose bumps marched in ranks down Susanna's back as she chattered to an unwilling Bobby about school. "I'd rather ride my horse," he said.

"Just think, Bobby," Susanna said "While you're waiting for spring, you can learn a few things."

She felt Mrs. Dunklin's eyes boring into her back. *Can we leave?* she pleaded silently to the post surgeon, wishing Major Randolph was susceptible to thought waves.

As the post surgeon started eyeing the door himself, Mrs. Dunklin stood up suddenly. "We're so pleased you are here to lead our children into knowledge," the woman said, sounding every bit as pompous as her husband. Then she frowned. "It's going to drive me distracted until I remember why your name sticks in my mind, Mrs. Hopkins. I'll figure it out."

"Is it too much to hope that Captain Dunklin be transferred before Monday morning?" Susanna asked as they walked toward the Reeses' quarters.

He said good-night on the porch. "If you're serious about an omelet at the Rattigans' tomorrow morning, I'll stop by at five-thirty to escort you. With eggs, of course."

She laughed softly. "Major, I never joke about omelets, or the weightier matters of our society. I'll be ready." She relished the sound of his own quiet laughter as he tipped his hat to her and continued on down the row.

Susanna was ready at five-thirty, waiting for the post surgeon's knock on the door.

When it came, she opened the door to Nick Martin, who held out a note to her. "'Nick's your escort this morning,'" she read, after ushering him inside out of the snow. "'I am doing my best to keep Lieutenant Bevins calm while his wife, a real trouper, labors on. Enjoy the eggs. Joe.'"

They crossed the parade ground quickly because the soldiers were assembling there, some of them still rubbing sleep from their eyes and yawning.

"What now?" she asked her escort.

"The corporal calls the roll, and then they go to breakfast," Nick said. "There's Sergeant Rattigan."

She followed Nick's pointing finger, the egg basket rocking on his arm, to see Maeve's husband, standing ramrod-straight for his corporal to finish the roll. Too bad the army didn't take into account that maybe Maeve needed Johnny more than some forty sleepy soldiers did.

Since Maeve's husband was on the parade ground, Susanna hesitated before knocking on the Rattigans' front door. It seemed a shame to make Maeve get up from her bed. She tapped lightly, and the sergeant's wife opened the door.

She could tell Maeve was better. With a smile, the woman opened the door wider. Nick tried to hand the eggs over the threshold and back away, but Maeve stopped him.

"Nick, since the major is busy, who will eat his portion of the omelet?" she asked. "Omelets don't keep well."

Nick handed the egg basket to Maeve, but came no closer than the porch. "I can wait out here," he mumbled.

"No, you won't," Maeve told him, her voice firm. Susanna decided she wasn't a sergeant's wife for nothing. "It's too cold." When he still didn't budge, her eyes grew thoughtful. "Saint Paul, how will you even keep up your strength for another missionary journey, without an omelet?"

"I do believe you are right," he replied, and came indoors.

By now, Maeve was leaning on the chair Susanna had left yesterday beside the armchair. Susanna took her arm. "Saint Paul, if you could bring that smaller chair into the kitchen, Maeve can sit down while I cook."

He did as she said. "I will bring in wood."

Maeve sat down thankfully. "I thought I could do this."

"I can help," Susanna said, taking off her overcoat and putting on the apron hanging on a nail by the dry sink. "Major Randolph is delivering…" She stopped, unwilling to remind Maeve Rattigan that other women had babies at Fort Laramie.

Maeve put her hand on Susanna's arm. "Mrs. Hopkins, life doesn't stop because of my misfortune," she said quietly. "I know he's delivering the Bevinses' baby."

"You're right," Susanna said, struck by her words. It was true that life hadn't stopped for her, either. Maybe she could learn something, if she chose to.

"I doubt it's any harder than your own situation, widowed at a young age."

I don't want to continue that lie, but what can I do? Susanna asked herself.

By the time the omelet was ready for the skillet, Nick had brought in more wood, and Sergeant Rattigan was stamping snow off his boots on the front porch. Susanna glanced at Maeve, charmed at her sudden animation. *I want to love like that someday,* she thought.

"Saint Paul, you're mighty handy," she said, as Nick put the wood by the stove.

The sergeant helped Maeve back to the big chair. He covered her with a blanket, kissed her forehead and then opened the oven door for another warm blanket.

"I'm staying here today, Sergeant," Susanna said.

"Thank you. I appreciate it."

"I don't mind at all," she replied, turning the omelet carefully and holding her breath until it was cooking, whole, on its other side.

"Very well." He put the warm blanket against Maeve's back, then returned to the kitchen. The sergeant glanced toward the parlor. "Maeve tells me you are interested in teaching some of the wives to read."

"I am." Susanna gestured to Nick, standing in the corner,

to hold out the platter. "I'll see how that works in with my other duties, and then we'll begin."

Nick may have objected to sitting at the table when Susanna asked, but Sergeant Rattigan was made of sterner stuff, apparently. One leveling glance and Nick sat down, hands folded in his lap like a well-behaved child.

Toast and tea completed the meal. Susanna ate as little as she could, hoping that would leave more for Maeve. She noticed Sergeant Rattigan was doing the same thing; they smiled at each other like conspirators as Maeve ate a large helping, then closed her eyes in satisfaction.

"'Tis rare to have an egg," she said, her eyes still closed, but a smile on her face.

"The major gave us a dozen," Susanna said, which made Maeve open her eyes in amazement. "I saved three. I intend to make a cake this morning."

"Imagine that, Johnny," Maeve said.

Susanna could barely suppress her delight at something so simple as a cake earning a response almost reverent. "If you have some dried apples, I can make an applesauce cake. Maybe you and Maeve could have a party tonight. You know, invite some friends over."

"I believe we could," the sergeant replied. "Would you be up to that, Maeve?"

"Aye, Johnny. I'd like a party."

Maeve dozed then, her face calm, as Nick helped Susanna with the dishes. The sergeant sat by his wife, doing nothing more than watching her and touching her hand when she stirred. The cake was ready for the oven when he stood up quietly and came into the kitchen.

The sergeant nodded to Nick. "It's time we left these ladies to their own devices," he whispered. "There's guard mount, and I imagine the hospital steward could use your help, uh…"

"Saint Paul," Nick said with dignity.

"Saint Paul." He put on his overcoat, kindly waiting for Nick to remember where he was and put on his own coat. "You're doing a fine thing, Mrs. Hopkins," the sergeant said. "I am in your debt."

"No debt," she said, shy again. "I'll take good care of her."

His eyes filled with sudden tears, but he made no comment as he released her hand and left with Saint Paul. Susanna sat a long moment in the kitchen, grateful for quiet as Maeve Rattigan healed, and she felt her own heart at peace.

There wasn't anything more grand than a frugal sprinkle of sugar for the top of the loaf cake, but Maeve clapped her hands when Susanna set the cooling cake by the front room's only window. It did look festive on the little table.

"I would serve it with tea," Susanna told her. A quick look in Maeve Rattigan's lean-to had revealed nothing grander. Army rations weren't designed for even modest card parties.

"Tea it will be," Maeve said. "Sit here now, if you please, Mrs. Hopkins. Could you read me another story?"

They resumed their association with Mark Twain and the "Jumping Frog of Calaveras County" this time, Maeve listening, then dozing, then listening again until the story was done. Sergeant Rattigan came by once before recall from fatigue, doing nothing more than looking at his sleeping wife, and nodding to Susanna, gratitude in his eyes.

After he left, Susanna put the cool blanket in the oven to warm until her uncomplaining patient woke. She heard a small knock and Major Randolph came inside. She put a finger to her lips, and he nodded.

He sat down beside Susanna, watching his sleeping patient as her husband had, his look both professional and fond. He got up quietly and tiptoed into the kitchen lean-to, gesturing for her to follow.

"All well here?"

Susanna nodded. "The omelet was wonderful and I saved enough eggs to make an applesauce cake. The Rattigans are going to have a card party tonight. I hope you approve of a party."

"It's an excellent idea," he told her. "Maeve can preside from her armchair, and her friends will laugh and have a good time."

Susanna couldn't overlook the wistful note in his voice. "Maybe you should do that some night," she suggested.

"I think I would, if I had a hostess as kind as Maeve," he said.

"Oh, I didn't mean to…" She stopped, her face warm.

"Remind me?" He shook his head and took her arm. "Mrs. Hopkins, you're eventually going to discover that life really does go on." He shrugged. "I'm not your good example, but the Rattigans are. A card party? I'll wager that Maeve cheats."

Susanna laughed out loud, then put her hand over her mouth. Her heart turned over when Major Randolph gently removed her hand from her face.

"That's the most spontaneous laugh I've heard yet from you," he said, his eyes merry. "Do it more often, Mrs. Hopkins. That's my prescription for you."

Chapter Nine

It was good advice, and she took it.

The week began well. When she opened the door that Monday morning, the room was already warm, coals glowing in the fireplace. She laughed to see on her desk bedraggled weeds crammed in a brown medicine bottle. There was a note, in a doctor's dubious handwriting: "No roses in January. Rabbit brush will have to do. Good luck!" It was signed, "Major Joe Randolph, M.D., U.S.A., and other letters of the alphabet."

When her pupils came into the classroom, Susanna wasted not a minute organizing them, although it came with an army surprise. Mystified, she watched them align themselves at desks in a way she had not considered. Three of the larger children sat in front, with some smaller ones behind, where they had to crane their necks to see her. Some boys and girls sat together, which also surprised her, remembering classrooms where boys and girls gravitated to opposite sides.

Susanna watched them until it dawned on her. *They have sat themselves in order of their fathers' ranks,* she thought, amazed. *Time to end that.*

She stood up in front of her desk, smiling inside to see

Nick Martin slip in and seat himself at the rear of the room. Some of the boys turned to look at him uneasily.

"Welcome to your classroom," she began. "I want all young children in the front row."

No one moved.

"I want you to move *now,*" Susanna said, putting some force behind her words, but not raising her voice. "Your fathers' ranks do not matter here."

Some students exchanged startled glances, but she had no doubt they would move. She looked every student in the eye until they did.

With help from the older boys, she arranged the younger children's desks to one side of the room and gave them the alphabet to copy. She sat among the older children, listening to them read. By the time the bugler blew mess call, the older students had their afternoon compositions assigned, and the young children were ready for her attention.

When the room emptied out quickly for dinner at home, Nick Martin looked at her with something resembling admiration.

"What is it, Nick?"

"Nothing, Mrs. Hopkins, except maybe you don't really need me, do you?"

She regarded him, sitting there so stolid, but his eyes alert. Susanna handed him the extra slate that she knew he had been eyeing while the little ones were writing on theirs. She pointed to the blackboard, where she had printed the alphabet. "Copy these."

"I'm not too old?"

"No one is too old, Nick." She smiled. "Or is it Saint Paul?"

His eyes didn't waver. "It's Nick. Just Nick."

She left him there in her classroom, carefully copying the alphabet, while she hurried to the Reeses' for lunch. She ate alone in the kitchen, because Emily was upstairs trying to coax Stanley into a nap not of his choosing. Even if her cousin was unsuccessful, Susanna knew she would remain upstairs, avoiding her.

Lunch soon over, Susanna pulled on her coat and hurried across the parade ground and the footbridge to visit Maeve, sure of a warmer welcome. Maeve opened the door, her eyes bright. She tugged Susanna inside, sat her down and brought tea.

Susanna told her of the pupils aligning themselves according to rank, and Maeve nodded. "When we change garrisons, the officers' wives and children travel first in the ambulances, and leave us in the dust behind them."

"It's hardly fair. What about women or children with asthma or other ailments?"

"Too bad for them," Maeve said. "It's the army way. You made their little darlings move back this morning, so you might get a protest."

"Too bad for them," Susanna joked, and they laughed together.

She stayed another five minutes, happy to see the sergeant's wife on her feet. "Maeve, when you feel up to it, ask your friends if they'd like to learn to read and write. There's no reason why we can't use my Old Bedlam classroom at night."

"Some might protest that, too," Maeve said.

"Then I will ask Private Benedict if we can use his classroom in the storehouse," Susanna told her.

She strode back across the parade ground with real purpose, head down against the perpetual Wyoming wind. She mentally rehearsed her afternoon's activities, then just stood still a moment, grateful for this chance to teach again.

No one objected to a composition on their favorite thing about Fort Laramie. She gave them ample time, and turned her attention to her littlest pupils, helping them sound out the letters they had copied that morning.

When she dismissed them after recall from fatigue, the older boys thundered out, while the girls followed more sedately, some stopping to help Susanna get the little pupils into their coats. One girl even whispered, "It's good to have school, Mrs. Hopkins."

"I agree," Susanna whispered back, warmed at the shy admission.

She swept the floor and banked the fire, while Nick Martin continued to sound out the alphabet and write on his slate. When he finished, he put it on her desk and left. She looked at what he had written. "'At, bat, cat,'" she read out loud. "Good for you, Nick."

She thought about him that evening as she sat at the kitchen table and prepared the next day's assignments, which would include recitation of the compositions and a preview of arithmetic. She half hoped Major Randolph would wander by to see how her day had gone, even going so far as to walk into the parlor and peer discreetly out the window, looking for him. Snow was falling and she doubted he would come.

But there was Emily, sitting in her rocking chair and staring at Susanna, while her husband snored on the settee. Susanna had felt her cousin's eyes boring into her back as she stood at the window.

"Yes?" she asked finally, tired of the scrutiny.

Emily couldn't look at her. "Several ladies have remarked about the time you are spending over on Suds Row."

"I suppose they would," Susanna said, her face warm at the criticism over something so minor. "Sergeant Rattigan's wife had a miscarriage and Major Randolph thought she might like to have someone read to her and keep her company."

From the shock on Emily's face, Susanna doubted anyone had ever said the word *miscarriage* aloud to her before.

"Maeve Rattigan just needed a friend, and…and maybe I did, too. Maeve's better now, but I'll have to warn you, I am planning to start a night school to teach some of the sergeants' and corporals' wives to read."

"Won't teaching during the day keep you busy enough?" Emily said.

Susanna wondered at the desperation in her cousin's voice, curious why the fort's wives seemed to think she was worth gossiping over. "I'm an educator. I want to help others."

"I think you shouldn't" was Emily's lame reply.

"It's a kindness to teach people to read and write," Susanna insisted. She left the room, angry, stood in the hallway a moment and decided to go to her classroom.

Her anger dissipated as she lit the lamp and sat at her desk, looking at the empty desks and mentally repeating the name of each student. Even though the room was cold, her contentment returned.

"Penny for your thoughts?"

She looked up, surprised. Major Randolph stood in the door in a buffalo overcoat and leather gloves, his muskrat cap pulled low.

"There's a lot of ignorance to stamp out," she said. Then she clasped her hands together on her desk. "Nick Martin told me he could not read or write, but he had no trouble copying the spelling words. Was he injured when you found him?"

Major Randolph started to shake his head, but stopped. "There was evidence of an old injury on the side of his head."

"I wonder who he really is."

"Welcome to the mystery."

The next day was even better. Shy at first to read aloud, the older students read their compositions about life at Fort Laramie, impressing Susanna with their knowledge of the area and the Indians. The young pupils contributed their mite, which made it easy to move into a discussion of local flora and fauna. Bobby Dunklin showed a real flair for drawing animals on the blackboard.

When they came back from luncheon, the air was charged with excitement that Susanna could almost feel through the floorboards. The little ones could barely sit still.

"What has happened?" she asked. "One at a time," she said with a laugh as every hand went up.

She called on a lieutenant's daughter, who stood up to answer, as Susanna had already taught them. "Mrs. Hopkins, it's the most wonderful thing!" she began, practically dancing. "A supply wagon came through with boxes and barrels from back East. Christmas is finally here!"

The story came out in an excited jumble. Apparently a boxcar had been uncoupled at a Nebraska siding and then forgotten as the snow rose higher. A high wind uncovered it and the boxcar arrived in Cheyenne, where the U. S. Army unpacked it and sent belated presents in large crates to Fort Laramie and Fort Fetterman.

"Tonight everyone will unpack what should have arrived weeks ago?" Susanna asked.

It was simple to turn these good tidings of great joy into a composition, with older children to speculate on what might be in the boxes, and the younger ones to draw possible gifts. She let them out twenty minutes early; to have kept them would have been inhumane, in her mind.

"When you come back tomorrow, be prepared to tell me whether you were right or not," Susanna called after them. She corrected the morning's work, humming to herself. When she finished, it was still early enough to hurry to Private Benedict's classroom in the commissary storehouse.

He was doing what she had just finished, if the stack of slates on his desk was any indication. He looked up, his smile genuine.

"I sent mine home early, too," he told her. "Who can think about adding and subtracting when there is greater game afoot?" He sighed. "You never know about the army. One day it's a ten-year supply of raisins or foot wash, and another it's Christmas presents only a month late."

"I sent my students home early after they wrote a quick composition on what they are hoping to receive, with the challenge to share it, in writing again, in the morning," Susanna told him.

He nodded. "I did something similar, but don't quite know what to do with the young ones who don't read or write."

"They can draw. Tomorrow, while the older ones are writing their compositions, you sit with your little ones and put together one composition, with all of them contributing something to the writing."

"I should have thought of that," he replied, shaking his head.

"You'll learn."

She stayed in the storehouse a few minutes more, but the private was obviously eager to return to his own quarters and see what might wait for him there. She knew there was nothing coming for her, so she walked up the hill to the hospital, where Major Randolph stood in his office, reaching deep into a crate filled with wood shavings. As she watched, he pulled out a black box.

"From your relatives?" she asked.

"Oh, no. They disowned me after I decided to stay with the Union," he reminded her. "I bought myself a present."

He set the box down carefully on his desk and unhooked the latches. He lifted up the sides to reveal a microscope. Susanna gasped and clapped her hands.

"Would you even consider letting me bring my older students up here to look through the microscope at something disgusting?"

He laughed out loud. "With pleasure. I'll find a pair of my old socks. Maybe what I had for breakfast."

"I was thinking more of water from the Laramie River when the ice breaks," she said.

"Killjoy."

He looked in the eyepiece and promptly forgot she was there. Susanna left the hospital and started down the hill, pleased that the wind wasn't blowing so hard, and wondering what compositions she would get tomorrow about overdue Christmas presents.

She was planning the rest of the week's lessons in her mind and nearly overlooked Nick Martin, trudging up the hill. He looked so cold that her heart went out to him. She touched his arm as he passed her.

"You need to be indoors," she said.

"That's where I'm going," he replied with considerable dignity. "Major Randolph tells me to clean out the ashes in your classroom and sweep the floor."

"I wondered who my benefactor was," she told him, pleased to see him smile.

He shivered and she waved him on, wondering how his mind worked. She stood still a moment after he passed, thinking of Maeve Rattigan with her own sorrows, and the cheerful Katie O'Leary, inured to snubs from other officers' wives. *Everyone bends and we try not to break,* she told herself, looking back at the hospital and thinking about Major Randolph and the heartbreak of his life.

"I suppose no one is immune to misfortune," she told the wind as she hurried down the hill and into the Reeses' quarters, where Stanley was riding a new hobbyhorse, and her cousin was looking through a stereopticon, her mouth open with the wonder of it. Susanna smiled to think that in homes all over the garrison, Christmas had finally arrived.

* * *

Every student had a story to tell the next morning. Susanna set aside her routine and gave everyone an opportunity to describe new dolls with eyes that blinked, and a wind-up train with enough track to stretch from the front hall to the kitchen in a standard four-room quarters.

She wanted to compliment the Dunklins' son on his excellent drawings of yesterday, but he was not present. She remarked about that to Emily over luncheon on new china— only three pieces arrived broken—that Captain Reese had ordered for his wife.

"That reminds me," Emily said. "Mrs. Dunklin has invited you to a meeting at her quarters tonight." She found the invitation, and held it out to Susanna. "She wants the parents to have a chance to meet you. Isn't that kind? I don't think the Dunklins have ever given even a card party before, and now this."

"But their boy must be ill, so I wonder why she would do that," Susanna said. She glanced at the clock. "You're not invited?"

"No." There was no denying the relief in Emily's eyes, which made Susanna wonder even more. "It's only the parents of students." Her cousin frowned. "Does she mean to invite you to a house filled with contagion?"

"I doubt the matter is quite that drastic," Susanna said. "Still…"

She thought about it when her older pupils were preparing their afternoon recitations and her little ones were attempting the alphabet without benefit of any help from the blackboard this time. Her mind was no easier when Major Randolph stopped by the schoolroom after her students had filed out, to invite her to accept his escort to the Dunklins' that evening.

After spending an inordinate amount of time trying to decide between green wool and black bombazine, Susanna settled on the black, which struck her as more sober and teacherly. In one of his better moments, Frederick had remarked how nice she looked in black, with the contrast of her blond hair. Perhaps Major Randolph would feel the same way.

He did, apparently, if the look in his eyes when she opened the door to his knock was any indication.

"Mighty fine, Mrs. Hopkins," he said.

Susanna blushed like a schoolgirl, and turned the conversation, remembering the microscope. "Have you made any earth-shattering discoveries with your microscope, Major?" she asked.

"No. A few years ago, I read a paper in a French journal about Louis Pasteur's theory of germ disease. I thought a microscope of my own was in order, after that."

"Why should that embarrass you?" she asked, curious because he seemed suddenly shy.

"I'll share my little secret. I want to study germ theory in Paris with Louis Pasteur."

"How did that come about?" Susanna asked, curious.

"My interest was always there. I was a long way through medical school before I admitted to myself that my favorite classes were the ones using microscopes, pond water and mold."

"But you're a good doctor of…of people."

He bowed elaborately, which made Susanna smile. "Thank you! It's theory that intrigues me the most, however."

"Why didn't you take that road instead of the practice of medicine?"

"A sensible question. After the Confederacy fired upon Fort Sumter, no one needed theory. I finished my last year of medical school in six months—we all did—and went into the army."

"I think you should go to Paris," she said, as he helped her into her coat. "Perhaps someone in the medical department would send you there, courtesy of the U.S. Army."

He shook his head. "Such plum assignments require patronage in Washington, something a son of Virginia has not. I would have to do it on my own dime."

"Well? What is stopping you?"

He seemed in no hurry to reach the Dunklins' quarters. He stopped, obviously contemplating her question.

"I suppose nothing is stopping me. I have enough funds. Maybe when this summer's Indian campaigns are over."

"Only don't do it until my teaching term is up, Major," she said impulsively, then felt her face grow warm again. "I mean, I think you are my only ally."

He patted her hand and started them in motion again. "You have several allies, but we could not consider the Rattigans or the O'Learys as possessed of patronage, either, could we?" He stopped again. "What *are* the Dunklins up to? I own to some uneasiness. You already know your students' parents. I saw to that."

"I'm uneasy, too," she agreed quietly, and told him that Bobby Dunklin was home from school today, and the Dunklins had chosen to give a party, anyway.

"Let's not take one more step toward the Dunklins'. In fact, I…"

He stopped, because Captain Dunklin opened the door, gesturing them inside. She saw through the front window that the parlor was full of people.

"No," she whispered, suddenly fearful. But there was Captain Dunklin, waiting.

"I'll stay close to you," Major Randolph promised. "What could have changed since yesterday, when you were everyone's favorite teacher?"

Chapter Ten

Captain Dunklin took their coats and walked away with them, leaving Susanna looking at his retreating back wistfully. Every instinct told her to run, but the last time she had done that had led to total ruin. She tried to swallow, but her throat was dry. The parlor door opened and there was Mrs. Dunklin, her smile as insincere as her husband's.

"Mrs. Hopkins, we've been waiting for you. Major? How nice to see you."

Terrified, Susanna looked around the parlor. Only the parents of her students were there, wearing expressions ranging from curiosity to hostility. Her bowels felt suddenly liquid, so she took several deep breaths.

Mrs. Dunklin just waited until her husband returned from hiding their coats somewhere. Susanna glanced at his bland face and swallowed again. She waited for him to speak—it was his house, after all—but he only gestured to his wife, who cleared her throat and picked up a crumpled newspaper. Everyone seated themselves and Susanna looked around for a chair before she fell down. There were none. She and the major were left to stand there.

"Do you have a chair, Mrs. Dunklin?" Major Randolph asked.

"No chairs. She won't be here long."

"Then we're leaving," Joe said.

Susanna shook her head. "Get on with it, Mrs. Dunklin."

Silence. Mrs. Dunklin looked around, a smirk on her face. "I had been racking my brain to remember why your name was familiar, but couldn't come up with anything. Then when our Christmas box arrived, I found this balled up in the newspapers used as packing material. Take it."

She thrust it at Susanna. The newspaper rattled in her hand, so Major Randolph took it from her.

"You read it then, Major," Mrs. Dunklin said, "if Mrs. Hopkins is too much of a coward."

The look he gave Mrs. Dunklin could have cut through lead. The woman stepped back involuntarily.

He read it. Susanna watched the blood drain from his face and then surge back. He handed it back to Mrs. Dunklin.

"You are sorely in need of honest facts, Mrs. Dunklin, before you do something that might ruin a life."

"I know what I know!" the woman snapped. She glared at Susanna. "You came to us pretending to be a war widow."

"I didn't," Susanna said, wishing her voice was strong right now, like Major Randolph's. "Someone else started that story and—"

"Liar!"

"I don't lie," Susanna said. She wanted to back up against the post surgeon, but knew that would give this vicious woman ammunition for other charges.

Mrs. Dunklin thrust the newspaper at Susanna. "To think we trusted our children to a woman who abandoned her own child!"

The room was absolutely silent. Susanna forced herself to look at the faces staring at her. In this closed society, she would see these faces again and again until she figured out some way to escape Fort Laramie. She was trapped with people she could not escape.

Mrs. Dunklin snatched the paper back. "It's all here, how you abandoned your child, and your poor husband was forced to sue you for divorce! And then you come here, playing on our sympathies by posing as a war widow. For shame!"

Susanna forced herself to look around the room again, knowing she was looking at officers who had fought in the Civil War and seen their friends on both sides of the conflict die in battle. She expected no sympathy and saw none.

"That rumor was started right here by one of your own," Major Randolph said.

Mrs. Dunklin turned her vitriol on the post surgeon. "And who could ever trust a word out of your mouth, you son of—"

A lady gasped.

"—Virginia," Mrs. Dunklin concluded. "I know General Crook doesn't trust you. Why should we?"

"Please don't excoriate Major Randolph because he's from Virginia," Susanna said, stung by the unfairness of it. "He's not your target. I am." She took a deep breath. "Yes, I fled my home, but only because my former husband, quite drunk, pushed my face into the mantel and I was bleeding. When I tried to get back in, he wouldn't let me—"

"That's not what the paper says," Mrs. Dunklin interrupted.

"No, it isn't." Susanna felt her courage peeking out again from a dark place where it had hidden, even though she couldn't stop shaking. "It also doesn't say how Frederick Hopkins bought up all the lawyers in Shippensburg, Gettysburg and even Boiling Springs, so no one would represent me. It doesn't say that, does it? The editor of the Shippensburg *Sentinel* is a drinking friend of my former husband."

"You're being ridiculous. Such a thing wouldn't happen

in Pennsylvania," Captain Dunklin said, sounding more self-righteous than fifty saints.

"It happened to me."

"Mrs. Hopkins, say no more," Major Randolph said. "It won't make any difference."

She knew he was right, but she knew this was her only opportunity to speak. "I know," she told him. "My side deserves a hearing, even if none of you listen." Little spots of light started dancing around her eyes, and she blinked to stop them. "Whether you believe me or not, and I fear you do not, I had the choice between being beaten to death that night or running away to find medical help. I don't see well out of my left eye, because there is only so much doctors can do."

She didn't bother to look for sympathy. "All I wanted to do here was teach," she said simply. "I'm an educator and—"

"Not anymore," Mrs. Dunklin said, producing another piece of paper. "This letter states that none of our children will attend school until we have a new teacher, and it has been signed by everyone here present."

Major Randolph stepped between Susanna and Mrs. Dunklin. "That's enough," he said.

"This is wrong."

It was a quiet voice, a lilting Irish voice, and Susanna looked around to see Captain O'Leary on his feet.

"Thank you," she said simply.

"Rooney will still be in your classroom tomorrow, Mrs Hopkins."

"Then I will be there, too," Susanna said, finally teasing courage out of its hiding place and holding her head higher.

"He'll be alone!" Mrs. Dunklin said.

Captain O'Leary shrugged and headed for the door. "All the better to get the total attention of one good teacher, eh?"

"When the rest of us withdraw our support for this creature, will you pay her entire salary?"

"I can't afford that, and you know it. Rooney will go to the enlisted men's school then." He smiled at the gasps in the room. "Should have done that last year. Mrs. Hopkins, come visit Katie anytime you want."

He left the room without a word to his hosts.

"Mrs. Hopkins, what do you say we follow? Witch hunts scare me," Major Randolph said. "Captain, our coats, please?"

The sparkles were back around her eyes. She shook her head to clear them this time, which made her lose her balance and stagger. The post surgeon steadied her.

The room was starting to revolve. Susanna took another deep breath, which ended in a ragged note. She turned to her hostess.

"Mrs. Dunklin, whether you believe me or a slanted newspaper article is your choice. I can tell you it was death or divorce." She kept her voice low, deriving her only mite of satisfaction from watching the others lean forward to hear. "I chose divorce because I wanted to live, but you'll be pleased to know that I chose death, too. Every morning when I wake up, I die when I remember that my son is not with me and never will be."

She stood there, silent, wondering if Captain Dunklin had taken their coats to the opposite end of the parade ground. *Breathe in and out,* she ordered her body.

After what felt like years, Captain Dunklin returned with the coats. In absolute silence, Major Randolph guided her arm into each sleeve, since she could barely move. He pulled on his own coat and took a firm grip on her, coaxing her into motion in that forthright way he probably used to get patients ambulatory.

She didn't think she could manage the steps, but she did. She got as far as the board sidewalk. For the first time in her life, she fainted.

She returned to consciousness almost at once, embarrassed

and terrified to be lying in the snow at the foot of the Dunklins' porch. Major Randolph had gathered a handful of snow and placed it on her forehead, which did the duty of smelling salts. And there was Nick Martin, helping her to her feet.

"Can you walk, Susanna?" Joe Randolph asked.

"I think so. It's not so far," she said, embarrassed. "Forgive me."

"Don't apologize for something you cannot control," he said promptly. "Forgive me for not taking you out of that den of vipers immediately."

"As you say, it hardly matters," Susanna reminded him. "If it hadn't been tonight, it would have been tomorrow." She sobbed out loud, and put her hand to her mouth. "I swore I had cried my last tear over this!"

Without a word he clapped his arm around her shoulders and pulled her close as they walked along, him holding her up more than she was standing. He seemed so furious she was almost afraid to look at him. When she did glance his way, she saw all the anger in his face, and knew it couldn't be just for this alone.

She stopped walking, and he was forced to stop, too. Gently, she disengaged from him.

"I was wrong to think I could escape this."

"Now you're going to blame yourself?" he exclaimed.

She shrugged out of his grasp and continued on by herself. She looked back at him standing there, puffs of winter steam coming from his nostrils. He was angry, but she knew in her bruised heart it wasn't at her.

"Will it ever warm up here?" she asked in a normal tone of voice. She went into the Reeses' house and closed the door behind her, wanting to lock it and never allow anyone in again, except it wasn't her house, and the enemy was here, too.

Standing right in front of her, in fact. Susanna regarded her cousin's white face.

There was so much she could have said then, none of it pretty. Suddenly Susanna was more weary than she been in months, tired of accusing faces and dead ends that brought her no closer to her son and toward no path leading back to respectability. Frederick had seen to that. If there was a greater evil than alcohol, she had no idea what it could be. All these thoughts went through her tired mind as she started up the stairs to her space behind an army blanket, the only refuge left to her in the world.

"Did you tell them I started that little untruth?" Emily asked as Susanna neared the top of the stairs.

Susanna shook her head, sad that her cousin felt no pity and no concern for her, beyond her own wish not to be part of her ruin. Susanna turned around to take a good look at her cousin, and mourned the loss of what could have been a friend. Perhaps Emily had meant well. Someone more intelligent would have understood how terrible a lie like that would appear to veterans of the Civil War, and that person was not Emily Reese.

"No, I did not tell them you started that lie. If I had even a little money I would be out of here tomorrow, to spare you any further embarrassment."

She knew sarcasm was wasted on Emily Reese, who probably thought she was serious. Susanna pulled aside the blanket, then let it fall behind her. She lay down to stare at the ceiling. She thought of how Joe Randolph had questioned her decision to remain silent. Obviously, neither of them had known how bad this would become. *I haven't a brave bone left in my body,* she thought. *I should have said something.*

She lay in perfect stillness until the house grew quiet and everyone in it slept. Because the walls were thin, she couldn't help but hear Katie O'Leary's tears through the wall.

Susanna went down the stairs a step at a time, careful to

make no noise. She didn't bother with her coat; she was only going next door. She knocked and waited.

Captain O'Leary opened the door and pulled her in quickly.

"You'll catch your death out there, Mrs. Hopkins," he told her, and put his arm around her shoulder. "Katie," he called up the stairs.

Her friend came down quickly, gathering Susanna close when her husband released her, and leading her into the parlor.

"What terrible thing is this?" Katie asked, a sodden handkerchief in her hand.

With her own hands so tight that her nails dug into her palms, Susanna told them the whole story of Frederick's descent into drunkenness, his brutality and degrading treatment, and her desperation the night she'd fled from her own home, blinded by her blood.

"He ruined me," she finished simply. "Emily thought to call me a war widow to spare her own embarrassment." She looked at Katie and held out her arms. "Katie! Joe wanted me to tell the truth to Major Townsend, but I was afraid! Am I always going to be afraid?" She started to sob.

Katie held her close, and looked at her husband. "Jim, is there anything we can do?" She kissed Susanna's forehead. "My dear lady, we have no credit here, either, or not much. Jim, please…"

Susanna wiped her eyes when he handed her a dry handkerchief. He looked at her for a long moment.

"I think I will tell Captain Burt tomorrow what you have told me." He managed a ghost of a smile. "He's infantry, but I trust him more than anyone here except Major Randolph."

Susanna shook her head. "He and Mrs. Burt were in that meeting, too! They both signed that letter!"

"I know," he replied, taking her hand. "But he's a reasonable man, is Andy Burt. I may not convince him, but I can plant a seed."

Susanna nodded, unconvinced, but determined not to say so to these kind people. "That will be a start," she said. She stood up and looked at the O'Learys. "I hope you will forgive me for not calling out that lie immediately. I think I have lived in fear so long that I don't know anything else." She touched Katie's shoulder. "I couldn't bear to lose your friendship, although I do not deserve it."

"You have never lost my friendship," Katie said quietly. "Never."

Susanna shook her head when the O'Learys tried to coax her to stay the night in their parlor, and went next door again, letting herself in as quietly as she had left. She climbed the stairs as though she wore lead boots, then lay down to sleep.

She was alone, at liberty to contemplate her ruin in a small society she could not escape until she earned some money to leave it. For the first time in the whole ordeal, she considered the merits of walking out the door and onto the open field behind Officers Row. She could take off her clothes and keep walking until she froze to death, which wouldn't take long. She discarded the idea; with her bad luck, she would likely encounter a sentry who would save her life.

Never mind. The O'Learys had assured her their son would be in the classroom in the morning, so Susanna would be there, too. The whole debacle probably would be over after one more day. Mrs. Dunklin would find a way to end the school.

Susanna lay on her cot, silent, relaxing gradually after she heard the O'Learys in their bedroom through the wall. She had heard them reciting the rosary on other evenings. This night, it was balm to her wounds, not because she had any idea what the Latin words meant, but simply because she knew there were good people through the wall.

She thought of the Rattigans, finding comfort in each other, and then of Private Benedict with his classroom in the commissary warehouse. Her mind lingered longest on Joe Randolph, who shouldered burdens even worse than hers.

As always, she thought finally of Tommy, home asleep in the big house in Carlisle, where life, if never completely pleasant, had been tolerable before Frederick Hopkins decided to fortify himself with alcohol and make his family suffer.

She did what she always did each night, whispering favorite nursery rhymes, then humming songs to Tommy far away. "Be a good son," Susanna whispered, as she always did before closing her eyes.

Joe Randolph couldn't help but feel that his constituents had failed him greatly that night. Not one of them came asking for help with babies due, or croup, or any little or large ailments that often kept him busy in those winter hours when Fort Laramie slept. After four years with Sherman's army, and then Melissa's shocking death, he had grown used to sleepless nights. Here he was, wide awake, and the only person who needed him would never ask.

Joe lay in bed, still dressed and still aghast at the cold-hearted ruin of Susanna Hopkins. The monstrosity of what he had witnessed in the Dunklins' parlor made the bile rise in his throat, until he had to get up and walk it off. Back and forth, from room to room, he tried to wear himself out. Instead, he revisited his own role in the deception, wondering if he should have gone immediately to Major Townsend and spelled out Emily Reese's original lie. He concluded it would have made no difference, once Mrs. Dunklin—damn the woman!—had found a tale to bear and a bone to gnaw on.

Joe concluded that all he could do in the morning was go to Major Townsend after guard mount and lay the whole nasty matter before him.

"What will he do, Joe?" the post surgeon asked himself out loud as he made another circuit of his own parlor. "He will say it is none of his business, that this was a matter between a few families and the educator they contracted. He is right. God, how it galls me!"

Joe walked until his feet began to hurt. He threw himself down into his favorite armchair, relieving his legs—oh, surgeons and their legs—but getting him no closer to sleep than he had been hours ago. Grim, he watched dawn come, relieved to hear reveille finally.

Silent, he shaved and changed his shirt, then made his way up the hill for sick call. He was not inclined to suffer fools gladly that morning, which meant that the malingerers whose creativity he sometimes secretly admired found themselves snapped at and returned to duty almost before they had a chance to recite their ordinarily diverting symptoms.

Guard mount offered none of its minuscule attraction. Since even colder weather had clamped down, the band remained in the music hall and the time-honored ritual of guard relief and guard mount seemed to go in double-quick rhythm, to Joe's tired eyes. Scarcely anyone moved across the parade ground, once the morning business concluded. Joe watched Sergeant Rattigan, in company with his corporals, hurrying toward the footbridge to Suds Row and their own families for breakfast.

A few minutes after the new guard had retired to the guardhouse and the cold soldiers had retreated to their mess halls, Joe saw Nick Martin leave Old Bedlam, where he must have started the usual fire, to warm up the classroom. Hands shoved deep in his pockets, Joe stood at his front window and watched Mrs. Hopkins leave the Reeses' quarters and make her way along the icy sidewalk to Old Bedlam. A few minutes later, both Captain and Katie O'Leary left their quarters, Rooney between them. From habit, Joe regarded Katie professionally, and decided he would be called upon soon enough to usher another army dependent into the world. God bless the O'Learys to give him his favorite army duty.

He stood by the window as the O'Learys returned. Joe noticed Katie's head against her husband's shoulder, his arm around her, consoling her. The sight made him angry all over again, which was probably a better emotion than the grim disgust at meanness that left him so hollow. Maybe it was more. Joe felt a strong urge to console Susanna Hopkins much as Captain O'Leary was consoling his wife.

"But here I stand, a coward," he remarked to no one except himself.

He watched as Jim O'Leary left his quarters and went down the row to Captain Burt's home. He wondered what business Jim had there, and shook his head. The Burts had signed that pernicious letter, too.

Next he watched Mrs. Dunklin leave her quarters and stride with great purpose toward the admin building. Joe sighed to see all that misguided umbrage on the loose. He watched until the woman returned to her quarters, then it was his turn.

The snow squeaked and crunched underfoot, advertising just how low the mercury had retreated. He looked up at the snow dogs overhead, another frigid advertisement to January on the northern plains. January was the month when the Northern Roamers were commanded by Washington to move their families to reservations not far from here in Nebraska. *That will not happen and there will be premeditated war,* Joe thought. *No one will care that a competent teacher has been forced from her classroom by meanness.*

Major Townsend was waiting for him. Joe nodded to him and shut the door behind him. All Townsend did was hand him the letter that Mrs. Dunklin must have carried to him that morning, the one with all the signatures of indignant parents on it, except the O'Learys.

Joe barely glanced at it. "What happened shouldn't have happened, Ed," he said, calling on his years of friendship with the fort's commanding officer to keep this painful discussion informal. "The Dunklins only have half the story, and their half is lies and character assassination."

Edwin Townsend regarded him for a long moment, and Joe felt his heart sink even lower.

"She had no business trying to pass herself off as a war widow."

"Emily Reese started that lie, heaven only knows why," Joe countered.

"Mrs. Hopkins had every opportunity to deny it."

"Did she? I earnestly believe she wanted to spare her cousin embarrassment. Ed, did you ever try to unbake a cake? Bring someone back to life after the autopsy? You can't do it!"

"Sit down, Joe."

The post surgeon sat. He hoped Ed would sit next to him in the empty chair, but the major sat behind his desk instead, choosing command over friendship. Silent, he rummaged through a stock of correspondence on his desk and pulled out one of the twice-folded documents with the government stamp.

"It's already begun. General Crook and Colonel Reynolds will be here in February to lead a winter campaign against the Roamers. I'll need that room at Old Bedlam for temporary quarters, so I probably would have evicted her, anyway."

"Ask General Crook if he'd like to stay with me," Joe said. "I know what it feels like to have lies and character assassination dished my way."

He hadn't meant for his voice to rise. He was going to be calm about this, except he couldn't, not with Susanna Hopkins's stricken face before his, and then the death of hope in her eyes that he understood all too well, because he had a mirror over his bureau.

Major Townsend couldn't look at him. He indicated the Dunklin letter again, which lay between them like a rank specimen in a pathology lab.

"Joe, I have no control over this situation," Townsend said, his voice firm, even if he couldn't look his friend and war comrade in the eyes. He jabbed the paper. "These families contracted with Mrs. Hopkins, and they are at liberty to break the contract, as they have done."

Joe took his time. "I suppose that as this year's administrative council head, you want me to shut her down. She's teaching the O'Learys' boy right now."

"I'm sorry. What can I do?"

Joe contemplated his friend, remembering their shared Civil War fights. "Not much, obviously," he said. He went to the door, wanting to jerk it off its hinges. As he stood there, Joe made up his mind. He looked back at the major, who was watching him now, wary. "I'm resigning my commission, Major Townsend."

"Save your breath. You're turned down, Major Randolph," his commanding officer replied, biting off his own words. "We're at war with the Sioux Nation, as of two weeks ago. You're not allowed to resign."

Joe walked to the hospital, head down. He mishandled paperwork until recall from fatigue, then walked down the hill to discharge his awful duty.

Mrs. Hopkins made it easy for him. As he approached Old Bedlam, she was coming out with Rooney O'Leary, holding his hand. She walked past Joe and took the boy up to his front door, giving him a hug and an affectionate swat on his backside when Katie O'Leary opened the door. Susanna shook her head at what must have been an invitation to come inside, then left the porch to stand by him on the boardwalk.

"Major, I have banked the fire and gathered the books on

the desk," she told him with the steely calm he wished he could have used in Major Townsend's office. "Please return them to the officers' families."

"Susanna, I…"

She only shook her head, and her expression was kind. "Thank you for trying, Major."

"It's Joe," he told her, feeling stupid and lame and impotent.

She shook her head again, her eyes still gentle. "I think not, sir. Friendship with me will not further your own cause. Good day."

She walked past him and up the steps of the Reeses' quarters. Miserable, he watched her as she stood a long moment, her forehead against the door, as though trying to work up her courage to turn the handle.

"Susanna, I know what it feels like to be where you are not wanted," he said distinctly, so she could hear him.

"Perhaps you do, but you're a man and you have the ability to change your situation," she told him as she went inside and closed the door quietly behind her.

"No, I do not," he whispered to the closed door. "I can't leave this place, either."

Chapter Eleven

I will leave that lady alone, Joe told himself for three days. It wasn't difficult, he decided, even though he felt ashamed of his attitude. Maybe if he was not popping in to offer whatever puny commiseration he thought useful, Susanna and her cousin Emily would finally start to talk.

To his gratification, even though it hardly mattered now, Jim O'Leary told him of Susanna's midnight visit and her confession. "She's been too frightened to speak up," O'Leary said.

His voice low, he told Joe what Susanna had said of her husband's mistreatment of her. "She just took it, until she feared for her life," he said, appalled at that kind of brutality.

Jim had told him of his visit to the Burts, where he minced no words, either.

"What was their reaction?" Joe asked.

"Shock. Revulsion. Uncertainty. No one knows what to believe," Jim said. "People have to know, though, even if Susanna is the last one who would ever tell such a sordid story."

It *was* a sordid story, Joe knew, after Jim O'Leary bared that kind woman's shame. He should have gone to her then, but it was easy enough to stay away because duty called, the kind of duty that he could cure with stitches or medicine. Susanna's wounds were different. With something approaching relief, Joe treated a nasty forefinger avulsion in the stables, which would more than likely cause an infection that led to amputation; a trying childbirth on Suds Row; and a more pleasant one just down the row at the O'Leary household, which resulted in a lively little redhead much like Katie O'Leary herself. Then his contract surgeon left unwillingly for detached duty at Camp Robinson, and Captain Hartsuff decided he needed another week in Cheyenne doing God knows what. By the fourth morning after Susanna Hopkins had returned the key to the classroom, Joe began to worry.

He was thinking about it over breakfast—lumpy oatmeal with everlasting raisins—when he heard a timid knock at his side door, the one that dependents used when they needed his services. It was Emily Reese. He didn't feel like looking at her, but Hippocrates overruled him as usual, and he ushered her inside.

"Mrs. Reese, what can I do for you?" He couldn't resist himself then, because he knew his ill-mannered joke would fall on stupid ears. "Did Stanley choke on a bar of soap after too much cussing?"

"Stanley is fine," Emily said. She clutched Joe's arm. "I haven't seen Susanna in five days."

"What?"

He hadn't meant to shout. He took a deep breath. Surely he hadn't heard her correctly. "You share a four-room house. What do you mean?"

She seemed to think *he* was the idiot. "I haven't seen her."

He thought about that before reacting this time, even as he felt a chill down his spine. "You must see her for meals, at least. And everyone has to, well, void, now and then. Surely you've seen her."

Emily shook her head, and he noticed for the first time that her lovely eyes were wide with worry. "I have heard her go downstairs late at night and early in the morning, but she is always behind that blanket, otherwise, and there is never any food missing."

"She's your cousin, Emily," Joe reminded her. "You couldn't just pull back the blanket?"

Emily's eyes filled with tears. "I'm afraid of what I will find now."

Joe didn't bother to grab his overcoat. He ran out of his quarters, his mind intent on what *he* would find. He took the steps two at a time, not even breathing heavily as he yanked back the blanket so hard that it fell from its rod.

Her hair a terrible tangle, and her face pale almost to parchment, Susanna looked back at him, startled. Without a word, she turned on her side and faced the wall. Joe took her gently by the shoulders and turned her around again. When she closed her eyes wearily, he pried them open with his fingers, to reassure himself that they hadn't started to settle back in her eye sockets just yet.

"Go away," she whispered, her voice a croak.

"Not a chance, Susanna," he said, his voice full of command. "Put your arms around my neck."

To her credit, she tried, but she was too weak. He scooped her up anyway, standing still a moment to steady himself. He realized with a pang that she barely weighed anything.

Emily stood at the bottom of the stairs, crying. Joe watched her a moment. She started to twist her hands, as though trying to clean them of something—responsibility, remorse. He didn't know, and he suddenly didn't care.

"Mrs. Reese, you're useless," he snapped as he carried Susanna out the open door.

Joe stopped on the porch, wondering what to do. He couldn't take her to the hospital, because his one small ward was occupied with soldiers. He thought about the Rattigans, and knew she would be welcome there, but he didn't relish carrying her across the parade ground under everyone's pry-ing eyes. There was only one place for her, and the odd humor of the situation took over.

"Susanna, I'm going to ruin your reputation and take you to my quarters," he told her as he hurried along the icy side-walk. "But you have no reputation to ruin, and neither do I. Any objections?"

She had none. In fact, her eyes were closed in exhaustion.

"I thought not."

He set her in his armchair, the old thing that M'liss had threatened not to take along, on their last journey together. Without a word, he covered Susanna with a blanket, felt her forehead and then hurried to his dependents' clinic across the hall.

Susanna offered no protest when he unbuttoned her shirt-waist, pulled aside her chemise and pressed his stethoscope at her heart. Her heartbeat was slow and steady, which reas-sured him. Her pulse was a little too slow to please him, but at least it wasn't thready. He had felt worse.

"Thirsty or hungry?" he asked, his voice gentle. The last thing Susanna Hopkins needed was one more bully in her life.

"Let me die," she said finally.

He shook his head. When he spoke, his words were so cheerful that he even surprised himself. "Sorry. You can't do that on my watch. It's not allowed."

"I am tired of being told what to do."

"I don't doubt that for a minute, but it's too bad. I'll get you some milk. When you finish that, I'll have my warmed-up oatmeal for you."

"You're not listening," she said, clearly irritated.

"I never do when my patients talk twaddle," he assured her. "Susanna, you are going to live and thrive." He leaned closer until his lips brushed her ear. "I'm surprised someone as bright as you never learned that living well is the best revenge."

He left her there, angry at him, and spent enough minutes in the kitchen to produce warmed milk, courtesy of Gale Borden, and some thinned oatmeal, well sugared.

"I'm no cook," he told her when he returned, happy enough to see that she hadn't bolted from his quarters. But where could she go? He handed her the mug of warm milk, holding his breath. He let it out slowly when she drank it down without a pause.

She took the oatmeal from him with no comment, spooning it down. She handed back the empty bowl and shook her head when he offered more. It took her another moment, but she finally looked him in the eyes.

"After two days, I wasn't really hungry." She shook her head sorrowfully. "It was easier not to face anyone." She put her hand on his arm and he felt her tremor. "All I wanted was to start over."

"I know," he said, covering her hand with his own. "You're not asking for the moon. Shall we try again?"

"Not here."

"Yes, here."

He was acutely aware that she was a single woman in a single man's quarters, even though he was a physician. For all he knew, word of what had just happened had spread all over the gossip-prone garrison, where so little happened that even the smallest deviation would be talked about for weeks. This was no small deviation. But, as he had pointed out earlier, she had no reputation to worry about.

He stood up, ready for action, even if it did embarrass her. "I am going to draw a bath for you in my kitchen. You need one. When the water's ready, you'll go in there and bathe. I'll get a change of clothing from the Reeses and leave it here in the parlor."

He glanced at her, happy enough to see spots of red in each cheek, where before she had been almost ghostly white. "While you are doing all this, I'm going to talk to Major Townsend."

"He will not listen," she said quickly.

"He will," he replied, sure of himself. "I left him feeling guilty this morning. My dear, great are the uses of guilt!"

Joe glanced at her again, just in time to see a fleeting smile. "I am going to make Major Townsend let you to teach in Private Benedict's school."

"I won't!"

"You will, if I have to drag you there," he assured her.

"You are as bad as everyone else!" Her voice had some bite to it now.

"I am worse," he said, relieved to hear some fight in her. "I will not waste a perfectly good human life. What would Hippocrates say?"

Joe concluded it wasn't going to be much of a bath, but she was smaller than he was and could fold more of herself into his tin tub. While Susanna glowered in the parlor, her arms folded across her chest, he found a clean towel and washcloth, and his last bar of soap. He draped the towel over a chair in the kitchen and set the soap in a saucer.

Susanna's militant expression had not changed.

"Up you get, madam."

She ignored him. He jerked the blanket from her with one motion and started on her buttons. With a gasp, she pushed away his hands and went into the kitchen, closing the door louder than he usually closed it. A smile on his face, Joe listened outside the door until he heard her step into the tub. Good.

Emily would probably have given him her cousin's entire wardrobe, so great was her own guilt.

"Just a change of clothing," he said. "Take it to my quarters and leave it in the parlor. I have business with Major Townsend." He jabbed his finger at her. "Don't you *dare* utter one word about this to anyone!"

Terrified, Emily shook her head.

Joe couldn't overlook the wary expression on Major Townsend's face when he sat down again in the post commander's office. Calmly, Joe explained precisely what had happened, starting with what Susanna had told the O'Learys and ending with her sitting in a tub in his kitchen. "Mrs. Hopkins tried to starve herself to death, rather than have to face anyone—anyone!—in this garrison."

"I can't change people's minds," Townsend protested, but there was no denying the shock on his face.

"I'm not asking you to change anyone's mind, Ed," Joe assured him. "What I want you to do is authorize Mrs. Hopkins to teach with Private Benedict in the commissary storehouse."

"Joe, you know general funds only cover one teacher for the enlisted men's children, and it's paltry enough. Government regulations."

"I know. *I'm* going to pay her salary. It'll come out of your office every month, and you won't say a word about this to anyone," Joe told him. "Since I cannot resign—something I should have done years ago, by the way—I'll just have to make things better here."

"People will talk."

"Not if you keep this financial arrangement silent," Joe replied. He couldn't help himself; he pounded on the major's desk, feeling the heat of anger on his own face. How many years had he just been existing? "Mrs. Hopkins has lost everything—her dignity as a wife, her child, her home, her respectability. We are going to change that woman's luck."

His commanding officer stared at him. "Why do I have

the feeling that you would do this even if I did not give my permission?"

There was only one reply. "It's the right thing to do. That's all."

Both men looked at each other. Ed Townsend looked away first.

"Very well. What will you pay her?"

"Twenty dollars a month," Joe said. "It's far less than the contract, but she already knows how much an enlisted man gets for teaching at Fort Laramie. Paying her more would make her suspicious. She must think the U.S. Army is paying her salary."

Joe stood up. Without a word, he turned on his heel and left Major Townsend's office. Outside, he breathed deep, catching just a whiff of rot from the venerable sinks behind the enlisted men's barracks. He reckoned it was a sign of spring, when he would have to authorize a general police of the old place to discard the outhouse rubbish of winter. He thought about Paris and studying with Pasteur and realized, as he stalked back to his own quarters, that for the first time since M'Liss died, he was making plans.

Susanna sat in the tin tub, her knees drawn up to her chin, even more angry with Major Randolph than with Mrs. Dunklin.

Rational good sense finally triumphed. She washed herself thoroughly, embarrassed now that a man had seen her in five-day-old dirt, she, the most meticulous of persons. Come to think of it, he had seen her at her worst from Cheyenne on, she reckoned, and scrubbed harder. Then she just sat there, her forehead resting on her drawn-up knees, because she was too tired to move.

After some effort, Susanna stood up, frightened at her own weakness. She wobbled there in the tub a moment, then wrapped the towel around her, shivering even though the small kitchen was warm. It chafed her that she had to lean on the chair to step from the tub, but that was the consequence of thinking she could starve herself to death. She sat there and decided she had done enough foolish things.

She was still sitting in the chair, towel wrapped around her, when she heard the post surgeon open his front door. Even though the kitchen door was closed, she felt a little puff of cold air around her bare ankles. She wanted to stand up and dress herself, but her clothes were still in the parlor, where Emily must have dropped them off.

"Susanna?" he called.

When she didn't answer promptly, he opened the door to the kitchen and stood there, giving her what looked like a professional appraisal.

"I didn't have the energy," she said finally, her face hot with humiliation for him to see her in a towel.

"I'll help you."

She shook her head, embarrassed at her weakness. "If you'll just get my things…"

He went into the parlor and returned with her clothes draped over his arm. He set them on the small kitchen table but did not leave the room. "I'm going to turn my back on you and create the specialty of Chez Randolph—cheese sandwiches made with army cheese and army bread. It is my sole accomplishment in the kitchen. You will eat one sandwich. I will not leave you alone."

True to his word, he turned his back and started to slice the bread. "If you need help, you only have to ask. I know what women look like," he said, his voice so noncommittal that he might have been telling her a straight line was the shortest distance between two points.

With a sigh, Susanna dropped her towel and dressed herself. At the same time, Major Randolph, imperturbable, kept up a commentary of Fort Laramie news, spending the most time on Katie O'Leary's delivery of a daughter. "I believe they are going to name her Mary Rose," he said. "I suggested Josephine Randolph, but Katie gave a most unladylike snort at my idea. Where is the gratitude, I ask you?"

Susanna laughed softly, surprising herself that she could still laugh. Light-headed, she sat down on the chair, her stocking in her hand. "Major…" she began. "I just can't bend over to do this. Makes me dizzy."

"Call me Joe," he said as he turned around and pulled her stocking up one leg, and then the other one. He did it with some expertise, which made her smile. "You can do the garters, Susanna," he said, handing them to her and turning back to the bread. "I had some butter for these sandwiches, but I think it has gone rancid."

"This is a strange conversation," she said as she finished dressing.

"No stranger than any conversation I have ever had with Nick Martin," he told her, setting the sandwiches on tin plates. "Incidentally, he asked me quite seriously if he could set fire to the Dunklins' quarters."

Susanna gasped. "I hope you discouraged him!"

"I did. Told him you would be very disappointed in him. He agreed finally, but I could tell his heart was not in it." Joe indicated the sandwiches. "This, Susanna Hopkins, is what passes for luncheon in my quarters. *Bon appétit.*" He smiled then, his eyes kind. "I plan to brush up on my French. Perhaps you can help. How is your French? I will resign my commission when this latest Indian war is over." He struck a pose that made her smile again. "I intend to travel to Paris and study with Pasteur! You have inspired me to blow the dust of gossipy, hypocritical army forts off my boots. I am in your debt." He bowed then, and sat down, handing her a sandwich. "Army cheese, Susanna. Let's see…*fromage?*"

Amazed at him, she accepted the sandwich. "This is wretched," she said after several bites. "How can you mess up a cheese sandwich so completely?"

"It's a mystery." He chewed and swallowed. "I only eat to stay alive. I hear there are excellent restaurants in Paris."

Susanna stared at him. "You are the strangest man," she murmured.

"Standard issue, that's all," he replied. He leaned his elbows on the table, and there was no mistaking how tired his eyes looked.

"Do you ever sleep?"

"Not much." He finished half his sandwich. When he looked at her, his expression was serious. "I went to Major Townsend this morning, and told him to hire you to work with Private Benedict."

"I'm too ashamed to walk across the parade ground, let alone teach," she said.

"You will. All I ask is that you be brave a little longer. Please. Private Benedict needs your help, and company funds will cover the cost. Maeve Rattigan has rounded up three other women who would like to learn to read. Perhaps you can teach them two evenings a week. I doubt you will make more than a dollar a week with the evening classes. Private Benedict's school is scheduled to run until the end of May, the same as yours was."

He returned his attention to his sandwich.

"Didn't you just hear me say I wouldn't do it?" she asked.

"I ignored it. This would be better with butter." He finished his sandwich as she fumed. "By May you will have a hundred dollars, plus whatever you earn from evening classes. That will give you enough to get to Cheyenne, and maybe beyond."

"To go where?" she asked, setting down her half-finished sandwich.

He put it back in her hand. "That will depend upon you."

* * *

Joe felt like a bully as he sat there, making sure she finished the miserable sandwich. He bullied her into another bowl of breakfast oatmeal and warm canned milk with cinnamon. By the time fatigue call sounded and the fort began afternoon duties, she had finished eating, and brushed her hair. He hadn't thought to ask Emily for a hairbrush, but it cost him not a single pang to get Melissa's hairbrush from the chest where he kept those articles of her life he could not part with.

Susanna took the hairbrush and just looked at it for a long moment, her eyes troubled. She opened her mouth to speak, then closed it. She brushed her hair, and he felt his own heart lift, as though that simple, womanly gesture had brushed aside years of cobwebs.

"What was her name?" was all she asked.

"Melissa Rhoades. She was from Ohio and very pretty."

Susanna smiled, her eyes not so troubled. "Would you… would Melissa have any hairpins?"

She did. He took them from the cedar chest and returned to the kitchen, as Susanna finished braiding her blond hair and coiling it into the black hairnet that Emily had thought to include. With Melissa's hairpins, Susanna Hopkins was tidy again, but still unwilling to leave his quarters.

Joe helped her to her feet anyway, steadying her. He had second thoughts about hauling her across the parade ground. Maybe she was still too weak. He appraised her as a physician. Her color was good, her eyes lively. She trembled a little, but she stood erect.

Then his mind took a sudden, great leap and he looked at her as a husband would. He asked himself if he would have treated his beloved Melissa this way. He could arrive at no conclusion, beyond the obvious fact that while Mrs. Hopkins was too thin, she was so lovely. He could see something in her eyes that looked a little bit like resolution; maybe a thin, wavering resolution, but resolution. Where it came from, he had no idea, considering how beaten down she was.

He took a chance then, and folded her in his arms, pushing her head gently until it rested against his chest. To his relief, her arms went around him and she clung to him. Whether it was from exhaustion or emotion, he couldn't tell.

"I just want to put the heart back in you, Susanna," he whispered. The thought struck him that maybe she was doing the same thing to him, probably without even knowing it. "Can you make it across the parade ground? It matters."

She pulled away from him, her hands on his chest now, not forcing him back, but steadying herself. She looked like a woman tired of the fight, but a woman not quite ready to concede, if she thought she had an ally.

"I believe I can," she said. "If you insist."

"I do, but this will be the last time I insist you do anything."

"What do you mean?"

"There is a job waiting for you in the commissary storehouse. It will be up to you to decide if you wish to take it, after spending an afternoon with Private Benedict."

Joe knew he had not convinced her, but he could tell he was close. "Does Private Benedict know I am coming?" she asked.

"I told him you might. By the way, his first name is Anthony. Are you up to it?"

She flashed him a look of irritation, which pleased him, because it was not a bland look of someone on the point of surrender. "I told you I would! Don't you listen?"

The parade ground was deserted because it was too cold for outdoor activities. They walked slowly, Susanna looking straight ahead, her sights fixed on the commissary storehouse. She closed her eyes once, so Joe stopped until she had command of herself again.

It wasn't a big parade ground, as parade grounds go, but he knew it taxed her. He was on the verge of turning around with her, except that her straightforward gaze never wavered. She stopped again, and he knew she was exhausted.

"I suppose you've heard my story from Captain Reese," he said. "Since there was no real reason to cashier me, George Crook used his influence to have me removed from the Army of the Potomac and sent to Florida. I've never been so humiliated. General George Thomas rescued me. I owe him a debt I cannot repay, because he is dead now. I'm paying that debt today. We're almost there."

The commissary storehouse was warm and there was no mistaking Susanna's sigh of relief. Joe helped her off with her coat, steadied her again and walked with her to the last bay in the long storehouse, their destination. A sideways glance at the woman who walked beside him showed her lips set tight in a firm line and her eyes looking into that distance he knew very well from warfare. She amazed him.

Private Benedict offered her a chair, which she sank into immediately. He looked at his students. "We have just become extraordinarily lucky," he said. "Mrs. Hopkins is thinking about joining me here to teach. Let's be on good behavior so she will agree. Major Randolph, thank you for escorting her. We'll take over from here."

Joe had never been so adroitly dismissed by a private, and he thought about it as he nerved himself to leave Susanna there: tired, weak, discouraged and not entirely certain she wanted to stay. He decided the private was right. Joe nodded to Benedict and touched Susanna's shoulder lightly.

"I'll be back for you at recall from fatigue, Mrs. Hopkins." *Please look at me,* he thought. *Let me know I'm not a fool.*

To his immense gratification, she did. The resolution he saw put the heart back in his body.

Chapter Twelve

It would have taken a much sterner teacher than Susanna Hopkins not to be charmed by Private Benedict's students. She sat there too tired to move, and grateful for a warm place. By the time an hour had passed, she was involved. By the end of two hours, she had gathered the smaller pupils around her, ready to teach them.

She had no idea what Major Randolph had told him, but Private Benedict acted as though worn-out women came into his classroom every day. He handed her a McGuffey's Reader, helped her to another seat farther away from the blackboard, where he was teaching multiplication tables, and channeled the little ones in her direction. She started to read to her students, transferred so seamlessly from him to her that she didn't even realize it until she heard recall from fatigue.

She looked up then and smiled at Anthony Benedict, who was watching her with a smile of his own. After he dismissed the class, her pupils brought her their coats, mufflers and hats for help, as though she had been their teacher since the first day of the term. When they left, she sat there barely allowing herself to feel what she felt.

"What do you think, Mrs. Hopkins?" the private asked, sitting beside her.

"I can do this, if you'll have me."

The look he gave her didn't need words—it was a combination of relief and agreement that she remembered from her early teaching days, when she had been the novice.

"I'll expect you here every morning after guard mount," he said. "I like to go Saturday mornings, too, and just read to them."

She nodded, overwhelmed. Private Benedict got up to give her a cup of tea, and some bread and butter. She accepted them gratefully.

"Major Randolph arranged for my own stash of food, in case some of my pupils come here unfed," he said, sitting down with a cup of coffee. "Maybe it's for teachers, too, although I expect you to have breakfast every morning."

It was gentle reproof from someone with little rank, much younger than she was, and no real teaching skills beyond willingness and interest, but she took it to heart, grateful for his kindness.

"I'll bring my own lunch," she said with playful dignity that made him laugh.

They were sitting there discussing lessons for tomorrow when Major Randolph made his way through the warehouse to them. Private Benedict watched him.

"I never met a better man," he said, his voice low.

"I'm not sure I have, either," she whispered back. "He wants me to succeed."

"Then I expect you will."

Susanna thought about Private Benedict's comment as she put on her coat and bent her head a bit, even before the major held open the warehouse door for her. She knew the wind was coming.

Surprise. The afternoon was still for a change and there

was something indefinable in the air. She glanced at her escort. "Dare I mention the word *spring?*"

"No. This is the January tease," he said. "Seize the moment, I say, because that's all it will be." He extended his arm for her and she took it. "We've been invited to dinner at the Rattigans'. I don't know what your plans are, but you've seen me at work in my kitchen, and I never turn down meals fixed elsewhere."

"Wise of you," she murmured. "Besides, I am not certain I can face my cousin yet. Maybe after dinner."

"I'll go with you. No sense in facing Emily alone."

Susanna stopped, overwhelmed again at his kindness.

"Is something wrong?" he asked, all solicitation in a way that seemed both professional and friendly at the same time.

She shook her head, not even certain she could put into words the sheer pleasure of having someone who wasn't bent on destruction take an interest in her. "It's hard to explain," she said, as they walked toward the footbridge spanning the Laramie.

"Try."

She thought a moment as they strolled across the footbridge. "You're not measuring me for a coffin."

"I couldn't possibly," he replied promptly.

"Would Hippocrates revoke your oath?" she teased.

"Hippocrates has nothing to do with my regard for you," he said suddenly, then looked at her as if he was as surprised as she was by what had come out of his mouth....

We're both too old to blush, Joe thought as Sergeant Rattigan showed them into his parlor and Susanna beat a hasty retreat to the kitchen, where Maeve was putting the final touches on dinner. Happy not to contemplate his impulsive comments of mere moments before, Joe sniffed the air appreciatively.

"Sergeant, I could live on this planet far beyond my alloted three score and ten, and my kitchen would never yield such fragrance," he said.

"It might if you remarried, Major," Rattigan said.

Joe had heard this from others, with such a statement usually followed by more embarrassment, and apology, as everyone tried to step carefully around his widower status. Not Sergeant Rattigan, drat the man, who regarded him calmly, puffing on his pipe with a thoughtful expression not owed entirely to the comfort of tobacco.

Rattigan's expression changed from thoughtful to tender when they heard the women laughing. For a moment, Joe envied the sergeant his charming wife.

"There aren't any spare Maeve Rattigans," Joe said, which might have sounded like bald envy, except he knew Rattigan understood.

"True," the sergeant said. "Mrs. Hopkins is equally charming. Don't you agree?"

Joe Randolph could not deny he had been considering the matter, on some level or other. Trust a sergeant to slice through the Gordian knot of convention and platitude, laying the matter bare. That's what sergeants did.

Joe was spared a reply by the timely arrival of Maeve herself, who set a concoction of government beef and other anonymous ingredients on the table in the front room. He took a deep breath, appreciative. Susanna carried in biscuits and that was dinner. Joe hoped there would be plum duff, that homely dessert of the military, and Maeve did not disappoint.

The whole meal was larded with the conversation of people who shared the same profession: the coming campaign, the latest gossip from Omaha Barracks, what late-winter oddities from the commissary department lurked for the unsuspecting. Joe had spent most shared meals in similar chat, but this was different. He glanced at Susanna Hopkins, who seemed to blossom before his eyes, because no one intimated anything concerning the last few horrendous days. He wondered how long it had been since she had enjoyed dinner and conversation.

He did want to turn the conversation her way. "Maeve, were you able to recruit any friends for a night school? Mrs. Hopkins gets bored easily if she's not teaching someone something."

Maybe he had blundered. After all, he hadn't even asked Susanna if she was going to accept his offer to teach with Private Benedict. "At least, I believe she has her work cut out for her in the garrison school," he added.

"I do," Susanna said, to his relief. "I promised Private Benedict that I would arrive tomorrow with my own lunch in my own lard bucket. My evenings are quite free, Maeve. Find me ladies to teach."

"I already have three. Is that enough?" Maeve asked.

"Even one is enough," Susanna replied promptly. "Shall we begin tomorrow night? You name the time and place."

Joe couldn't help himself. Or maybe he didn't try. Without a word, he leaned over and kissed Susanna's cheek. "Bravo," he said, then returned to the plum duff in front of him, as though he did that every evening.

Maeve started to giggle, then Susanna. The women were still chuckling when they gathered up the dishes and moved back to the kitchen, that female sanctuary. Sergeant Rattigan wisely turned his after-dinner conversation to the upcoming campaign. By the time Joe ushered Susanna back across the footbridge, all was calm.

"Lights out any minute," he told her as they walked more and more slowly across the parade ground, Susanna unconsciously moving at a snail's pace, the closer they came to Officers Row. "You have to be in a classroom in the morning, looking chipper. I'd be derelict indeed if I monopolized any more of your time tonight."

She stopped. "Thank you from the bottom of my heart," she whispered.

"Just doing my job, as head of this year's administrative council," he said. They stood in silence as the bugler played taps. As the last note still lingered, he started her in motion again. The wind was picking up and winter had returned. "I'll stop at the O'Learys, and tell them that you'll be happy to escort Rooney to the enlisted men's school, if you're game."

"I am."

They were on the porch now. "Do you want me to come in? I could explain…"

She put her hand on his arm. "Thank you, no. This is for me to do." She looked at the front door, as though it were the gaping jaws of hell, and went inside.

Stay with me, he wanted to say, but did not. He had nothing to offer her on the spur of the moment that was acceptable in any society, especially one as censorious as this one.

He stood a moment on the porch, then segued a few steps to the O'Learys' front door, where he stood a few minutes with James O'Leary. The captain assured him that Rooney would be ready for school in the morning.

Joe returned to his cold quarters. He lit a fire in the parlor's potbellied stove, because he expected a visit from Sergeant Rattigan. A whispered comment as Maeve and Susanna were kitchen-bound, and a nod from the sergeant, had assured him of that.

It was going to be a touchy subject, but maybe he had science on his side. Heaven knows, nothing else had worked for Maeve Rattigan. He was seated at his desk in his home office, looking at the *Journal for Homeopathy,* when he heard Rattigan's knock.

Sergeant Rattigan gave Joe all his attention as the post surgeon fired the only shot left in his puny medical arsenal, an 1854 article from an obscure British medical journal. Professors at the University of Maryland had scoffed, but Joe had never forgotten it.

"I'm going to intrude in a monumentally intimate way, Sergeant," he said. "You can stop me at any time and there will be no hard feelings. I mean that."

The sergeant nodded. He stared at his well-polished shoes. "Please don't expect us to abstain, Major. I don't think we could."

Joe thought of his own wife. *Neither could we,* he remembered. *Tread lightly on Sergeant Rattigan's heart. Maeve's, too.* He sat back, then came around to the other side of his desk, to sit beside the sergeant. His professors in medical school had always encouraged distance between physician and patient, nonsense Joe had discarded right after the Battle of Bull Run.

"I won't ask you to abstain. How could I? Here are the facts, Sergeant—every few months, your wife suffers a spontaneous abortion. Technically, it's not a miscarriage, because she is not far enough along for that. It's wearing her out, body and soul. If this continues, your darling Maeve will become a name on a gravestone that you have to leave behind when the regiment moves on."

Sergeant Rattigan groaned out loud. The heartbroken sound shot a chill down Joe's back, reminding him of other Irishmen keening after death of comrades in battle. The unearthly sound had haunted him many a night.

"I fear for her life. She is unquestionably anemic and this is taking a terrible toll," Joe added for good measure.

Rattigan looked at him then, and Joe absorbed all the pain and worry into his own heart, because that was part of medicine.

"Sergeant, would you try something?" He opened up the

journal, ragged from being hauled from post to post, along with his other medical books. "This treatise by George Drysdale was published in London in 1854. I came across it in medical school. No one took it seriously. I do."

Rattigan's expression had changed from devastated to interested.

"I have no idea why Maeve suffers so. I doubt I will ever know, but try this. Confine your marital congress to directly *after* her monthly flow. Say, up to ten days after the cessation of menses, no more. Don't resume again until after her next monthly."

"What will that prove?" the sergeant asked.

"I think she will not get pregnant. Maybe others scoff, but as Maeve's surgeon, I am desperate to help her. By God, I will grasp at any straw!"

He hadn't meant to sound so adamant, but there it was, the practice of last-ditch medicine, the kind of medicine he seemed to practice all too often. He was almost afraid to look at the sergeant, but he did, and saw shock, followed by interest.

"It's like this, Sergeant—the longer her body can rest and heal, the better Maeve's overall health." Joe held up his hands to stop the question he knew was coming from an Irishman. "I understand the tenets of your faith, but how could this possibly affect them? I am suggesting nothing artificial. Besides, after years of this wretched pattern afflicting the dearest person in your life, how could God be upset with you?"

Tears started in the sergeant's eyes. He bowed his head and cried. Joe hesitated not a moment before putting his arm around the big man and holding him close. "Just try it, John," he urged, disregarding rank. "Please. I don't know what else to do."

They sat together until the sergeant dried his eyes and blew his nose on the handkerchief Joe handed him. He held out the journal, too. "Read the article. Some of it you probably won't understand—I barely do. Talk to Maeve. I believe Drysdale's science is sound."

"We're never going to have children, are we?"

The words were wrenched from the sergeant like an inflamed molar. Probably he had never voiced that dread before.

Joe shook his head. "No, you're not," he said softly, "but it doesn't follow that you have to be miserable. Try it, just try it."

Sergeant Rattigan stood up. He managed a faint smile, and then he saluted. "You'll know we're successful if there aren't any more late-night notes tacked to your message board. I promise we'll try it."

Joe let out an enormous sigh when the door closed quietly behind the sergeant. He just sat there, then nodded to his bust of Hippocrates, scarred and banged around from travel between garrisons. "Well, Hip, there you are. What am I going to do about Susanna Hopkins? Any ideas? I think I love her."

I have to live here until I earn enough money to move on, Susanna thought as she stepped into the Reeses' entry hall. She wished she had agreed to Major Randolph's willingness to stand by her, but this was for her to do. She took a deep breath and walked into the parlor, where Emily sat frozen in place, dreading whatever Susanna was going to say or do. With a shock, Susanna recognized that look. It was the same look she used to direct toward Frederick Hopkins when he frightened her. She resolved that no matter how badly her cousin had used her, she would do nothing more to cause fright.

"Emily, I didn't mean to frighten you," she said immediately. "I'm sorry for what I did." Her glance took in Dan Reese, sitting almost as still as his wife. "I was just so discouraged that I thought I wanted to die. I won't do that again."

Susanna sat down beside her cousin. "I am going to be teaching in the school for enlisted men's children. I will also be teaching reading and writing several nights a week to some of the enlisted men's wives." She waved off the comment she knew was coming. "It doesn't matter that your friends talk and think me past redemption. I promise that when I have earned enough money to leave this place, I will."

Cautiously, Emily nodded.

"In no time at all, you'll forget I was ever here!" she said, unable to resist a little smile, because she knew it was true. "Do this for me, cousin, even if you have to pretend. Just… just entertain the notion that maybe I am not entirely at fault, and maybe you *haven't* heard the whole story. Just do that, dearest, and we will manage. Can you?"

Emily nodded again, though not willingly. Susanna rose.

"That's all I ask. If you have a spare lard can, I'd like to use that for my lunch bucket."

"Could you find something more dignified?"

Susanna sighed inwardly—Emily and her appearances. "I have nothing," she said with all the dignity she could muster. She nodded to them both and went to the stairs.

Someone had reattached the blanket that Major Randolph had ripped down that morning. It seemed so long ago now. Susanna stepped behind it and closed her eyes, tired and still weak. She prepared for bed, grateful the upstairs was warm. On impulse, she looked out the little window over the porch and saw Sergeant Rattigan walking back across the parade ground. He must have come from Major Randolph's quarters, and she hoped Maeve hadn't taken a sudden turn. No, he would be hurrying, and Major Randolph would be with him. It was more the stroll of a man with something on his mind.

For the first time in well over a year, she knelt beside her cot and prayed, first for Tommy, and then for the Rattigans and the O'Learys (she could hear an infant's wail through the wall, and it warmed her). It was easy to pray for Private Benedict and his school that was hers, too, but less easy to pray for Major Randolph, who sometimes looked as though he carried the weight of the world on his shoulders. She told herself it was foolish to be shy about prayer, since her words were probably going nowhere, and she was whispering into her pillow. "I pray not to be a nuisance to him," she concluded. "That's enough to ask."

Chapter Thirteen

Susanna Hopkins woke up early. There was that moment of panic when she wondered where she was—whether Frederick was drunk, sober, demanding, compliant, suddenly sad or bent on mischief. Once the moment passed, she lay there and made a raft of decisions.

The first one was the most important, because she knew it affected all the others: on that morning in a place where she never thought her life would take her, Susanna decided to forgive her cousin Emily Reese for being stupid. She decided to overlook the enormous lie that Emily had concocted to make her divorced cousin somehow more palatable to censorious people who knew too much about each other. Emily was too stupid to think of consequences, and she had probably meant well.

"I can live with that," Susanna mouthed more than whispered, not wanting to wake anyone. Of course, the only people awake were the O'Learys through the wall. She smiled and listened to the baby's tiny wail, and then silence, followed by two parents talking softly to each other. The voices were indistinct, but they were a mother and father sharing a moment with Mary Rose O'Leary, the army's newest dependent.

Susanna lay there and reminded herself that for a time,

she and Frederick had done that after Tommy was born. She reminded herself that those had been wonderful, drowsy moments, shared with a baby she was getting acquainted with, created with a husband she loved. Matters may have gone terribly wrong five years later, when business concerns started to collapse and rye whiskey became an enticing substitute for reality, but they hadn't always been bad.

"I can live with that," she murmured again. "We had good times." She soothed herself with the fact that she never would have married a man she hadn't loved. There was a time when Frederick Hopkins would have made any woman look twice. She knew, even now, that if he had not pushed her face into the mantelpiece, and blind instinct hadn't made her flee for her own safety, she would be there still, protecting Tommy, as if nothing was the matter. She suspected there were many women in precisely her position.

"I can live with that, too, even though it is unfair to women," she whispered. She had heard stories about women crusading against "Demon Rum," and been aghast at such unladylike behavior. Didn't those rabble-rousing women know that a woman's sphere was the home? She understood that kind of courage now. Liquor had probably destroyed more homes and hopes than marital infidelity, and wives often suffered in silence. *Bravo to the brave crusaders,* she thought.

Time passed and both duplexes were silent now, Mary Rose back to sleep, maybe slumbering between her parents. On her side of the wall, Susanna heard Daniel Reese snoring, the sound more comforting than grating. She decided to forgive him for being light-headed, too. He loved his son and wife, and was probably a pretty good commander of a company of infantry, out here in the wilds of Wyoming Territory.

She took her thoughts to another level, right down into her own hesitant heart. She had begun her journey from Pennsylvania with hope and the promise of a useful life. Events had taken a terrible turn, but she was still alive, her brain was agile and she was beginning to suspect that she was a resourceful woman. She had a skill people needed. There were six young children in a commissary warehouse, sitting at packing crate desks, who needed her. There was a private teaching a school for fifty cents extra duty pay a day, and in over his head, who needed her. There was a post surgeon with sorrows at least as great as hers, perhaps greater, who was determined she would not give up on his watch. And there was Maeve Rattigan, denied the one thing she wanted most, who cared to read and write.

"I can live with this, because I have work to do," she murmured, and closed her eyes, content. When she woke later to the sound of reveille, Susanna Hopkins made a conscious decision to live well. Maybe Major Randolph was right; maybe living well *was* the best revenge. Or maybe it was the right thing to do.

It was not so hard to make small talk that morning with her cousin, who only wanted to forget her disastrous part in Susanna's ruin. She told Emily her plans for the garrison school, and her night school for women. "I came here to teach." She said it firmly and not defensively, and in the saying, believed it.

Emily found her an empty lard bucket and made her laugh by drawing a flower on the tin lid. "To make it more genteel," Emily said, with a grin that Susanna remembered from years ago, when they had been much younger. Bread and butter, dried apples and the everlasting raisins that made them look at each other and giggle went into the bucket, along with a cloth napkin and two small pieces of chocolate from Dan Reese's secret stash.

"Thanks, Emily," Susanna said after guard mount, which they watched together, Stanley between them, from the warmth of the parlor window. She put on her coat, wound her muffler tight and went out to slay dragons.

The task was made much simpler, because Nick Martin escorted her to the warehouse complex south of the parade ground.

"Major Randolph told me to make sure you got there and that's all," he confided. "I'd like to learn, too, but he needs me to sweep out the ward."

We all need to be needed, she thought, touched. "I understand, Nick." She looked at him more closely. "It *is* Nick, isn't it? I expect Saint Paul is busy on those missionary journeys."

"I expect he is," Nick said. "I'll ask him someday."

Susanna thought about that. She nodded and looked back at Officers Row. The major in question stood on his own porch. He lifted his coffee mug to her and she waved.

Before she married Frederick and left the teaching profession, Susanna had taught at a private school in Carlisle. Her classroom had come with brocaded draperies, a carpet on the floor and hand-turned desks bordering on elegant. She discovered that day in her warehouse school that packing-crate desks had a certain utility, and the fragrance of dried apples and raisins, stacked in kegs next to coffee beans, reminded her of favorite kitchens.

With all her heart and mind, she concentrated on her six pupils, finding out what they knew, and creating a term full of lesson plans in her head. At first, she knew Private Benedict was conscious of her quiet presence in the back of his classroom. By mess call, he had turned all his attention to his older students, and looked up with surprise when he heard the bugle.

"Compositions and recitations this afternoon," he called after his pupils as they hurried home for lunch. He took his own back to her corner after she had ushered out her little ones and sat down again with her lunch. "I have permission to eat here, instead of in the mess hall," he explained. "Sometimes there are children who stay."

They spent the hour eating and discussing the morning's work. Private Benedict had a few questions she answered, and he liked her suggestion that they teach together in the afternoon occasionally.

"I noticed in my…my first school how well-tuned to the local flora and fauna these children are," she said. "Let's have them tell us what they know, and build some lessons around it."

Private Benedict looked at her with an expression she recognized: that of an educator with an idea. "We could spend a day or two outlining interesting topics such as buffalo, wolves and Indians, and have our students compose letters on these subjects to their friends in the States."

"Bravo, Private Benedict," she said. "That's certainly more interesting than a mere composition! My pupils will draw and we can put together a letter of our own."

She observed him then, investing more than just her mind in what he had said. Something in his face drew her attention, and there was no sense in hanging back, now that she had decided to live. "Private Benedict, something tells me you already send letters like that home to…"

"Connecticut," he said, and there was no overlooking the blush that rose from his neck. "There's a young lady in Hartford who gets letters like that."

Susanna nodded. "I thought so. I hope she saves all of them. Think what a wonderful look at the West you are providing."

"She sends them to the newspaper." He stopped, his face fiery-red now. "Well, at least part of them. It's become a regular column—*Life and Times on the Frontier.*"

"Bravo again!" Susanna said, delighted. "Tell me, is she a teacher, too?"

The look he gave her nearly took her breath away. There was everything in it of pride and gratitude. "So you really think I am a teacher?"

"I know you are," she said quietly.

He drew a deep breath, and there was no overlooking that Private Benedict was a man in love and a man with a plan. "Yes, she's a teacher. My enlistment is up at the end of summer. I'm going to attend the normal school in Hartford, after I marry her this fall."

Susanna clapped her hands, then handed him one of Captain Reese's prized chocolates and popped the other one in her mouth. She smiled at him in perfect charity and something else: for the first time in a long time, she was happy.

The post surgeon knew he should probably apologize to Hippocrates for his morning's inattention. At least he had not splinted the wrong leg on a streetwalker, as one of his unfortunate fellow medical students had done at the University of Maryland. Joe still remembered the look of astonishment on the poor woman's face as she swore a round oath worthy of a sailor and raised her hands in an appeal to the Almighty to protect her from malpractice. Joe's malpractice that morning had amounted to no more than prescribing a purgative to the patient in bed three with the runs. Luckily, raised eyebrows from his hospital steward had rectified that wrong. Joe had been big enough to apologize to his steward later, and thank the gods of medicine that his steward had been good enough to follow him after Appomattox to Reconstruction duty in Louisiana, then exile to Outer Darkness in the Department of the Platte.

No doubt Joe had been woolgathering. Nick had told him earlier that Mrs. Hopkins had walked across the parade ground that morning with a certain spring in her stride.

"She's a short one, but I had to hurry to keep up with her" was how Nick had put it.

Nick hadn't been aware, but Joe had watched her, too, standing on his porch, a mug of his awful coffee in hand. He had admired at a distance Susanna's pleasant sway and the purpose with which she moved. This wasn't the frightened woman in the Shy-Dead depot; it wasn't even the woman of yesterday with no hope in her eyes. This was a woman with a plan.

The notion nourished him all morning. Thanks again to his steward, the hospital ran like a top. After his early blunder, Joe had repented with a good save in what he always considered his specialty, debriding a nasty burn from Company A's mess kitchen. At least, the look his steward gave him— the man hated debridement—had redemption written large upon it. Joe could retire to his office redeemed and at liberty to woolgather, when he should have been finalizing the list of pharmacopoeia for Omaha.

Other than that moment watching the poetry of a woman's hips, Joe's morning had two more gems in it. The first one came from Sergeant Rattigan, who returned his copy of George Drysdale's article. The sergeant actually made himself at home in the office, less formal than usual. Well, the topic *du jour* was certainly not government issue; why be formal?

"I read the article to Maeve last night," the sergeant said. "I didn't know a lot of those words, but the meaning was clear—" he gave a self-conscious chuckle "—as Maeve so kindly pointed out to me. She's a shrewd one!"

"We always knew that," Joe said. "She'll keep you on your toes, once Mrs. Hopkins teaches her to read. And?"

"We'll do it, sir. We…we need each other, but I'd do anything to spare my darling Maeve one more heartache."

The sergeant said it simply, but Joe heard every syllable of love. "I thought you would," he told the man.

The sergeant smiled, stood up and snapped off one of his usual salutes, more precise than nearly anyone ever executed at Fort Laramie. He stopped at the door. "If you see Mrs. Hopkins today, tell her we're expecting her for class in my parlor tonight, and we'd be pleased to serve her supper, too."

"Include me in that invitation, and I'll tell her," Joe said.

"You're included, sir, although I've been told by herself to vacate the premises for the evening. See you tonight, Major."

The next gem of the day might have been called a milestone, if Joe had felt so inclined. After a satisfying hour standing around mostly idle while the capable wife of an Arikara scout presented the army with its newest Indian dependent, Joe had walked back to the hospital in that pleasant sort of euphoria that a successful birth always provided. It carried him into his office, where he loosened his collar and wrote a letter to the lycée in Paris where Louis Pasteur taught.

He had written such a letter once or twice in his head, and then on paper three times in the same number of years, only to scrap it. This time he wrote the entire letter, describing his medical training, his subsequent career, the war years and his own interest in microbiology. He had concluded with the hope that Pasteur might allow him entrance into the lycée in the autumn. He signed his name with a flourish, addressed an envelope and hurried the letter to the post office in the post trader's complex before he lost his courage.

He had his first attack of nerves when John Collins, postmaster along with his post trader duties, raised his eyebrows at "Paris, France" on the envelope.

"Long way from here." Collins tapped the letter. "Making some plans, sir?"

Joe had never known the post trader to pry, but he supposed it wasn't every day that a letter to Paris crossed his desk. "I believe I am," he said.

There was a small argument with Nick Martin after recall

from fatigue, when the quiet man announced his intention of escorting Mrs. Hopkins back across the parade ground. Joe's hospital steward intervened, claiming Nick for his own, which allowed the post surgeon to head for the commissary warehouse by himself.

He arrived just as the door opened to allow a flood of escaping students. A smile on his face, Joe watched as Susanna knelt by her little charges, making sure each one was buttoned, mittened and scarved against the omnipresent wind. He couldn't help observing the smooth line of her hip and leg and then the pencil stuck at random in the bun of her untidy hair. Teaching took its toll on coiffure, obviously. Hardly mattered; blondes had a certain indefinable something.

As he stood in the door, letting in all that cold air, she looked at him, and took his breath away with the width of her smile.

"Close the door, Major," she said in her teacher's voice that allowed no argument. He closed the door, then helped her up. Her hand was warm and he wanted to hold it forever.

He didn't, of course, but he noted with something approaching glee that she hadn't been in a hurry to release his, either.

As he waited, she spent a few minutes in conversation with Private Benedict. Joe helped her into her coat when she joined him, relishing the feel of tendrils of her escaping hair on his hand.

"A good day, Susanna?" he asked as they faced into the wind toward Suds Row.

"A very good one," she assured him. "Tomorrow we will take some time during luncheon to construct lesson plans."

"Sounds like you are teaching the teacher."

"I am, but he has a fine natural instinct for the profession."

It was harmless, innocuous conversation and it took them across the footbridge. He yearned to tell her of the letter he had written that day, and finally blurted it out as they approached the sergeant's quarters. The result was most gratifying. Susanna turned her beautiful brown eyes full on him and touched his sleeve. She didn't say anything, but the pleasure on her face made words unnecessary. Her obvious approval made him realize how much he had missed sharing the details of his life with a woman.

"It's well and good, but I have no way of knowing if Monsieur Pasteur will even consider me as a student," he said. "My French is barely workable."

"Perhaps I should teach you this spring, Joe. I know a little."

She knocked on the Rattigans' door because he seemed to have forgotten. The mention of his name on her lips had sent him into a schoolboy sort of euphoria.

Supper was over too quickly. Sergeant Rattigan kissed his wife's check and ushered Joe out the door.

"Maeve is so excited," the man confided as they crossed the footbridge, Rattigan to return to his company's barracks and continue his own school of instruction for the coming winter campaign to his lads. After a quick check on Mary Rose O'Leary, who was already putting on weight, Joe returned to his quarters to pace the floor for an hour and a half before returning to the Rattigans to escort Susanna home.

He was accompanied this time by Nick Martin. Susanna's school may have changed venue, but the man seemed determined that his mandate to assist in every way possible would continue. It gratified Joe to watch the enigmatic fellow show his own loyalty to a lady others had been only too willing to cast off.

They went first to Company A barrack to collect Sergeant Rattigan, who had been sitting there, a palpable presence requiring good order. Joe knew that many of the married sergeants did just that in January and February, when restless privates grew more tired of each other, and fights were common. Joe appreciated the effort, since it relieved him of patching up men who had nothing better to do in winter than plague each other.

"Sir, something is different about Mrs. Hopkins today," the sergeant began as they walked toward the footbridge, Nick trailing along behind. "At least, that's what I think I noticed over supper."

"I, too, Sergeant. Perhaps she is just glad to be teaching where she is appreciated."

Whatever had happened to spark Susanna Hopkins must have continued during her first teaching session, Joe decided, after a few minutes of polite chat with the Rattigans, and then their own retreat to the other side of Fort Laramie. Susanna's exhaustion was stamped all over her face, but something more remained.

"Tired?" he asked her, hoping she would hear the professional tone, and nothing more.

"I am worn-out, but, Joe, you should have seen the ladies! They are so eager to learn."

"Then you're not tired at all," he said, offering her his arm, which she took.

"It's all I ever wanted to do here," she said simply. She looked over her shoulder at Nick, who trailed along. "Nick, Private Benedict told me that you are welcome to sit in the back of the classroom, if you'd like to learn."

"Maybe, if the surgeon doesn't need me."

"Come when you can." Susanna increased the pressure of her hand on Joe's arm. He even thought she leaned into his shoulder a little. "Joe, I did a wise thing this morning. I decided to forgive my cousin for being stupid."

He couldn't help a chuckle, even though what she said

touched him. "You're a lady of considerable forbearance! I'm not sure I could do that."

"Then it's a good thing the matter didn't fall to you," she said. "Seriously, I decided I could live with what happened. People like my former husband have a way of muddying their nests. I don't know when, but eventually the whole matter will come out. I am a patient woman."

He heard the hesitation in her voice, amazing himself how aware he was of every nuance from Susanna Hopkins, almost as if he studied her. The idea charmed him. "What more?" he asked, raising his voice a little because the wind was strong. Never mind; he knew Nick Martin would tell no tales.

"A few nights ago, I told the O'Learys everything and asked their forgiveness for the lie," she said.

No need for her to know that Jim O'Leary had already told him, not when the subject was so frank and terrible. "I'm certain they assured you that you had nothing to ask forgiveness for."

"They did. How kind they are," Susanna told him, almost as if it still amazed her. "After the ladies left tonight, I...I told Maeve, too." She sighed. "She just hugged me."

"What else, Susanna?" he asked, some instinct telling him there was more.

"I decided there is only one thing I cannot live *without,* and see no solution at present." She took a deep breath. "My son. He should be with me."

Joe had nothing to say to that. They walked in silence to Emily Reese's front door, where he said good-night.

He doubted she would say more, suspecting her thoughts were of Tommy Hopkins. She surprised him. He had released her arm, but she took his hand and looked him in the eye. He knew how much that cost her, since she was a reticent woman.

"Joe, I am glad you sent that letter to Monsieur Pasteur," she said. "And I meant it about French. I brought my textbook with me, thinking perhaps there would be a pupil advanced enough to learn a little. Maybe it will be you?"

"Oui, madame," he replied, and raised her mittened hand to his lips. The result was a laugh.

"We can learn more than that, *monsieur,*" she said. "Name a night and I will bring my textbook to the hospital."

Joe was a long time getting to sleep that night.

Chapter Fourteen

Susanna fell into the rhythm of work, fitting her mind to the never-changing routine of an army garrison. The regularity of bugle calls and order was a balm to her soul. Now that she had made her personal peace with her cousin, she discovered how little it mattered to her what anyone else felt.

She called it victory the morning Elizabeth Burt brought her younger son to the garrison school. "You'd have my other two, as well, except they are back East with my sister for their education," Mrs. Burt told her.

The woman also had the courage to apologize for signing that letter. "I shouldn't have done that," she said quietly. "Forgive me." She opened her mouth, closed it, then spoke. "Major Randolph told us what had happened to you. I have passed on what he said to some others. What will be the result, I cannot say, but please believe me when I say Andy and I are sorry."

No other families unbent enough to send their children to the warehouse, but Susanna was not one to search for grand success. Life had taught her how unlikely that was. Her heart warmed to know that Joe had her interests at heart.

The pattern of each day moved into the next with soothing regularity: breakfast with Emily in the kitchen; stopping to pick up Rooney O'Leary; a brisk walk across the lower parade ground with Nick Martin, her self-appointed guardian; the bliss of school; lunch and ideas with Anthony Benedict; a walk back to Emily's or to Maeve Rattigan's, depending on the day; night school with two Irishwomen, a German lady and one Polish woman, all eager to read; French lessons one evening a week with Major Joe Randolph. Once a week she wrote to her son, telling him about her pupils, and enclosing some of their drawings and small attempts at writing. Once a week she gave the letter to Nick Martin, who carried it to the post office. She had no hopes that Tommy received her letters, but she persisted.

French lessons were the most unpredictable part of her week, mainly because illness or injury always trumped *parlez-vous francais*. On those nights when there was a note tacked to his office door—"*Diarrhea*" or "*Bone to set*" or the everlasting "*Catarrh*"—she went to the ward, supervised by Theodore Brown, and read to the patients. At first she wondered why the post surgeon did not tack such a note to the Reeses' door, and save her the effort to go to the hospital. Then she realized he wanted her there, visiting his patients.

She had dredged up volume one of *Little Women* for herself in the fort's library, but none of the men objected, especially since it was all she had with her that first night, except for Joe's French textbook. When she was well into *Little Women,* with no volume two in sight, she had suggested they read something else, since there was no way to know the ending. The storm of manly protest surprised her, so she kept reading and overlooking, to her private amusement, the sniffles and nose blowing that had nothing to do with illness.

"Your patients are a bunch of softies," she told Joe one night when he was actually in his office for a French lesson. "Do you realize that even the men you have discharged keep returning to hear the story? I confess we all cried when Beth took a turn for the worse. I tell you, Joe, that these men can read, but they keep returning! We've run out of chairs, so they sit on the floor."

"Aren't you aware how much *fun* it is to be read to?" the post surgeon had asked. "I'd sit in there, too, but you'd probably frog-march me back to my office to conjugate another verb. I know you would!"

She had laughed long at that. What did bring tears to her eyes in February was the evening one of the discharged patients, a former tough from New York's notorious Five Points, presented her with volume two. He had been on detached duty at Fort Russell, and confessed to "lifting" the copy from that garrison's library. She made him promise to return it, but not until they finished the book. He assured her it would go back on the shelf as quietly as it left, and no one would know. "I'm good at that," he confided.

"I am aiding and abetting criminals," she told the surgeon, and he only grinned.

She noted that he had nothing to smile about as the end of February brought troops from other forts to Laramie, preparing for the Powder River winter campaign, and then General George Crook from Omaha arrived, not so much to lead the expedition, but to watch Colonel J. J. Reynolds lead it.

"What will he do, ride along and peer over Colonel Reynolds's shoulder?" she had asked Joe one night, when she'd returned a much-corrected French essay to the surgeon.

"Basically, that's as good a description as any. Georgie does like to be in charge," Joe said, wincing at the red marks on his essay, and changing what was obviously an unpleasant subject. "Susanna, is there any hope for me? Will I have to take you with me to the lycée to sit in class and translate in my ear?"

"I'm a woman. They would never let me near Monsieur Pasteur's classroom!" had been her retort, even though the idea of being in Paris with Major Joseph Randolph gave her something to think about that evening as Nick Martin escorted her back to Officers Row.

The arrival of more troops and companies to Fort Laramie meant that the flats by Suds Row suddenly blossomed with tents, even in the cold days and still-longer Wyoming nights of late winter. Inadequate housing meant cases of frostbite and more catarrh, so she was not surprised when Joe suspended his French lessons.

"I haven't time," he told her. "Do keep coming to read to the men, though. I have it on good authority from my steward that some of my patients and former patients are placing bets on whether Laurie will marry Jo, or whether Professor Bhaer will carry off the palm there." In a surprising bit of spontaneity that charmed her, he nudged her shoulder. "No one wants to think what will happen to Beth!"

She did as he said, suffering through Beth's illness and death, overlooking everyone's sniffs by keeping her eyes on the blurry page, and promising the men that their next book would be a comedy.

She wanted to laugh, until she looked in Joe's office one night. She had finished reading and wanted to say good-night. She was going to knock on the door, but it was open a fraction, so she merely opened it wider, to see the major slumped forward, his hands over his eyes.

Her first instinct was to tiptoe away. But then her face grew hot with shame as she thought of what might have happened to her if this man, sitting there so sadly, had ignored his instincts after that disastrous encounter at the Dunklins. She opened the door wider and walked in quietly, determined to help if she could. She put her hand lightly on his shoulder.

He started, then looked up at her. She couldn't help her

sigh; she knew what that kind of misery felt like. She pulled a chair up beside him and just sat there, her hands in her lap now.

With a great effort, he sat up straight. She silently handed him her handkerchief and he blew his nose. He looked at her again.

"Susanna, I treat his men for frostbite, I patch and stitch where needed, but George Crook can never overlook that moment when I turned my attention from a dying soldier in blue to a living one in gray, no matter that fourteen years have come and gone. Hippocrates himself could argue with him, and it would make no difference." He smiled faintly. "Crook will punish me forever, but you know how that feels, don't you?"

Susanna nodded, not trusting herself to speak, until she had taken several deep breaths. "You told me that living well is the best revenge. Is that a lie?"

He shook his head, and his expression went from sorrowful to rueful. "I have it on good authority that Crook is still trying to get me cashiered from the army."

"No!"

"Yes. Luckily, no one listens to him on this matter, and I practice good medicine, no matter what he thinks." His smile was no smile. "I suppose I have stayed in the army mainly because I do not want General Crook to think he drove me out." Joe grasped Susanna's arm. "A good gambler knows when to fold a bad hand, but I don't gamble any better than I cook."

"All the more reason for you to improve your French," she said, covering his hand with her own briefly. "When the letter comes from Pasteur himself, admitting you to his lycée, you can walk away with no regret."

"I can," he said, after a moment's reflection. "I had better study my French."

"Mais oui, monsieur."

* * *

To her relief, Colonel Reynolds and General Crook led four troops of horses north to Fort Fetterman in early March, including Dan Reese's and Jim O'Leary's cavalry companies. Susanna listened to both wives crying through the walls, silently took her cousin by the hand and walked her next door. Her eyes red, Kate O'Leary opened the door. She swallowed her amazement and opened her arms wider, folding her difficult neighbor into her generous embrace.

"Good!" Susanna exclaimed, and closed the door on them, clutching each other and crying. She went back to the Reeses' quarters, cooked Stanley a toasted cheese sandwich and spent the evening, shoes off, reading to him in his bed. By morning, all was serene.

"I'm glad you're infantry, Private Benedict," Susanna said that morning, as they stood at their classroom door—set apart from the rest of the warehouse by flour sacks—and ushered in their students, some of them uncharacteristically sober because their fathers had ridden away.

"If the summer expedition goes as planned, you'll have the whole classroom, because even the infantry will go, which means yours truly," he told her. "I think that's why the army favors school terms that end in May, when summer campaigning starts."

"Could I keep the school going this summer?" she asked him.

"If the administrative council says yea, why not?"

What am I thinking? she asked herself later, as her little ones concentrated on simple addition and subtraction. *I'm going to be gone from here by June. Where, I do not know yet.* It would keep, she decided, returning her attention to her pupils.

Not long before recall from fatigue, Susanna looked up to see Majors Townsend and Randolph in the flour-sack doorway. Standing behind them, hat in hand, was a man she did not know.

"Oh, please, no," she said, suddenly terrified, thinking of Tommy and Frederick.

Joe crossed the room in a few steps and put his arm around her shoulder, holding her close to him. Major Townsend raised his eyebrows but said nothing.

"It's not bad news," Joe told her.

Townsend nodded to Private Benedict, who quietly dismissed the students. Susanna couldn't help both her pride and relief when they marched out like little angels. Private Benedict saluted smartly and Susanna brushed the chalk dust from her dress, even as Joe continued to hold her close.

When Major Townsend and the strange man came into the classroom, Susanna exchanged an "Are we in trouble?" look with her fellow teacher. He gave her the slightest shrug.

"I'm all right now," she told Joe, not wanting him to let go, but not willing to give Major Townsend any fodder for gossip. "Just for a moment… You know what I thought."

Major Townsend turned to the civilian. "Private Benedict and Mrs. Hopkins, this is Jules Ecoffey. He, uh, owns the Three Mile Ranch with Adolf Cuny."

Susanna could not help noticing the look that Private Benedict exchanged with Joe.

Anthony Benedict cleared his throat. "Major Townsend, I know I'm the lowest man on the totem pole in this room, but should Mrs. Hopkins be party to a conversation involving Three Mile Ranch?"

Silence. Susanna looked from man to man, mystified. Her gaze lingered longest on the post surgeon, not a man slow with cues.

"Private, the matter concerns Mrs. Hopkins most of all, because there is a potential pupil at Three Mile." Joe glanced at Jules Ecoffey. "Jules, better explain Three Mile Ranch, if you can, or should I?"

"You do it."

"Mrs. Hopkins, let me put this as plainly as I can, even though the matter is offensive. Among other more legitimate enterprises, Ecoffey and Cuny run a hog ranch." He smiled, because he seemed to be reading her mind. "It's not what you think. It's a whorehouse, located three miles from the fort."

"Oh," she said, and felt her face grow warm.

"I occasionally have the unenviable duty of treating prostitutes and soldiers for venereal diseases, although I am not certain that mercury does the slightest good. Apparently one of the, uh, practitioners of the art of Venus has a daughter, age six, that Mr. Ecoffey would like to see in school."

"She should be in school," Susanna said. She looked at Major Townsend. "Sir, I have no objection, and I doubt Private Benedict has, either."

"Not one, sir," Anthony said. "We have room and Mrs. Hopkins is an exemplary teacher. But how…"

"How will I get her to you?" Ecoffey asked. He glanced at Major Townsend, too. "I propose to deliver her to this classroom every morning. Afternoons are more difficult, but if someone can see her to the Rustic Hotel, I can pick her up from there."

"The Rustic…" Susanna looked at Ecoffey.

"It is the hotel John Collins is constructing, a quarter mile from here," Joe explained, when Ecoffey said nothing. "Is it open?"

Ecoffey nodded. "Just barely. If I can retrieve Maddie from there, it would give me time to get back to the ranch for…" He paused, his face red now. "…the evening's activity."

"Heavens, where does the child go in the evening?" Susanna asked.

"She sits in my office until…until it quiets down," the man said.

I am appalled, Susanna thought, unconsciously edging closer to her fellow teacher. "Such a place! Couldn't we just keep her here?" She hadn't meant to blurt it out, but the idea of a child at Three Mile Ranch made her blood run in chunks.

The look Jules Ecoffey gave her was a kindly one. "I know what you are thinking, but Maddie has a mother who loves her. Perhaps if you have children, you understand."

She did, with a clarity that sliced right through her shock and disgust. "We will do the best we can, if…if…Major Townsend and Major Randolph allow it."

"I can think of a hundred objections," the post commander said. "There might be a huge outcry from the parents of these students, or from the officers' families. Major Randolph?"

"I can't think of a single objection," he said firmly. "Would you be willing to pay some tuition?"

"I would," Ecoffey said promptly. "Only name it."

"Might I ask why you are doing this?" Susanna asked. "How long has…"

"Maddie Wilby," Ecoffey said.

"…been there? And why?"

"She came with her mother from Denver before Christmas." Ecoffey shrugged. "I did not know of the child until Claudine Wilby arrived. Why am I doing this?" He shrugged again. "Perhaps I care." He glanced at the post surgeon. "There is more. We will talk." He bowed to Susanna. "Madam, she is a charming child."

"Is she your daughter?" Susanna asked, her voice soft.

Apparently not surprised by her question, even though Major Townsend stared in amazement, Ecoffey shrugged again. "I knew Claudine briefly in Denver. Who can tell? Good day, Mrs. Hopkins."

The three men left. Susanna stared at Private Benedict. "I

used to teach at an exclusive girls' school in Carlisle, Pennsylvania," she said.

"And I clerked in a store in Hartford, Connecticut," Anthony said, his voice equally mystified. "Who knew the army would be so interesting? How much do you think Major Randolph will charge for tuition?"

"I rather hate to think where the money is coming from."

She thought about Maddie Wilby while her night class members sounded out words to each other. When they left, she stayed in Maeve's warm parlor, telling the sergeant's wife what had happened that afternoon.

"Do you think the other families here on Suds Row will have objections?" Susanna asked.

Maeve shook her head. "What business is it of theirs? Poor child."

My own child has no mother, Susanna thought. "Maybe not so poor. Maybe we should remind ourselves that she has a mother who loves her." It was food for thought.

She was glad Joe Randolph came to escort her home by himself, without Nick.

"I put Saint Paul in charge of counting sheets in the linen closet," Joe said as they started across the parade ground. "I wanted to talk to you."

"What else did Ecoffey tell you?"

"He wants me to visit Claudine Wilby. Apparently she is ill. Will you come with me?"

"Me? Now?"

"You. Now."

"I'm afraid."

"You're Maddie Wilby's teacher. Let's meet her."

God knows he didn't want to keep bullying Susanna Hopkins, but there was no overlooking her fright as they sat in the ambulance, bumping over the bad road between Fort Laramie and Three Mile Ranch. Maybe if he kept up some informative chatter she would be less intimidated.

"I hardly need to tell you that Three Mile Ranch is off-limits to all military personnel, but the boys have a way of sneaking off."

Her faint smile encouraged him. "I'm surprised you could dredge up enough iron-willed soldiers to accompany this ambulance," she said in a faint approximation of a joke.

"Ah, that is the beauty of having our cavalry troops gone north to fight Northern Roamers. Those men riding alongside are mounted infantry, and they are doing their dead level best to stay in the saddle. I also showed them several textbook pages of diseased organs before I got into the ambulance. I anticipate no trouble."

"Major Randolph, you are amazing," she said.

"Merely desperate," he assured her. "Let me tell you about this place. Jules Ecoffey, an enterprising Swiss, runs it with his partner Adolf Cuny, another enterprising Swiss. They also operate Six Mile Ranch about…"

"Six miles from here in another direction," Susanna said.

"My dear, you are wise beyond your years," Joe teased. "Precisely. Both establishments have a legitimate purpose of supplying miners headed for the Black Hills. Prostitution is a side venture, apparently started a few years back when business was slow. I visit both places to stitch up bar fight wounds and treat the clap. I hope you are not too disappointed in me to know that post surgeons are the only persons at Fort Laramie officially allowed here. Al Hartsuff takes his turn, when he is here. Our contract surgeon, long gone, was too squeamish."

"Have you visited Claudine before?" Susanna asked, then put her hands to her face. "Oh, you know what I mean!"

"Of course," he replied with a chuckle. "No. Jules said she

has been here only a month or two. I do not know what I will find." *But I suspect,* he thought.

The ambulance driver took them directly to the large adobe building that Joe knew housed the saloon, restaurant and office. He held out his hand to help Susanna from the vehicle, and did not let go of it as he led her into the building.

It was early evening, and the saloon was nearly deserted. Joe had his own private chuckle to note how quickly the two men at the bar left the building. Those were two cases of drunkenness he would probably not have to treat tomorrow at sick call.

Jules Ecoffey appeared through a door beside the bar and gestured to them after a courtly bow so out of place in a hog ranch. Joe glanced at the woman who clung to his hand with a death grip. She was pale, but her eyes were filled with resolution. *Would I be this brave, were our situations reversed?* he asked himself. He doubted it supremely.

Jules ushered them into a tiny office, the desk overflowing with papers. In the corner sat a little girl with a doll in her lap. Joe smiled to see her, a child with big brown eyes, auburn hair neatly arranged and that look of patience he was familiar with from children in fraught situations. He had seen that look many times during the Civil War.

Susanna went to the child immediately, kneeling beside her chair, exercising those fine instincts of woman, mother and teacher he already appreciated, perhaps never with the intensity he did now.

"You're Maddie Wilby?" she asked. "What a lovely doll. I am Mrs. Hopkins and I will be your teacher."

He left the office quietly with Jules. They went to the adobe building next door that housed six prostitutes.

"I put her and Maddie out here because each crib has two rooms."

Big of you, Joe wanted to say, but knew better.

Ecoffey knocked and then opened the door.

Only a blind man wouldn't have seen the woman's resemblance to the lovely child in the office. Only a blind man couldn't have diagnosed her immediately. Joe didn't even need to put his hand on her forehead. One look at her pale skin and exquisite frailty told him everything. He silently gave her a month and not one day more.

He sat beside her anyway, calling "Mrs. Wilby," until her eyes fluttered open in surprise, perhaps that he knew she had a last name. "I am Major Randolph, Fort Laramie's senior post surgeon. I brought a Mrs. Hopkins with me. She will be Maddie's teacher. They are together in Mr. Ecoffey's office right now."

He should have been prepared for the tears that filled Claudine Wilby's brown eyes, but he was not, compelling him to admit to his own prejudices and judgments around prostitutes. *She loves her child, you idiot,* he reminded himself, as he dabbed at the woman's tears. He doubted she was much beyond her middle twenties, aged prematurely by the hard life he wouldn't even have wished on so vile a woman as Mrs. Dunklin.

He took his patient's hand and squeezed it. She tried to return the gesture, but could do no more than curl her delicate fingers around his for a brief moment. Her eyes closed again, signaling that minuscule effort had exhausted her. He revised his estimate and gave her two weeks, no more.

"Maddie will be in good hands in Mrs. Hopkins's class," he said, his lips close to her ear now. "You needn't worry about her. Save your strength. I'm going to prescribe some powders for you."

She nodded, then opened her mouth to say something. Nothing came out except a sigh, which relieved him of telling her that his puny powders would be monumentally ineffective against last stage consumption. Not that he would have; he could lie with the best of physicians, when confronted with death. He knew from experience that she might even rally a bit, thinking the medicine was doing some good.

She did not open her eyes again while he handed a packet to Ecoffey and instructed him in its use. To his credit, Ecoffey didn't even blink when Joe insisted that the poor woman see no more clients.

"Can your other girls take turns sitting with her?" he asked, after pulling the coverlet higher on wasted shoulders.

"They already do," Ecoffey replied, with considerable dignity. "And no, Major, she has seen no clients since the middle of January. We are not entirely devoid of feeling here."

Joe accepted his quiet words as a well-deserved rebuke, and said nothing. As they walked back to the main building, Joe turned around when another door opened and a woman walked into Claudine's crib. *Look out for her,* he thought, *and for heaven's sake, leave this deadly profession when you can.*

He returned to the office to see Susanna sitting in Ecoffey's swivel chair, reading to Maddie, who was snuggled on her lap. When she saw him and Ecoffey, she kissed the top of the child's head and closed the book.

"We'll have time for more reading tomorrow," she whispered. Susanna spoke to Ecoffey. "Send her with a lunch, and a slate with chalk, if you have such things here. We'll give her a good place to learn."

Susanna waited until the ambulance door had shut behind her before giving Joe her spectacles and covering her face with her hands. She shivered and shook, beyond tears, as he held her close. He told her what he had seen in the crib, and his diagnosis and prognosis. By the time they arrived at Fort Laramie, she had regained her spectacles and her composure, but made no objection to his arm around her slim shoulders, which were weighted with their own burdens.

When he helped her from the ambulance, she held his hand again for a long moment. "You say two weeks to a month?"

"No more."

She turned to look into his face, giving him the full power of her own beautiful eyes. "I say more. No woman willingly surrenders a child, even for so unkind a visitor as death."

He did not doubt her own prognosis.

Chapter Fifteen

Maddie Wilby fit into Susanna's classroom as easily as though she had been there all term, reminding Susanna how flexible children could be. Maddie knew her letters and numbers already. By the end of the third day, the self-possessed child, obviously used to the company of adults, was helping the younger pupils with adding single columns.

"Monsieur Ecoffey lets me look at his ledgers," Maddie had explained to her, in her matter-of-fact way. "Each morning I check his totals from the night's business—two, four, six, eight, ten, twelve."

"That's a questionable way to learn to count by twos," Susanna told Joe when she came to the hospital a few nights later to finish *Little Women*. "Joe, those women aren't paid very much for services rendered."

She knew she had shocked him with such a statement, but that he would see the humor of it. "Susanna, do I see before me a rabble-rousing reformer?" he asked.

"I'm just a teacher," she assured him.

"Just." He took her hand, raised it to his lips, then turned back to the paperwork on his desk, as if such a gesture was something he did every day of his life.

"Are…are you practicing for Paris?" she asked, wishing she did not sound so breathless.

He just shook his head as a slow smile spread across his face. "Leave me alone. Go read to my vile patients! I love it when hardened veterans cry over Beth and worry about Amy."

Susanna hoped every morning that Jules Ecoffey would be true to his word and get Maddie to school. And he did, depositing her at the warehouse and admonishing the child in quiet French to do her best for her mother's sake.

The afternoon transfer was less reliable. Hand in hand with Rooney O'Leary, who had whispered to her earlier that he thought Maddie was pretty, Susanna walked the O'Leary's son home, and then continued the quarter mile to the Rustic Hotel, a raw building that more than lived up to its name. She read to Maddie or sometimes just held her on her lap, until Ecoffey arrived.

He was invariably late. After the second day, Nick Martin accompanied her and sat with her as darkness fell. By the end of the week, the post surgeon came along, too, when Nick was busy. Once he rode out with Ecoffey and Maddie. When he came back hours later, he slipped a note under the Reeses' door for her. "Claudine is holding her own," the note read. "I believe your prognosis is better than mine. JR."

In all the turmoil, Maddie Wilby held her own, too, calling no attention to herself, but capable in a way that made Private Benedict shake his head in wonder. She always came to school as neat as a pin, her hair arranged beautifully in styles too old for her years, but lovely. To her amusement, Susanna observed two distinct styles of coiffure, which made her suspect that at least two of the Three Mile Ranch women were competing.

Maddie's clothes were equally lovely. Only the sharpest of needlewomen could have detected they were cut down from larger sizes, or so Maeve Rattigan told Susanna when they stopped at the Rattigans' for an after-school cookie.

"There must be plenty of willing hands at Three Mile," Maeve whispered to her. "So stylish."

The cookie habit had begun almost as soon as Maddie arrived. After school one day, Susanna had walked both of her after-school charges to Suds Row to visit Maeve, who had been pulling cookies from the oven when they arrived. After two days of this, the children just naturally veered to the Rattigans', and Maeve did not disappoint.

Susanna knew Joe made visits to Three Mile Ranch as Claudine's condition worsened. He stopped by the Reeses' quarters a week later, long after taps.

"I know it's late." He nodded to Emily, whose eye were full of fright. "Now, now, Emily. No news from the field," he soothed. "I just wanted give Susanna something. Rest your mind."

Susanna lowered her voice. "Is Claudine still alive?"

He handed her a note with delicate, spidery handwriting.

"'*Merci*,'" Susanna read. "That's all?"

"It took all her strength, Fifi said."

"Fifi?"

"One of the girls," he replied, and held out a book. "This was at the hospital addressed to you, and it's from a more dignified source."

Puzzled, she took the book and let out a whoop that made Emily look up from her knitting in surprise. "*Little Men!* Oh, my! Is there a note?"

"Look inside."

She did. "'I have heard through the infamous army grapevine that you just completed *Little Women*,'" she read. "'We just finished this at our house, and it's the book that follows Jo March's adventures. Keep it as long as you need it.'" Susanna ran her finger over the signature. "'Mrs. Andrew Burt.'" She looked at the post surgeon. "She is so kind."

Emily looked, too. "Susanna, do you have a champion?" she asked, amazement in her voice.

"Just a nice lady. That's all," she replied quietly, when she really wanted to dance around the room. "Please tell her thank-you for me, Major."

"Tell her yourself," he said, as he opened the door again. He touched Susanna's nose. "I *told* you it was just a matter of hanging on a little longer."

"You did," she agreed, wishing he would stay there. She put her hand on his arm to detain him. "We've heard rumors of battle, and Emily and Katie are on edge. If you know anything…"

"I'll tell you immediately," he whispered back, his eyes on Emily sitting with her knitting, staring at the wall. He kissed Susanna's cheek quickly. "Chin up."

She tried to be severe with him. "You would do better to conjugate a French verb or two, rather than kiss me on the cheek like a Frenchman."

"To be proper, I should kiss the other cheek, too," he whispered, and did just that. "Do you know, Jules Ecoffey—whose French is excellent, if not his good taste—loaned me a scurrilous book of naked women and French text. It looks like more fun than conjugating everlasting verbs. So glad I didn't hand you the wrong book just now. 'Night, Susanna."

Amazed, she stood in the open door, watching his jaunty walk as he crossed the parade ground. In another moment, he was whistling.

After school the next day, Susanna worked up her nerve to visit Elizabeth Burt. It took all her courage to knock on the door, and to her relief, the infantry captain's wife opened her door wide and welcomed her.

"I was hoping you would visit me," Mrs. Burt said. "Would you like some tea?"

Susanna was so terrified she didn't think she could swallow, but she nodded. In another moment, she was seated in the parlor, teacup in hand.

"I wanted to thank you for the book," she said, and took a sip. Peppermint. Just the way she liked it. "The men liked *Little Women* so well, and they are enjoying its companion now."

"I thought they might. My husband blew his nose a lot when we were reading *Little Women!*"

She talked of inconsequentials then, and Susanna felt herself relaxing. By the time she left, she wondered why she had worried at all.

Mrs. Burt showed her out, touching her hand. "Mrs. Hopkins, would you object to cards here some evening with a few of my friends?"

Susanna felt her face drain of color. "I shouldn't think…"

Mrs. Burt looked at her in a kindly manner. "You need never fear, in my home." She touched her again. "Think about it, all right?"

March dragged, mainly because escort service between Fort Russell in Cheyenne and Fort Laramie was reduced to vital messages only, since so many mounted soldiers were in the Powder River country. The December and January newspapers had been around the fort twice, and were finally relegated to lining shelves and starting fires.

When Colonel Bradley, commanding officer of the Ninth Infantry, arrived to relieve Major Townsend of duty, he brought mail with him, and a stack of newspapers. They followed the usual pecking order of rank, with dependents last, but Major Randolph brought Emily and Susanna one Pennsylvania paper on the sly.

"Captain Dunklin snatched the Gettysburg paper, but he

wasn't quick enough to grab the Carlisle one, too," Joe said as he presented the newspaper to Emily with a flourish. "What a dog in the manger. I'm glad I outrank him. Use it well and pass it on." He pointed to Susanna. "And *you* have a roomful of patients waiting to hear about Professor Bhaer's school for boys at Plumfield. Need an escort?"

"Do you have time tonight for more French verbs?" she asked as they walked to the hospital. Susanna took a deep breath and regretted it. "My stars, what *is* that odor?"

"That is the fragrance of spring at Fort Laramie. While you are reading to a roomful of eager listeners, I will be composing a stiffly worded memo to the effect that it is time for the garrison to turn out and police the grounds. Don't let me offend you—"

"You couldn't possibly. I have heard it all," she murmured.

"I'll be the judge of that. During this long, cold winter, everyone from private to major—I am the notable exception—has been tossing the contents of chamber pots out into the snow, knowing said contents will be covered by the next snowfall, and so on."

"I know this for a fact," Susanna said. "Pardon *your* blushes now!"

"It takes more than that to make me blush," Joe retorted. "We are now at that moment of reckoning. Spring at Fort Laramie brings with it the bouquet of raw sewage. Welcome to my public health world. It's even more fun than being a surgeon."

"I had no idea your position was so exalted," she joked. "Very well, you may write your memo. But there will be French verbs in your near future."

Joe was still laboring over his memo when she finished reading, but there was Nick Martin to deposit her at the Reeses' quarters, where Emily was still reading the Carlisle paper. Her eyes troubled, Emily gestured for her to come closer.

"What is it?" Susanna asked.

"Look."

Susanna looked where Emily pointed, read it, and read it again. "Do you believe me now?" she asked finally.

Emily nodded. "I almost overlooked the article. It's so small. 'Frederick Hopkins of Hopkins Carriage Works has filed for bankruptcy,'" she read, taking the newspaper back. "There is such a list of creditors! But that is not the worst part." She turned to another page and jabbed her finger. "Look at this letter from one of his creditors, blaming 'the grain and the grape' for his dereliction!"

"I was not wrong," Susanna said quietly, but there was no victory, not with her son facing ruin, too, and her so far away. She pulled on her coat and grabbed the newspaper from Emily, running up the hill to the hospital to arrive at Joe's office, out of breath and her hair tugged out of its pins by the wind.

Nick stopped sweeping. Startled, Joe looked up from his paperwork. He was out of his chair in a moment, his arm around her, as she calmed herself. She still couldn't talk, but she handed him the Carlisle newspaper and pointed to the article. He read it, and then she turned to the editorial page with the condemning letter. They stared at each other over the paper.

"Is there anything I can do, do you think, to get my son back?" she asked.

"We need a lawyer."

She stared at him, still out of breath and wondering if she had heard him correctly. He set down the paper and put his hands gently on her face.

"I know what I said. *We* need a lawyer." He glanced at Nick, who stood there leaning on his broom, looking at the article. "Nick, could you see if there is any of my bad coffee left in the ward?"

Joe sat her down and took the chair opposite her. He made no other move to touch her, but his expression seemed to reach out and caress her heart.

"This…this isn't your fight, Major Randolph," she said tentatively and formally, so unsure of herself.

"I rather believe it is," he replied.

She tried again; the man needed to be reasoned with. "Major Randolph, I'm the scapegoat and bad example of this entire garrison."

"Not lately," he countered. "The people who matter know better. I happen to be one of them."

He looked up when Nick returned with coffee. "Thanks. You might as well retire now, my friend."

Nick shook his head. "She's in trouble? I don't like that."

"I don't either, Nick," Joe said, speaking carefully to the big man. "It's her son who could be in trouble, back in Carlisle. Susanna is fine."

No, I'm not, she thought, almost as a reflex, then let the matter work on her brain as a great feeling of relief covered her. And there was Nick, her champion, looking so concerned. "I *am* fine," she told him, meaning it with all her heart, because it was suddenly true. "My son is in a difficult position because his father is facing ruin." She put out her hand to Nick. "The wheels of justice move slowly, my friend."

Nick nodded and left.

"You'll have to reassure him. He *is* my champion, isn't he?"

"I'm another one, Susanna," Joe replied. "Casual travel between forts is so unsafe right now, but when things loosen up, we'll go to Cheyenne for a lawyer. Coffee?"

She took the cup from him, sipped and made a face. "You haven't a clue what to do in your kitchen, or a hospital kitchen, or probably over a campfire."

There was a long silence that Susanna knew better than to interrupt. She saw before her a man whose heart was as hesitant as her own, who years before had watched, powerless, as the dearest person in his life died a terrible death. *You need time,* she thought, as she set down the cup and rose.

"I'll go back to Emily now. We'll…we'll worry about an attorney later."

The look in his eyes told her he knew she wasn't talking about attorneys. He nodded, then put his arms around her, holding her close until her arms went around him, too. They stood that way, her head against his chest, until he kissed the top of her untidy head and stepped away, professional again.

She hadn't even removed her coat, so she waited while he put his on and doused the lamp. She followed him into the hall and waited while he walked into the ward and spoke to his night steward. Then, arm in arm, the two of them walked slowly, silently, down the hill. She noticed that his steps slowed as he passed his own quarters, almost as if he wanted to take her inside.

Not yet, Joe, not yet, she thought, relieved when his pace quickened again, because she did not want to tell him no.

The light in the Reeses' parlor was still burning, so she asked him in. Emily just sat in her chair, knitting in her lap. She looked at the newspaper in Joe's hand.

"Can we rectify a terrible wrong?" her cousin asked, surprising Susanna with her concern.

Joe looked her in the eye and shook his head. "I'll circle those articles and leave the paper on the Dunklins' stoop. I know from long experience that some are unable to give up a prejudice. We can try, but some minds won't change. Good night to both of you lovely ladies."

After the door closed, Emily and Susanna just looked at each other. Emily broke the silence first. "Cousin, my feet are cold every night and I know yours must be, too. What do you say we share my bed, like we used to when we were little?" Her voice faltered. "Until my darling returns."

After a good cry with her cousin, Susanna had the warmest night's sleep in recent memory. Cuddled close to Emily, she thought of Major Randolph in his solitary quarters and wished herself beside him.

Word of battle seemed to come from everywhere and nowhere. Garbled word filtered down, probably carried in some way known only to them, from Indian to Indian until it reached the Arikara scouts at Fort Laramie: big fight. Village burning. Horse herd captured. And that was all anyone knew.

To Joe's surprise, he who thought he knew human nature, it was Emily Reese who gathered women at the hospital to roll bandages and scrape lint, preparing for the troops' return. "Thank you for keeping us busy," she told him one afternoon.

He wanted to visit Susanna, but she was busy all day with school, and then night school, and then reading twice a week to his patients. Organizing and policing the filthy grounds occupied him, and he chafed at his duties, where before he would have just accepted them.

As the tense days passed, he examined his heart, trying to make scientific sense of his emotions, because that was how he worked. Probably since that awful night in the aid station when he had turned from a dying man to save a living one, and sealed his future, he had allowed a callus to grow around his heart. He knew that was scientifically impossible. In his yearnings to turn to Susanna Hopkins now for comfort, he understood what he had done to himself. The callus was gone now and he ached inside, because he wanted to love that lady. He was in pain, where he had been numb. Numbness was better, in some respects, but as a physician he knew pain might mean healing.

She seemed to see him differently, too, in the few moments they had to look, talk and say nothing remotely close to what they wanted to say. He made his peace with that, because larger concerns loomed.

One concern that *embarrassed* him was the disappearance of Nick Martin. Perhaps *embarrassed* was the wrong word, he told himself, the morning he found Nick gone from the military reservation, along with two hundred dollars, the entire contents of his special fund. Joe endured a scathing rebuke from Colonel Bradley for being so careless around an idiot, and knew that his pride was more wounded. It was an easy enough matter to assure Bradley he could make good the loss with his own money.

Mostly he missed Nick's help around the hospital, and his escort for Susanna and Maddie to the Rustic Hotel every afternoon. He discovered he missed Nick for a lot of reasons; maybe he missed his strange friendship.

"Gone? You mean as in *gone?*" Susanna asked that afternoon as he walked her and the child to the Rustic Hotel.

No wonder he loved her. She had the good sense to laugh at herself, which gave him permission to laugh, too, because it was the funniest thing he'd heard in days.

"Yes, *that* gone," he teased, which earned him a slap on the arm, which made Maddie laugh, too.

"Any idea where?" Susanna asked.

He could only shrug and suggest that Nick had followed the increasingly large number of miners now using the iron bridge that took them to the Black Hills and lots of gold, or so they hoped. Amazing that just the thought of gold seduced otherwise reasonable men to take a chance on Indians, accident, ailments and other calamities.

For a change, Jules Ecoffey was there on time at the Rustic, worry etched all over his face. Susanna saw it, too, and distracted Maddie with another cookie purloined from the generous Maeve.

"Is Claudine dead?" Joe whispered.

"No, but hemorrhaging. Could you come? I brought an extra horse so you wouldn't have to take the time to get one."

"Let's go."

Susanna was so well in tune with him that he didn't do more than wave his hand. She nodded, kissed Maddie and handed her up to Jules. Joe looked back once to see her still watching them.

When they arrived at Three Mile, one of the women took Maddie with her, and he followed Jules to Claudine's crib. He knew what he would see, but he was never prepared for it. No one should suffer as consumptives suffered. She had bled so much that she was impossibly white, her eyes large and terrified.

Once the blood was cleaned up, he helped Fifi dress Claudine in a clean nightgown. He held her frail body as another woman changed the bed, then carefully settled her between tidy coverlets, with a well-wrapped iron pig at her feet. He knew the hospital wouldn't miss it.

There was nothing he could do, so he sat with her, telling her about Maddie's progress at school, which lit up her tired eyes.

"She's a bright one, Claudine."

The prostitute nodded and struggled to speak. "Promise me…" was the best she could do.

"I promise you she will have an excellent home and all the education she needs to make a real difference in the world." Joe swallowed, amazed how his callus-free heart could ache so much for this prostitute he could not help. "Of course, she still has a fine mother. Claudine, you've done good things with Maddie."

The woman nodded, then slept, at peace in that strange way of patients who have reached the point of acceptance.

He rode back to Fort Laramie long after dark, thinking he

would just go to bed. He went instead to the Reeses' quarters, knocking softly on the door when he saw there was still a light on.

In nightgown and robe, Susanna let him in, her finger to her lips. "I couldn't sleep until I knew," she told him.

He sat in the armchair he figured was Dan's, wondering if he would have the energy to get up. "I'm not sure what she's using for blood now, because she lost so much. Hanging on, Suzie."

He had never called her that before. For all he knew, it was a nickname her former husband had used. Her smile told Joe otherwise, which relieved him, because he had wanted to call her that for ages. "I just sat with her and made her all kinds of extravagant promises for a rosy future for her daughter. She believed me, and maybe I believed me, too."

"I'd be willing to sit with Claudine."

He shook his head. "No. I won't have you risking infection. I'm not totally sure how consumption travels, but I take no chances with people I'm…fond of."

There. He wanted to say more, but he still had his doubts about himself, not Suzie. "If I'm speaking out of turn…"

"You're not, but that will do for now," she said, her voice equally quiet. "I would suffer if the, um, good people of Fort Laramie ostracize you if you are…fond of me."

Ostracism? Child's play. He tried out her nickname again, noticing how her eyes lit up. "Suzie, I've been ostracized by masters, and I include my own family, may you never meet them. I'm always amazed how ostracism ends when someone in garrison needs a doctor and all they have is little ol' Virginia me."

She started to say something, but there was Emily at the top of the stairs, alert, her voice full of panic.

"Susanna! Please don't tell me it's bad news!"

Joe got up quickly and went to the stairs. "No fears, Emily.

It concerns Maddie Wilby's mother, who is fighting a pretty good fight. Go back to sleep."

He sat down again with a sigh. "The commanding officer often gives me the 'death walk,' I call it. I get to deliver sad tidings. All we know so far is that there was a fight, but every cavalry wife on this post has dread in her eyes when she sees me."

Susanna put her hand over his. "These are difficult times. Perhaps we had better just remain fond."

He thought it was a stupid idea and nearly told her so. A moment's consideration forced him to agree, because he knew she was right. Still, if everyone waited until the time was precisely right to marry, or even fool around, the earth would have ground to a stop eons ago. She looked so pretty in her flannel nightgown. If he made a move toward her, he wasn't sure if she would resist or yield. Better not test the matter. She was right; it was late.

"'Night, Suzie. Don't let the bedbugs bite."

Joe was right about the tension, Susanna decided, as another day passed. She felt the whole garrison's strain, and so did her little ones at school. One child, ordinarily so cheerful, burst into tears when the chalk broke against his slate. Another child glowered at her uncharacteristically when she said it was time to turn in her class work. Even Private Benedict had a sharp word for his best pupil, too distracted to diagram a compound sentence.

Taking her cue from her students' worry, Susanna abandoned her afternoon lessons and just read to them instead. Everyone eventually took a turn on her lap, and she dubbed them "page-turning monitors." The afternoon stop at Maeve Rattigan's quarters lengthened to include ample time for Maddie on Maeve's lap, or the sergeant's, if he happened to be home. Susanna noticed with a pang that Maddie's pretty hair was less tidy. Joe had told her how busy the other sporting women were, taking care of Claudine.

The odorous policing of the fort had begun, which meant the post surgeon was out at all hours, making sure the prisoners from the guardhouse scooped, shoveled and limed the ground. This led to a flaming row when one of the more lax infantry lieutenants took exception to his company's participation, and the major thought otherwise.

"I always win those discussions," he told her later as he passed the Reeses' quarters, headed for his own. "Amazing how rank can sharpen even a second lieutenant's intellect." He held up his hands playfully to ward her off. "Close enough, Suzie! I reek."

From a distance, he told her he had left the Carlisle newspaper for the Dunklins' perusal, but Susanna had no expectations. The only difference she noticed was that Mrs. Dunklin avoided her eyes now, the gloat gone. Susanna didn't look for more, especially since it was more pleasant to exchange a few words with Mrs. Burt, or spend an evening laughing with her night school students, some of whom could read better than their husbands now.

I could worry myself into an early grave, Susanna decided after a week of tension. It was a rare night. The house was her own, since Emily and Stanley had adjourned to the Burt quarters for an evening of cards and games—anything to create a diversion. Susanna had been invited, too, but that was a step she wasn't prepared to take yet.

She had adjourned to the kitchen table to write her weekly letter to Tommy, when she heard banging at the door. Her nerves practically humming, she listened. No, someone was kicking at the door. Her heart in her mouth, Susanna leaped to her feet, her mind crowded with Tommy first, as always, then Captain Reese, and now Nick.

"Yes?" she quavered, not about to open the door.

"Ma'am, it's Sentry Number 4. There's someone who needs you."

Confused, she opened the door. Her coat a mess and her shoes muddy, Maddie Wilby was held tight in the arms of a sentry who juggled his gun on one shoulder.

"Maddie!" she exclaimed, taking the sobbing child from the soldier, who stepped back in obvious relief.

"I found her on the flats by the Rustic Hotel," he said, his eyes full of concern. "I think she must have walked from Three Mile Ranch." He touched her head. "When I called out the password challenge, she started to cry. I have a little sister back in Indiana…." He shouldered his rifle again, nodded to them and left the porch.

His voice came out of the darkness. "Mrs. Hopkins, she told me you would help her, because you are her teacher."

"I am, Private. Thank you," she told him, then called after him. "Before you return to your post, could you please inform Major Randolph?" She turned her attention to the child in her arms. "Maddie, my dear, is your mother…"

Maddie nodded, clutching her tighter. "Everyone was crying. I couldn't see her. I knew you would help me."

"Yes, but mercy, you took a chance getting here," Susanna said, sitting down with her, trying to calm herself so she wouldn't show fear to a distressed child. She sat still a long moment, holding Maddie, wanting to hold her forever, since her own dear child was out of reach, perhaps never to be seen again. As her mind cleared, she knew she had to be brave. Someone else needed Maddie even more.

"My dear, I know just the place for you. Let me get my coat." She yanked it on, knowing that if she hesitated for another moment, her resolve would fail her. There was only one place for Maddie Wilby, one refuge. She picked up the child and ran toward the footbridge, running from herself, maybe, because she wanted the child for her own. Halfway across the parade ground, she wasn't sure if she had closed the door behind her. She hesitated and nearly turned back, but from some forgotten reservoir of courage deep inside her, she found determination.

Chapter Sixteen

Joe joined her at the footbridge, plucking Maddie from her arms. With another sob, the child wrapped her legs around him, her face in his shirt. He hadn't bothered with his uniform jacket or overcoat. Susanna looked down. His shoes were off and he wore moccasins. He must have been relaxing in his quarters when the sentry burst in.

"Joe, she walked from Three Mile Ranch!" she said, hurrying to keep up.

"Good God." He held the child close. "She has a guardian angel working overtime, this one."

"Are we doing the right thing?" she whispered.

"The rightest thing anyone has ever done, my dear," he assured her. "We're about to cure the common heartache."

"I want her, but I know she will be better off here," she said simply.

"Then bless your heart, Susanna Hopkins," he whispered. "You're one in a million."

While Joe soothed Maddie, Susanna knocked on the Rattigans' door. In his shirtsleeves and socks—Susanna had never seen him so casual—Sergeant Rattigan opened the door almost immediately, Maeve at his shoulder, her eyes anxious.

The moment she saw Maddie, Maeve held out her arms.

The child practically leaped into them, causing her to stagger backward until John Rattigan steadied them both. In a moment she was seated in her chair, rocking back and forth, crooning to the child.

"Thank God," Susanna whispered, finding herself in the post surgeon's grip now. As Maeve practiced her magic with Maddie, Susanna told the men everything she knew. "The sentry thinks she must have walked in the dark from Three Mile Ranch." She reached out to Sergeant Rattigan and he grasped her hand like a lifeline. She took a deep breath. "Sergeant, she needs to be here with you and Maeve."

Susanna never dreamed she would see a sergeant with tears in his eyes. "You thought right," he told her. "We'll keep Maddie." He bowed his head over her hand, unable to continue.

She looked at Joe, who was having his own struggles. "What a congregation of watering pots," she said. No need for them to know of her tears.

"I have to ride to Three Mile," Joe said.

"I'll come with you, sir," Rattigan said.

"As much as I love the infantry, you're not much of a horseman, Sergeant."

"No, I'm not, sir, but I can stay in the saddle and you shouldn't ride alone. Let me get my shoes. We'll stop by the barracks and pick up a squad of other terrible horsemen."

The men left in a few minutes. Susanna sank down on the sofa, her eyes filled with the sight of mother and daughter. She closed her eyes against her own pain of wanting to be with her son. Maybe Joe had spoken truly. As painful as it was for her, this did feel like the rightest thing anyone had ever done.

When she opened her eyes, surprised that she had slept, she heard Maddie and Maeve in the postage stamp of a spare room, moving boxes. She went to the doorway and watched them as Maeve made a pallet on the floor.

"We'll have a cot for you tomorrow, my love," Maeve said.

She kissed Maddie's untidy hair. "Or maybe we won't worry about this now. Let's just go to my room."

Maddie nodded, her serious self again, possessed of years beyond her childhood. "I'd rather not sleep alone tonight."

"Neither would I," Maeve said softly.

Nor I, Susanna thought. She knelt by Maddie. "Sleep tight, dearest."

Maeve followed her to the door. "You have done the kindest thing," she whispered. "I know you must want to keep her yourself."

Yes, a thousand times, Susanna thought. "I have a son. You needed a daughter."

Susanna stood a long time on the footbridge, watching the flowing water, seeing in her mind Maeve and Maddie cuddled together in bed. When Sergeant Rattigan returned, if there was still time before reveille, he would likely join them. They would probably sleep three to a bed, tight as mussels in a basket, until Maddie was ready to sleep alone.

The ice was breaking up and she knew there were fish below, freed from their winter prison and eager for spring. She had heard taps earlier, so it must be ten o'clock now, because the sentries were calling their "All's well" around the post. Her heart was troubled, but spring settled around her, anyway.

The front door was closed when she came home. She went inside to see Emily knitting. Susanna sat beside her cousin and told her what had happened.

"Maddie will have a good mother now," Emily said.

She had a good mother before, Susanna thought. She knew Emily wouldn't believe her, so she just nodded.

Emily resumed her knitting as Susanna hesitated a long moment, weighing the consequences of what she wanted to do. In an evening of deep breaths, she took another one.

"Emily, I'm going to Major Randolph's quarters. He is the

worst cook ever, and I'm going to make him some muffins and coffee. He'll be famished when he returns."

To her surprise, Emily continued knitting. "I rather think you should," she said. "Don't put any of those everlasting raisins in the muffins. I've been hoarding a handful of dried apricots. Let me get those. Just soak them a little while before you add them to the batter." She went into the kitchen.

Susanna took the apricots and kissed her cheek.

"And for goodness' sake, do try to return before reveille, and use the back door. You know how people like to spread rumors here. *I,* of course, will be as silent as the grave."

"Cousin, you know what I'm doing isn't right and proper," Susanna said.

Emily thought a long moment before she spoke. "We're grown women. Maybe life isn't just black-and-white, is it?" She held out her hand for Susanna to grasp.

Susanna walked two doors down to the major's quarters. She knew his door wouldn't be locked. Funny how a house with only a man in it could feel so empty. The lamp in the parlor still burned, so she sat in his armchair, tired to her bones. To her amusement, she saw he had tacked up the French words for *chair, table, bookcase, books* and *rug* by their namesakes. She went into the kitchen, and reacquainted herself with French for *sink, cookstove* and a variety of edibles. She laughed out loud to see the word *merde* scrawled on the wooden box containing raisins. Good thing Emily had given her apricots.

The rest of his quarters were wreathed in shadow, but enough moonlight showed her an orderly bedroom, where the dining room should have been. She shook her head over the strips from an army blanket tacked over the windows, probably to ensure darkness for daytime naps after nighttime duty. She knew she was the only one in the house, but she still tiptoed down the hall to peer into the clinic for dependents. There were other rooms upstairs, probably empty.

She went into the parlor again. No pictures, no paintings, only a calendar. The books were mainly medical texts, with some Dickens and Victor Hugo, battered and looking much like a veteran of the late war, when *Les Misérables* had been all the rage. Still, the armchair was comfortable. She curled up in the big chair, her legs tucked under her, and fell asleep.

When she woke, dawn had not yet come. She hurried to build up a fire in the cookstove, which would have received a failing grade in her own kitchen back in Carlisle. At least he had the basic army food: dubious sowbelly, but enough flour and sugar to make muffins with Emily's apricots. By the time Susanna found the baking powder, the small oven was hot enough. She knew better than to look for a muffin tin. She let herself out the back door and found one in Emily's kitchen.

While the muffins baked, Susanna brewed coffee, breathing in the soothing aroma. She located three cups, one with a drastic chip in it, which she threw away. She poured herself a cup, sipping and staring at a mysterious furry mound that might have been bread once. She wondered what on earth he ate.

The kitchen was filled with the aroma of cooling muffins and hot coffee when she heard the front door open. Suddenly shy, and doubting the wisdom of her good intentions, Susanna considered darting out the back door. "Tell me this isn't a mirage," spoken in the dark with a Virginia drawl, stiffened her spine.

"It's not," she said, coming out of the kitchen. "I thought you might want something besides horrid oatmeal."

He was indistinct in the dark because she had doused the parlor lamp. She came closer, still hesitant, taking her time.

Joe hadn't moved from beside the door, although he had closed it. Maybe he thought he was in the wrong quarters.

"You know, the muffins in the kitchen won't stay warm forever," she suggested, hoping to jog him into action.

"I'm so tired, Suzie."

That was all she needed to know. She unwound his muffler and unbuttoned his overcoat, helping him shrug out of it. She steered him toward the kitchen, where he sat down heavily.

"There isn't any butter, but I did find some honey," she said, putting four muffins before him and a cup of hot coffee, which he sniffed, then sipped cautiously. His smile was her reward.

The four muffins disappeared and were replaced with two more, and then one. He downed one cup of coffee and was starting on his second when Susanna decided he was patched together enough to talk.

"Well?"

He gazed at her now as though she registered in his tired brain. "I can't tell you how nice it was to open my front door and take a whiff of someone cares."

She smiled at that and sat down in the other chair, after removing the medical journals. She dribbled honey on her muffin, and he held out another for the same treatment.

"The…oh, let's call them ladies…were frantic with worry, so I reassured them that Maddie was in a good place and wouldn't be returning." He picked up his cup and stared into its depths for a moment. "No one objected to that. I wouldn't have cared if they had."

"Claudine is dead?"

"Apparently it was a more peaceful death than usual from consumption. I think her heart just gave out, which always trumps staring at blood dripping off your chin." He shook his head. "I'm sorry."

"Apology unnecessary, Dr. Randolph. I wish you could

have told her Maddie went to a wonderful couple who will love her forever."

He took her hand. "I did that anyway, sitting there beside her. I assured her that Maddie had a guardian angel or two. Fifi thought I was barmy. I told Jules Ecoffey he can bury Claudine here, if he is so inclined. I think he will do that. It's better that Maddie knows where her mother is."

Without another word, he pushed away the plate in front of him and pillowed his head on his arms, asleep in moments. Since he was asleep, she kissed the top of his head.

"You can't be comfortable," she murmured after a few minutes. She gently shook him awake and helped him to his feet.

He offered no objection when she steered him to his bed in the dining room and helped him out of his uniform jacket. She removed his shoes as he sat with his eyes closed. His suspenders came off next, but her nerve failed her then and she just gave him a push onto his back. He unbuttoned his own trousers, then turned on his side and extended his arm.

"Lie down a minute, Suzie," he said, his words slurred. "There's a coverlet somewhere."

She found it and did as he said, cautiously resting her head on his arm. He pulled her close and sighed. He sounded so satisfied that tears came to her eyes.

"I've missed this," he said quite clearly.

Susanna was content to lie beside him and enjoy his warmth. Reason told her that it was no different from the warmth Emily gave off, since they had been sharing her bed. His hand was firm against her stomach and the feeling was soothing, but with an edge she had not enjoyed in years.

When he was sound asleep, Susanna got up carefully and eased herself out of Joe's slackened grasp, making sure he was covered. It was still dark, but she heard reveille. Joe stirred a little and muttered something, but slumbered on, to her relief.

She knew Captain Hartsuff was back at the fort and available. Joe could sleep, if he would.

She went quietly out the back door again and into the Reeses' quarters. No one stirred yet, so she tiptoed upstairs, avoiding the squeaking tread, and lay down on her cot. She felt unreasonably content, considering that nothing was resolved in her life, the fort was tense and waiting news from Powder River, and she had no idea how her son was faring. Before Susanna slept, she wondered if Maddie could share her guardian angel with a child in Pennsylvania, now that she had found a safe harbor.

Susanna didn't expect to see Maddie in her classroom that morning, so took the opportunity to tell the other students her mother had died during the night. Little Eddie Hanrahan suggested they draw pictures for Maddie, so Susanna tossed out her lesson plans and they did just that. The commissary clerk dredged up a partly used ledger from 1864 and her students drew on the pages she tore out.

She hurried to the Rattigans' quarters during mess call. Maeve and Maddie sat close together as they looked at the drawings.

"Please tell my friends I appreciate their sentiments," Maddie said in that dignified way of hers.

"Major Randolph told me Claudine will be buried here tomorrow," Maeve whispered when Maddie turned her attention back to the drawings. "We'll go to that, and Maddie will be in school the day after."

"The sporting ladies from Three Mile will probably be there, too," Susanna warned.

"I expect they will be," Maeve replied, unperturbed. "I guess we won't be bothered by the ladies from Officers Row, will we?"

When school ended, Private Benedict ushered out his children and helped her with hers, telling Rooney O'Leary to wait for him this time. Puzzled, Susanna looked at him. He drew her aside.

"While you were having recitations, Major Randolph stopped in and asked me to escort Rooney today. The major needs you."

"What…why?"

Private Benedict moved closer. "Admin has the butcher's bill from Powder River. One of your boys' fathers is on the list and the major wants you to go with him to the home. He said it was your choice, though."

"I'll go," she said without hesitation, thinking of Joe's dangerous nighttime ride to Three Mile, when he already knew Claudine was dead.

She was sitting in her portion of the commissary storehouse classroom when Joe came. Without a word, he sat beside her and took her hand, pressing it to his lips. He looked so tired, and she suspected he hadn't slept much longer after she left.

"Tell me first—no bad news for Emily or Katie?"

"No, thank God. The captains are fine. Apparently General Crook even complimented James O'Leary on his coolness in battle." His arm went around her then. "There are four dead and six wounded, but here's the tough part—Colonel Reynolds withdrew and left two of the dead on the field. One of those was Corporal Hanrahan."

Susanna leaned her head against Joe's shoulder. "Eddie Hanrahan organized us to write little notes and draw pictures for Maddie."

"At times like this, the army doesn't pay me enough."

They sat together in silence for a few minutes more, then Joe pulled her to her feet. "We have to do this now, before word gets there before we do."

"I'm afraid."

"No, you're not, just hesitant. You'll know precisely what to do when Mrs. Hanrahan opens her door and sees me standing there, Major Grim Reaper. I'm counting on you to make *me* look good." He gave her a slight smile. "Did you ever meet a more selfish man?"

"Actually, yes," she told him, which made Joe give her a squeeze.

It was unnerving to walk with the post surgeon down Suds Row, and see women look out of windows and follow their progress with terrified eyes. Some crossed themselves, others turned away. Joe walked calmly, his face serious. She wondered how many times he had done this death walk.

When they turned in at Hanrahan's quarters, Susanna heard a wail inside before Joe even raised his hand to knock.

Joe was right, she decided later as she still sat in the Hanrahans' parlor, holding Eddie on her lap. When Mrs. Hanrahan collapsed, Susanna's arms just naturally opened for Eddie, and there was room for his little brother and sister, too. She held the children on her lap and cried with them as Joe revived Mrs. Hanrahan, and gave her the additional bad news that there would be no body to bury. Soon the room was full of other army wives, many of them Irish, keening. In a few minutes they had shut the door on the post surgeon, death's messenger unwanted.

Susanna stayed where she was, humming to the bereft children now, then talking to Eddie about books, and summer coming. She told him about her son, Tommy, and climbing trees, anything to distract him from the sorrow all around. She knew she was not successful, but she tried anyway.

The stars were out when she finally left the Hanrahans' quarters. Her back ached and she crossed the footbridge slowly. The river was free of ice now, and she thought she heard small birds. It would be April soon.

Emily was waiting for her with warmed-up dinner. "Major Randolph told me you'd be late," she said. Her face grew more solemn and there was suddenly nothing frivolous about Emily Reese. "Dearest, why do I feel guilty because my darling survived?"

"I don't understand, either, Emily," she replied. "Bless you, do you go through this every time he rides out of the fort?"

"Every time. No one talks about this before marriage. Then, it's all gilt buttons and swords."

Susanna gave her a brief smile. "Men are such deceivers."

Emily looked shyly at her cousin. "Major Randolph said he hoped you'd stop by his quarters." She blushed. "He told me thanks for the dried apricots."

Susanna knocked on his door, then opened it when no one answered. Joe Randolph sat in his armchair, staring at nothing. His eyes flickered to hers. Without a word, he held out his arms and she sat on his lap with no hesitation. His heartbeat was regular and reassuring; she closed her eyes.

"You realize that when Louis Pasteur accepts you as an intern—I'm promoting you beyond mere student—you won't have to make a death walk ever again. Emily told me the other deaths were single men, and the company commanders will write those family letters. No more death walk today."

He was a long time speaking. "The death walk isn't over, Suzie. Take a deep breath."

She gasped and leaped off his lap, backing away and staring at him. "Please, no. Not Tommy!"

Joe hesitated, and she felt her legs suddenly give out as though some cosmic hand had swept away her knees. For the second time in her life, she fainted.

When she woke up, she was lying on the post surgeon's bed, her shirtwaist unbuttoned and her corset stings loosened. Joe sat in a chair beside his bed, looking at her with an expression so tender she had to close her eyes.

"Please. You're too far away."

His shoes were already off. In another moment she was in his arms.

"Now you can tell me," she whispered, her face turned into his chest.

"I'm not quite sure what to tell you, Suzie," he began, "because there's an unknown here. Take a deep breath. I mean it. Keep breathing regularly, because there is more here than I understand."

The post surgeon took his own deep breath. "Along with the dispatch from Fort Fetterman, there were letters from Cheyenne. One came addressed to the commanding officer, but with your name under it. Colonel Bradley read it, then gave it to me." Joe kissed her cheek. "Your former husband, in a drunken stupor, tipped over a lamp and set fire to your house."

"Good God," she whispered.

"Frederick Hopkins died in the blaze, according to your uncle. He wrote that there were bottles all over the house. Hopkins was a drunkard and dangerous, just as you tried to tell everyone at the trial. As for Tommy, there was no sign of him. None at all. He simply disappeared. I'm sure he's alive, but no one knows where he is."

She cried into his chest, partly from relief and partly from sorrow at Frederick's wasted life. Joe's hands were warm inside her shirtwaist now, loosening her corset strings more, and then just massaging her bare back.

"That's all your uncle knows. The local constables searched and found nothing. If Tommy were dead, they would have found his body, the same as they found Frederick's. They didn't."

"Where is he?" she asked when she could speak.

She knew Joe couldn't answer that question. He pulled her even closer. "Tell me, is your son resourceful?"

She thought a moment. "I rather think he is," she said. "After all, he and I lived for years in the same house with Frederick and his mercurial moods. Tommy knows how to lie low." She burrowed her head into Joe's chest. "But he's barely twelve!"

"And resourceful," he reminded her. "All I ask you to do is hang on a little longer. Al's on duty tonight, and tomorrow we're going to get a raft of frostbite cases from Fort Fetterman as the men return. You won't see me for days. Stay with me tonight, Suzie. I'll hang on with you."

Chapter Seventeen

Joe helped her into one of his nightshirts in such a matter-of-fact way that she couldn't feel embarrassed. Worn out with worry, she was asleep before he even joined her.

Susanna woke up once in the middle of the night. She had thrown one leg over the post surgeon. She tried to slide away, but he pulled her back, kissing her neck.

"I'm not ready for any more than a kiss," she whispered.

"Good thing," he replied, surprisingly alert for the middle of the night. "Neither am I." He sighed and pulled her close again. "I did not want to sleep alone, either. I've been a long time without a woman, Suzie, but it doesn't follow that I'd ever do anything to you against your will. I couldn't."

"Frederick never minded, especially when he was drunk," she said in a small voice. "What could I do? I was his wife and that was my duty."

"Suzie, I'm sorry for that," Joe answered, his voice equally soft. "I don't care if the marriage ceremony says 'obey.' No wife should be forced against her will. It's not something I could ever do, and I suspect most men feel the same way. Frederick was an aberration."

She nodded, and returned to sleep in his arms. When reveille roused her, Joe was sitting in the chair he had vacated last night, observing her.

"You are such a pretty woman."

"Best seen in low light," she teased.

"Any light. I confess I never was partial to blondes until..."

"You saw me? How romantic." *Keep it light, Susanna,* she told herself.

He looked handsome in a nightshirt; maybe it was the stripes. She watched him sitting so close to her now, and held back from touching his leg, even though she found herself moved by the capable solidity of him. She took a chance then, and rested her head against his leg. His hand seemed to go automatically to her hair, his fingers twining her curls.

"There's no time, as usual, but I was sitting here, debating whether to tell you a thought I have," he said finally. "It might get your hopes up, but remember, it's only a supposition."

"As long as it doesn't break my heart," she said.

"Your heart's been broken enough," he told her. "Mine, too." He looked at his hand. "I wore my wedding ring a long time. Somewhere in the back of my mind, I used to hope I would turn a corner, and there M'liss would be." He shook his head. "Barmy, eh? I'll tell you how she died. Sit up, Suzie. It's probably better."

She did as he said. He put his arm around her. "I think you know what happened to her. After a day of seeing her suffer in horrific pain—my God, this was the woman I loved!— I administered a huge dose of morphine and killed her. She didn't live ten more seconds."

Susanna felt the breath go out of her. Her arm went around his back, until she had encircled him with both arms.

"Theodore Brown watched the whole thing. He just nodded and covered her face, because I couldn't. Is it any wonder that he is still my hospital steward? Ted told me years later that if I hadn't done that, he would have the next time I left her side. I know what a broken heart feels like." Joe looked at her, as if gauging her heart. "No one knows that except you now, and Ted. Am I a monster?"

"A monster to save your wife one more second of excruciating agony?" she whispered to him. "Oh, no."

He seemed to relax in her arms. "I wanted to tell you."

"It must pain you to even speak of such tragedy."

"It does," he admitted. "Doctors can get inured to suffering. Husbands? Never."

"I used to think no one could hurt worse than I do. How foolish I've been," she told him. "I look at the Rattigans, and now Mrs. Hanrahan...."

"But now the Rattigans are happy." Joe kissed her hair. "M'liss was carrying our child. Oh, damn...it's still almost too much to talk about." He collected himself. "I know you wanted to keep Maddie. In fact, Fifi told me that before Claudine died, she made her promise that the schoolteacher would have her daughter."

"Joe, I wanted her with every fiber of my heart!" Susanna cried, unable to stop her tears at this news. They just held each other until her tears stopped.

"Every step I took toward the Rattigans with Maddie broke my heart," Susanna said when she could speak.

"I thought it must have." He kissed her hand. "I'm not sure I'm that brave."

"But I did the right thing with Maddie," she said finally.

"I know you did, but I have some idea what it cost you." He shifted a little and she found herself on his lap. "Here's what I am thinking. Whether it's wise to tell you, I don't know."

"Let me judge."

"Very well. I looked everywhere for Nick Martin after he went missing. Finally I went to his cubbyhole off the storage room again and took another look. He had obviously cleared out, but under his cot was one of the letters you wrote to Tommy."

She considered the implication. "He has Tommy's address!"

"Precisely. I didn't say anything to you sooner, because it just seemed to be one more oddity about Nick. Now I'm wondering if he went back to Pennsylvania to retrieve your son, or maybe protect him." He smiled at her. "Nick always was your champion."

"You think Nick can even *find* Pennsylvania?"

"Hard to say." Joe shrugged. "We know so little about Nick Martin." He loosened his grip on her. "We'll just have to wait and see. Up you get now. You're going to dress and take that discreet route through the backyards."

She had to know. "Do you think Nick set fire to my house?"

Another shrug. "We'll have to wait and see."

That was no answer to reassure a woman who had lost everything, and Joe knew it. His own heart drooped lower when he told Susanna she had probably better not risk returning to his quarters again. "You know the gossips here," he reminded her.

The light went out of her eyes, but she nodded. "Emily and I had this discussion earlier," she said. "She understands, but we can't expect others to." She dressed quietly and let herself out the back door.

He missed sick call that morning, but it hardly mattered, because Al was there. Guard mount came and went, and still he sat on the end of his barren bed, staring down at the photograph of Melissa that he had tucked away with his wedding ring. He put his ring on again, looked at it, then removed it and replaced it next to the photograph. He lay down again and stared at the ceiling, trying to fathom how a man in love with his wife reconciles taking another wife.

That he was lonely, he had no doubt, but he had been lonely before. He had been a young man when he'd courted and won Melissa in the middle of a war, when he had even less time than now. He had yearned for Melissa Rhoades with a passion that surprised him, but there she was, lovely in her wide-hooped dresses that swayed so sensually when she walked. There was no more guile in her than in him, and she'd showed her heart on her sleeve, the same as he did.

After her death, his work had ferried him through a tidal wave of grief. The medical department mercifully reassigned him to reconstruction duty in Louisiana, away from Texas, where she had met her death. He took more risks there than he should have, not hesitating to volunteer for yellow fever duty. Truth to tell, it wouldn't have bothered him to have contracted the disease that seasonally roved up and down the Mississippi. He was almost relieved when he caught it, but damn, he survived. What was worse, he was now immune. Where was the justice?

He hadn't been eager to transfer to the Department of the Platte, but the transfer came with an overdue promotion to major. He had bowed to duty, as he always did, mainly because it didn't matter to him where he served or what his rank. His assignments took him to several forts, where friends tried to pair him with sisters or other relatives from back East who had come West specifically to find husbands among the officer corps. After a few years, no one tried anymore.

Joe dressed and walked slowly toward the hospital. For a change, the wind wasn't blowing. The small bird sounds he had imagined yesterday were real now. There was still the bite of winter in the air, but he had already walked past the post trader's store before he realized he had left his overcoat behind.

The sound of children reached him so he glanced toward the commissary storehouse, smiling to see Suzie outside with her class. He watched as she jumped rope, her skirts flying and her blond hair quickly loosed from its moorings. There would probably never be enough hairpins to anchor those curls. He knew how soft they felt, twined around his fingers. He had the strongest impulse—and he was not impulsive—to walk over there and turn one end of the rope, or jump with her.

He swallowed once and then again, and knew he loved Susanna Hopkins, the bravest woman he had probably ever met. He had tentatively suggested it earlier, then backed away from the idea. Only this morning he had watched the hope in her eyes dim when he'd said it wasn't wise of them to help each other through another night. It may have been proper, but all he wanted to do was discard duty and jump rope with his darling.

There she was, lovely and brave and funny. He thought about his feelings when they were together, and realized Suzie made him brave and funny, too. M'liss was gone now and not coming back in this life, at least. He was still alive, a healthy man. As he watched his newest darling, he knew in his heart that his first darling would be terribly disappointed in him if he wasted his life mourning her.

Joe stood there a moment longer, enjoying the sun finally warm on his neck. He counted Suzie's little class, picking out Maddie in her pretty red coat, probably cut down from something of Claudine's. He wasn't surprised to see Eddie Hanrahan. No doubt he had insisted he not miss school, because his mother had women to comfort her, and Eddie knew Mrs. Hopkins loved him.

Joe looked down. Soon there would be dandelions everywhere. For the first time since Texas, he knew that spring had truly come, because he felt it inside.

Claudine Wilby was buried in the military cemetery a half mile north of the fort. Susanna walked with the Rattigans,

Maddie between Maeve and James. To her surprise, she felt a little hand in hers halfway there, and looked down to see Eddie Hanrahan.

"My dear, you were sweet to come," she said, kneeling by him and tucking his muffler into his coat. "Does your mama know?"

"She said I should be here," he said. "Maddie's my friend."

Before they reached the post trader's store, all of her pupils walked with her, some with a parent, and others alone. She thought none of the residents of Officers Row would join their little procession, but there was Katie O'Leary with Rooney.

"I left Mary Rose with Emily," Katie said. "Rooney insisted we come."

Susanna knew Joe would be there, and he did not disappoint, coming to stand beside her. She didn't think she moved, but soon they were touching. She glanced at Maddie in Sergeant Rattigan's arms, her face turned into his uniform coat, her shoulders shaking.

Susanna hadn't meant to cry, but Joe had a handkerchief ready. "Believe me, Claudine is better off. And so is Maddie, although she might not know it yet."

"What about you, Joe?"

The question came out before she even realized it, and she knew she had startled him. Startled herself, too; she had never called him Joe except in private, and her question was impertinent. Or maybe it wasn't; she wanted to know.

He thought a moment before he answered, but she knew Joe was a deliberate man not given to impulse. A smile started to play around his lips, and she felt the rest of the callus around her heart dissolve. All the slights and vitriol, the humiliation and sorrow paled in significance as she watched his dear face relax, even though they stood in a military cemetery.

"I'm better off, too. Unlike Maddie, I already know it."

He said it so simply. He turned his attention to a corporal from Company H, Ninth Infantry, an ordained minister, who recited the Twenty-third Psalm, and the passage from Job about "men born unto trouble as the sparks fly upward."

"That would be Claudine," Joe whispered. "Come to think of it, none of us are wholly good or completely bad."

"I think you're wholly good," Suzanna said, discarding every fear that had ever controlled her. She made herself vulnerable.

Such a light came into the post surgeon's eyes that she stepped back, wondering at her own temerity. He came closer again, such a small distance to move, but one that made her heart beat faster. She knew her cheeks were red, but it was cold out. No one would notice.

"Wholly good? Not so, Suzie. Before you arrived with Eddie, I was admiring Fifi's assets." He looked straight ahead then, the very image of military deportment, as she struggled not to laugh at a funeral.

Only by bowing her head and cramming her fingers against the bridge of her nose could she control herself. Susanna looked up when she was firmly in charge again, this time to observe the four women who stood between Jules Ecoffey and a man who must be Adolf Cuny, his partner in commerce and vice. Fifi was easy to spot.

"Someone should take out your eyeballs and wash them with pine tar soap," she murmured out of the side of her mouth, and it was his turn not to laugh at a burial.

By the time the brief service ended, the wind had picked up, tossing around dead cottonwood leaves from last fall. She looked around for Eddie, but Katie O'Leary had his hand now, and Rooney's. They walked away, leaving her to stroll down the hill toward the hospital with the post surgeon only. He held out his elbow a little and her arm went naturally into the crook of his arm.

"I'm supposed to read tomorrow night at the hospital, but I don't have a book. We finished *Little Men* last week."

He shook his head. "Not this week, Suzie. We're expecting the wounded from the battlefield any hour now, and I know there will be frostbite cases, too. Al picked up a telegram from Fetterman's post surgeon to warn us what's coming. Looks like we will be performing at least one amputation, maybe two. Better you stay away for a few days. I'll be sleeping at the hospital." He sighed. "It was easy enough during the late war. Maybe I'm getting old."

Susanna took another chance, even though it made her blush to bring it up. "Joe, if you're at hospital, would you mind if I slept in your quarters for a few nights? Captain Reese will be newly home in one half of the house, Captain O'Leary in the other one. The walls are thin and I'm in the middle."

He threw back his head and laughed. "Suzie, you're more than welcome in my ever so humble abode! I'll be camping on a cot at the hospital. Give the lovebirds a couple of days." He grew more thoughtful. "I hate for you to sneak around, but no one will understand, if they see you in my place. Back door and after taps, all right?"

She did as he said. Private Benedict dismissed school early the next afternoon as the troopers rode into Fort Laramie, as dismal a bunch of campaigners as Maeve said she had ever seen. Susanna stayed for supper at the Rattigans, impressed with how quickly Maddie had taken over the duty of setting the table. Bless her Gallic heart, there were the first dandelions of spring flared out nicely in a teacup for a centerpiece.

"It didn't go well, did it?" Maeve asked John when he came home after retreat.

The sergeant shook his head, his eyes lighting up when Maddie held up both arms for his overcoat. She practically staggered under its weight as she took it into the bedroom. "She's a help, Maeve," he said, and kissed his wife. "No, it didn't go well, God bless the cavalry. The rumor mill says General Crook is preferring charges and specifications against Colonel Reynolds and another officer for neglect, mismanagement, and just about everything else Crook can think of except chilblains. The Northern Roamers are still free to roam, army men are dead and some left on the battlefield, and the Cheyenne have now allied with the Lakota." John shook his head. "It'll be a hot summer for campaigning."

"Must be nice to be an observer and take none of the blame, but dole out all the complaints," Susanna grumbled.

"It's no wonder he and his aide de camp took another route back to Omaha," Sergeant Rattigan said, then grabbed up Maddie when she came back into the parlor. "And how's my girl?"

Both your girls are fine, Susanna thought, as she walked back to the Reeses' quarters, where the captain, dirty and needing a shave, had his arms around Emily. Amused, Susanna told them where she was going for the night, and heard no objections. She laughed to herself and walked two doors down, careful to stay in the shadows.

The major had left a lamp burning. Glowing coals in the parlor stove welcomed her. There was a bowl of raisins in the kitchen. "*Eat these. Please. I insist,*" read the note. She did just that, taking the bowl on her lap, kicking off her shoes and sinking into the major's armchair, saggy in all the right places, sort of like the major. She read his threadbare copy of *Les Misérables* until her eyes grew heavy. She took a blanket from the end of Joe's bed and made herself comfortable on the packing crate settee in the parlor again, where the stove still shed its warmth. She knew sleeping alone in his bed would have made her sad.

After the fort slept and the sentries were occupied, Susanna stayed there two more nights, enjoying the solitude after busy days of teaching. She must have slept more soundly than usual, because there was a note pinned to her blanket on the third morning. "Joe, you are silent," she murmured as she opened the note.

"*Come up tonight, sleepyhead,*" she read. "*I have a good book that will make the men laugh.*"

The odor of carbolic, stronger than usual, tickled her nostrils as she opened the door to the hospital that evening. The single ward must have been full, because there were two hospital beds in the hall with portable partitions around them. She stood there, uncertain, until the post surgeon came out of the ward, still wearing his surgical apron, complete with mysterious stains.

It was his eyes that troubled her. He looked so tired. And there was Captain Hartsuff pulling aside one of the partitions, the same look on his face and a nearly identical apron.

"Did either of you sleep?" she asked, keeping her voice low.

The surgeons looked at each other and both shrugged. "We must have, ma'am," Al Hartsuff said. "Can't remember, though. I can stay, Joe."

"Nope. Get a good night's sleep and relieve me in the morning, Captain, and that's an order." Joe rubbed his hands together, and Susanna noticed how chapped they were. "Go to bed, Al."

Eyes half-closed, Joe ushered her into the ward, where every bed was occupied. "Croup, bronchitis, frostbite," he whispered. "We were a little late taking off one leg—how I wish Fetterman's surgeon had acted! It doesn't look good. He's in the hall now, probably dying, so there I must be, too."

Joe raised his voice so his patients could hear him, leading Susanna into the middle of the ward. "Here she is, gentlemen." He produced a book from his apron pocket, brushing off some flecks better left unexamined. "Give 'em two chapters, Suzie. That's all these wretches deserve."

Several of the more alert men laughed. Susanna seated herself and looked at the book, *Roughing It,* by Mark Twain.

"Very well, sirs! Your post surgeon thinks reading is a remedy for everything from dandruff to bunions," she said, pleased to hear low laughter. She cleared her throat. "Chapter One. 'My brother had just been appointed secretary of Nevada Territory—an office of such majesty that it concentrated itself in the duties and dignities…'"

She read through the first short chapter, pausing at the end to note some patients already asleep. Others regarded her with the inward contemplation of men in pain. She doubted half of them comprehended what she was reading, but she recognized their satisfied expressions, which mirrored those of her own little students when she read to them. Since the first chapter was so short, she read the second and then the third, with its stagecoach journey and camels. She looked around then; everyone slept.

"Perfect," she whispered. She ruffled quickly through the book, reading some of the subtitles, which made her chuckle. As she did, a piece of yellow foolscap fell into her lap. She looked at it idly, then stared.

"My goodness, Joe," she said softly. "What are you doing?"

Across the top, in his doctor's handwriting, she could just make out "Suzie Randolph." Her face grew hot and she put one hand to her cheek. Feeling like an eavesdropper into the most private part of a man, she looked at the page, which, to her relief, appeared to be nothing more than French sentences.

She looked closer in the dim light. It seemed that Joe had printed in English, and someone else had written in French. There appeared to be two different handwritings besides his, one firm and graceful, the other spidery and barely legible.

At the top, under "Suzie Randolph," Joe had printed, "How do I say 'I care for you'?"

"Je m'occupe de vous," Susanna whispered, not even needing to read what the firm hand had written.

She looked down another line to see Joe's printing. "More serious?" she read. It was followed by the spidery writing, *"Je t'aime."*

Scarcely breathing now, she read, "How do I say, 'Do you love me?'"

"You just ask me, Joe, and I'll tell you," she said softly.

"I'm not wasting my hard-learned French. *Est-ce que tu m'aimes?*"

Startled, she looked up, aware now that Joe was leaning over the chair. *"Mais oui,"* she said simply. "I do love you."

His hand was on her shoulder now. She looked at his chapped fingers, probably washed over and over with carbolic as he'd treated the wounded men from the monumentally unsuccessful Powder River campaign.

"I have some salve for your hands," she whispered.

"I can't say that in French yet," he whispered back, his lips close to her ear now, tickling it and causing the warmth in her chest to travel lower. "I did work on this next sentence, because it's important. Fifi helped me, and Claudine, when she could. Mostly it made them giggle. So nice to see Claudine happy. Let me try…. *Veux-tu m'épouser?*"

"You have a terrible accent," Susanna told him. "No wonder they giggled."

"Well?" he asked, kneeling by her chair now. "After fourteen years of nothing, it took me about four months to go from 'I worry about you,' to 'I care for you,' to 'I love you more seriously,' and now this last question. I can't imagine a less romantic setting, unless it might be the dead house out back, but that's the question. What's your answer? I'll take it in any language."

Susanna turned to look him in the eyes. He still wore that disgusting apron, and he had not shaved in at least three days.

"How have I lived this long without you?" she murmured, both hands on his face as the book fell to the floor.

"You're supposed to answer *my* question, not ask another one, knucklehead," he said. He sounded like a man who already knew what her answer would be. He sounded like a husband. It occurred to her that all Joe knew how to be was a husband—a good one.

"It's yes," she said. "Soon, *s'il vous plait*."

Chapter Eighteen

Susanna didn't care if all the patients were asleep as she kissed Joe Randolph. He smelled of exhaustion and carbolic and other nameless odors that she didn't intend to question. She breathed deep, and found him entirely to her liking.

Her spectacles got in the way a little, until Joe unhooked them from around her ears and set them on the floor as they both continued a remedy for heart pain not commonly found in an army ward. His hand was warm on her neck. When their lips parted, he rested his head in her lap, and she understood how supremely tired he was: tired of this medical emergency, tired of living alone, tired of wanting and not having. She understood him precisely, because she felt the same way.

After a few more minutes, he got up off his knees, handing back her spectacles and raising her to her feet. His arm around her, he walked her from the quiet ward. She glanced in the hall to see the partition gone from around a now empty bed.

He gave her shoulders a squeeze and started her toward the entrance. "In the middle of this month, would Private Benedict have any serious objection if you take two weeks off for a trip to Cheyenne? I'll have two patients fit enough to travel to Fort Russell by then. I intend to accompany them in an ambulance, and you will come along, if you haven't decided I'd make a terrible husband."

"I will come along."

"Rumor says there will be a court-martial—the first of General Crook's victims from Powder River—and I will be needed for court-martial duty. Before that boring job, you and I will find a justice of the peace. I trust you won't be too bored waiting for my sorry carcass to show up each evening in the hotel. What do you think? It's hardly the honeymoon of a woman's dreams, but welcome to the army."

"I have fairly low expectations."

He laughed softly. "Good thing. You've seen my kitchen, and you already know I have a lumpy bed."

"I thought it was fine."

"So did I, actually. Change your mind now, if you're going to."

He waited, his tired eyes as lively as they were going to get, without at least eight hours of sleep. She kissed him.

"I won't change my mind." She hesitated, watching his face. "There is one thing."

"You can have anything up to half my kingdom, which right now is a plantation in Virginia where my unforgiving relatives squat. I own it, by the way. Paid enough damned taxes to carpetbaggers."

"I want to ask an attorney what...what my rights are, if we find Tommy."

"We'll find him, and we know where he belongs."

He said it quietly, but the conviction in his voice stayed with her down the hill, into the Reeses' quiet quarters, and to her own bed. She made herself drowsy by trying to decide which of her shabby dresses would be the best wedding dress. She smiled in the dark. It had probably better be the one with the least chalk dust on the sleeves.

* * *

They were married two weeks later in Cheyenne by a justice of the peace who seemed to find their shyness somehow endearing, no matter that both of them were above and beyond thirty years of age, previously experienced in the snares of Venus, and endearingly besotted with each other. The JP had sharp eyes.

Or so he told Joe, while spending a moment with him, examining the certificate Joe had composed as attending physician, and registered after Melissa's death. He spent more time over Suzie's more voluminous divorce decree. To Joe's relief, he had no editorial comment to make about divorce. He only offered one piece of advice.

"Major, treat her as you would the Queen of Sheba," he said as he pulled on his more official black frock coat. "Ladies are a rare commodity in Wyoming Territory, and a pretty one like your future wife should keep you on your toes."

"I'll treat her as kindly as the army allows."

The justice of the peace winced at that doleful bit of news. He regarded the post surgeon in silence a moment, his eyes kind now. "Major, did you have a good first marriage?"

"I did. No complaints except that it was too short."

"Then you should have another good one. Those things tend to follow one another."

They nodded to each other in perfect agreement.

Joe didn't think Suzie could have any surprise for him, but there she was in the justice of the peace's parlor, almost breathtaking in a deep green dress that he thought he remembered Katie O'Leary wearing at a dinner a year ago. The dress had an exquisite lace collar similar to one he had noticed Mrs. Burt wear at the enlisted men's Christmas dance two years before the O'Leary dinner. He definitely recognized the paisley shawl as Maeve Rattigan's.

"You're well rigged out, Mrs. Hopkins," he whispered

when he took his place beside her and offered his arm. "Did you borrow a nightgown from Fifi?"

She looked down, then gave him a sidelong glance. "Major, I didn't even bother with a nightgown."

That rendered him speechless until his "I do," which amused his new wife no end.

He had collected himself by the time they stood in the street again. "Why are you not flustered and taking shallow breaths?" he asked, surprised at his wife's calm demeanor.

She gave him another look, one that set his mind at ease. She leaned toward him. "You mentioned a few weeks ago about curing the common heartache. We've just done that again." Two men walked by and she lowered her voice. "I love you, Major Randolph. I never thought I would love anyone again. I was wrong." She patted his arm. "You may take all the time you need to decide. I already have. And now, where is that attorney's office?"

His fingers propped together in a steeple, the lawyer heard what both of them had to say without interrupting, writing down his questions to ask when each finished. He sat a long moment, looking at his list, then leaned back in his chair.

"Mrs. Randolph, to your knowledge, your former husband, now deceased, had no living relatives?"

"None."

He smiled at them both. "Frederick Hopkins's death renders this court decision void. Nowhere do I see any evidence of another party authorized to step in. I hope you find Thomas. I would certainly advise at least one of you to return to Carlisle and consult with the local authorities. Little boys don't just disappear."

"No, they don't just disappear," Joe said as they walked back to the hotel. "I'm convinced Nick had a hand in it."

"We're putting a lot of trust in a man who showed up from

nowhere, thinks he's Saint Paul, and stole two hundred dollars from your medical fund," Suzie replied.

Joe put his arm around her, even though it was a forward thing to do on a public street. "I just have a good feeling about Nick Martin. Always have. He was helpful and very much your champion." He pressed the worry line between her eyes. "And now I'm your champion."

In shy silence, they ate roast beef far better than government issue in the hotel dining room, with mashed potatoes and gravy.

"Can you make gravy as good as this?" he asked at last. It seemed such an inane filler, "And mashed potatoes?"

"Better," she assured him, then laughed softly. "Joe, anything I cook will be better than what you're used to." She leaned closer. "I fibbed about the nightgown. I did bring one, but it's just old flannel."

It was just old flannel, faded from numerous washings. Without her usual armor of corset and stays and petticoats, she looked smaller and almost fragile, but he knew looks were deceiving. She was going to braid her hair before bed, but he stopped her, sat her on his lap and brushed her hair. It crackled in the dry air and turned into a blond nimbus around her face. He took off her spectacles and left them on the bedside table. He touched the dimple below her eye.

"What do you see out of this eye?"

"Not much. Blurry images." She folded her hands in her lap like the well-mannered lady he knew she was. "The physician said that was all I could hope for."

"I expect he was right. Magnification from the lens doesn't make much difference, does it?"

"None that I can tell," she confided, leaning against him. "It seemed to make my physician happy to think he was doing something, so I didn't argue."

"You don't need to wear spectacles then, do you?"

"Probably not."

"Then don't. If you feel eyestrain, then you should wear them."

"Yes, Doctor."

His lips were close to hers now. "Yea or nay tonight, Mrs. Randolph?"

"How about hallelujah?"

He grabbed her around the waist, breathing in the wonderful fragrance of her hair, which excited him as much as her softness. Her arms were tight around him, and she kissed him. He wondered at first if she would feel like M'liss. She did, in the basics, but she didn't. Melissa had been tall and well-built, and Suzie wasn't. He decided to be as gentle as possible, because he knew Frederick, drunk or sober, hadn't cared much about the niceties. Joe realized after a mere minute that Suzie was as hungry for him as he was for her.

He wasn't sure where her nightgown went; probably in the same corner as his nightshirt. He lay on top of her, almost giddy with the feeling, smoothing her hair back with both hands as he kissed her neck and her breasts. She shifted a little, raised her hips, murmured his name, and the mating dance began. He hadn't forgotten any of the choreography and neither had she. Her breath came as rapidly as his, her hands warm on his back, then caressing him in a way oddly gentle, in the middle of tumult. It soothed him as much as it excited him. His last coherent thought before he climaxed was that perhaps he should reserve the hotel rooms on either side of them. Thank God his quarters at Fort Laramie were freestanding, and he shared no walls with anyone.

She came right after him, and her sigh went right to his heart. She kissed his lips so gently then, her legs tight around him, her hands, sweaty now, still caressing his back. He didn't move for a while, but raised up on his elbows to allow some lung expansion. She made no move to release him, so they stayed as they were until his eyes started to droop. He fought it; the last thing he wanted to do was sleep right now, even though biology made men so susceptible.

It was her turn to say something incoherent when he finally moved—easy enough, because her legs felt boneless. Totally content, he lay beside her, knowing he should tidy himself up a bit, but not inclined to that much exertion.

He discovered Suzie was more practical. She sat up. After a massive stretch that reminded him of a cat, she padded to the washstand and the pitcher of water the management had thoughtfully provided. He admired her backside and the marvelous slope from her shoulders to her waist. As he watched, interested, she took care of herself, and returned to bed with a warm cloth for him. He reached for it, but she did the honors.

"You're going to spoil me."

"No. We'll take turns. Women can vote here, you know, and I intend to."

He growled, grabbed her and held her in a bear hug. "That makes absolutely no sense."

"I don't care, Joe," she said. "Maybe I just want you to know from the start that this is a partnership."

"That *does* make sense," he agreed. "How about you just make yourself comfortable. Oh, yes, like that."

Suzie pillowed her head on his chest and put her leg over him. Both his arms were around her. He knew from experience that he'd have to shift eventually before his arms grew numb, but that was a while off, and he loved the feel of her bare body against his. He figured one of the mysteries of science was how soft women's bodies were, compared to men.

"Satisfied?" she asked.

"Need you ask? I've exceeded the legal limit of satisfaction. You're, uh, inspiring." He kissed her sweaty head. "My bed's not very comfortable at home, but we're probably stuck with it until we change duty stations."

"Or go to Paris."

He smiled in the dark. "You married me because you want to travel," he teased.

Her response was so serious that he almost felt a chill. "I married you because I love you. I don't even know when it happened."

He thought about his own epiphany. "I was watching you jump rope, and I wanted to jump with you. Silly, yes, but I knew."

She said his name so softly. He knew she felt safe with him, which aroused every protective instinct in his generous nature. This was a wife to treasure, just as M'liss had been.

Susanna was silent for a long moment. He knew she wasn't asleep, because he felt her eyelashes opening and closing against his chest.

"Yes, my lovely Suzie?" he asked finally.

"I'll try not to, but...but I usually end up crying myself to sleep or crying myself awake. I think of Tommy, and that's what I do. Now I don't know where he is, and I can't seem to help myself."

Joe felt her tears on his chest and he held her close. "I understand. I'll let you in on a secret—I cried myself to sleep for a long time after Melissa died. Tears don't scare me. I've seen plenty."

Her tears stopped in a few moments. She sat up, looking down on him. He scarcely breathed as she touched his face, outlining his nose and lips, her finger ending at his throat. She pressed her hand against his chest, as if checking him for soundness; maybe she was. She felt his stomach, lingered over his genitals, and ran her hands down his legs. He laughed when she tickled his foot.

"I'll be a good wife. I can't be Melissa, but I'll be a good wife," she said simply.

Tears started in his eyes then, and it wasn't from sorrow

or wishing Melissa back. It was from the absolute certainty that he was the most fortunate man who had ever lived. He wanted to tell her that, but he didn't know if she set much store by mere words. She had probably heard plenty of them. He would just have to show his appreciation.

"You already are a good wife," he whispered back. "Better go to sleep, because I intend to wake you up later on tonight."

"If I don't beat you to it," she said. "Remember? Partners?"

She beat him to it.

As she thought about the matter a week later, still in Cheyenne, Susanna decided that the greatest blessing of marriage to Joe Randolph so far was the certainty that no matter what happened, she wasn't by herself in times of trouble.

When she woke up in tears that first morning, he held her close, singing a ribald song he must have learned in the late war, so vulgar that she gasped and then laughed.

"It takes no imagination to rhyme *luck* and *pluck*," he joked. "Those Ohio regiments were full of farm boys with saucy tongues and vivid imaginations." His eyes grew distant. "I wish I could have saved more of them."

"You saved all you could, didn't you?"

"I did."

She knew Joe was a man of duty, but she had to chuckle to herself how he had to drag himself out of bed every morning to ride his borrowed horse to Fort Russell for the court-martial of a captain that Crook had found wanting during the Powder River campaign.

"I'd rather spend two hours just staring at your nice ankles than listening to fifteen minutes of why the army should slap this poor captain's wrist because he decided to dismount his men for a while on a freezing cold morning to boil coffee. It made no difference in the outcome of the battle. He convinced me; hell, he convinced all of us. Court-martial duty is a pain," Joe told her one evening, as he lay with his head in her bare lap.

And so it went. She recalled him to duty each morning, laughed when he grumbled, sent him out the door, and slept for another hour or two. A court-martial honeymoon was not for the faint of heart, she decided, at least for the major. For her part, it was idle luxury to lie in bed, think about the night before, then take a long soak in the tub down the hall and think about the night to come. She decided her husband had a certain talent. Maybe that came from knowing more about female anatomy than most men.

She spent her afternoons with more purpose, writing to her uncle in Shippensburg, asking to be kept abreast of attempts to find Tommy. Joe suggested that she compose a notice to be sent to Pennsylvania, Illinois, Iowa and Nebraska papers—following a probable path to Cheyenne—asking for the whereabouts of a tall twelve-year-old with a dark blaze in his blond hair, and brown eyes, with a mole on his cheekbone, answering to the name of Tommy Hopkins.

One night, lying satiated with her equally sated husband, Susanna composed the announcement, pausing a long time over Nick Martin's description. "We daren't mention Saint Paul, or no editor will print this, no matter how much money we send," she told her husband, who looked nearly comatose. "Joe, you are surely the most satisfied-looking man in the territory."

"I expect I am," he told her, all complacence. "Certainly the happiest man at the court-martial table. I show up every morning with a big grin on my face. They all hate me now." He took a nip of her neck and looked over her shoulder at her announcement. "'Tall, silent, long dark hair' should do it. We dubbed him Nick Martin. I wonder what his name is."

She took the announcement to the newspaper editor, who

promised to send it out. He looked at her with some sympathy. "Your son, ma'am?" he asked.

She nodded, unable to help the tears that welled in her eyes. She left the newspaper office as quickly as she could, and spent the next hour composing herself by feeding pigeons in a straggly park that was Cheyenne's attempt at gentility. The sun was warm on her face, now that it was nearly May.

She walked back to the hotel, suddenly wishing to return to Fort Laramie and the post surgeon's house, to cook for him, to smooth his way however she could, and to teach her pupils in the commissary storehouse. It was time to plan a year-end program for the parents, before the fathers had to mount up or march out for Montana Territory and a summer of campaigning. There would be recitations and maybe a play, and refreshments. She would plan and work and love her husband and try not to think about Tommy any more than most of every day.

She calmed herself, grateful that every night she would be in the capable arms of a man who knew her sorrows, knew his own, and who seemed to have no trouble comforting her. She couldn't help smiling.

He was waiting for her in the hotel room when she returned, surprising her. She was grateful she had spent some time composing herself, but he seemed to see right through what she thought was her calm demeanor.

"I thought it might be hard for you to go to the newspaper office," he said, putting down the paper he was reading and holding out his arms for her.

She sat on his lap. "How on earth did you get away early?" she asked.

"*I* requested an early adjournment," he replied, and chuckled. "You can imagine the ribbing I got, complete with suggestions on how I should spend my extra free time! They're so envious."

She poked him in the chest, then kissed him. "You're going to make it hard for me to ever meet these gentlemen without blushing. Why *are* you early?"

"I have an idea. I was sitting there, bored, doodling little blonde ladies with big eyes, when it occurred to me that I possibly have an ace up my sleeve—Allan Pinkerton."

"Of the detective agency?"

"The same. I knew him as Major E.J. Allen, when he was doing undercover work around Atlanta in '64. He had a rather nasty case of diarrhea."

"You are descriptive."

"Ah, yes. He owes me one or two. Mr. Pinkerton isn't active in the agency now, but his sons are. I came home early to get a bank draft—over there on the desk—and write a letter. We'll put the National Detective Agency on Tommy's trail." Joe kissed her. "Don't cry, Suzie. I'm just sorry it took me this long to think of it."

They put their heads together over the letter. An hour later Susanna had finished writing it, because she knew her penmanship was better than a physician's. Joe looked at the letter a long time.

"I know you've described him down to the mole under his eye, but I wish you had a photograph," he said finally.

She almost didn't want to tell him. She had promised herself she would never let it out of her sight. *Do you want him found or not?* she asked herself.

"I do have a photograph," she told her husband. "I carry it everywhere with me."

"We need to send it to Will Pinkerton, Suzie."

"It's all I have," she said as she took it from her carpetbag and handed it to him. "It was taken just before Frederick nearly killed me, and thank God Frederick had forgotten all about it."

Joe looked at the photograph a long time, a smile playing

around his lips. "He looks so much like you." He pointed to the picture. "That's interesting—he really does have that same blaze of dark hair on his temple like you."

"He's my son," she said simply. "Just make sure Mr. Pinkerton knows I must have the photograph back."

The court-martial ended two days later, to her husband's obvious relief. He came into the hotel room carrying a large pasteboard box and wearing a grin from ear to ear. "General Crook will be so disappointed," he told her, setting down the box. "All we did was issue a rather tepid reprimand, because that was all the matter deserved." He followed the trajectory of her expression. "And what is this, you're thinking?"

"It's too big for flowers, and you hardly seem like someone who would waste money on flowers," she said.

"It's for you, and you don't even need to do anything extraordinary for it."

When she said, "I already *did* that last night," he laughed and handed her the box.

She felt her breath catch when she took off the lid. Nestled inside were two dresses, one a dignified royal-blue and the other made of summery lawn, little purple flowers on a pale green background.

"You dear man," she whispered, shaking out the blue dress. It was simple, with long sleeves and a plain round neckline.

"There's a lace collar in the box, too," her husband said, his eyes lively. "I really liked the one you borrowed from Mrs. Burt for our wedding. I have a very nice opal necklace in my quarters that should go fine with the dress and collar."

"Only if you really want me to wear it," she said quietly.

"I do. One Mrs. Randolph wore it, and now another one should." He touched her face. "I have other pieces, too. What I have is yours."

She wrapped her arms around both dresses. "I don't have anything special for you!"

"*You're* my something special, Suzie. I don't need anything else. Try it on."

He didn't need to ask twice, unbuttoning the plaid dress she had worn several days now, and helping her step out of it. The blue dress buttoned up the front, but her fingers were shaking, so he helped her. It fit perfectly.

"How did…how did…"

"I asked Emily for your measurements." He was unbuttoning the blue dress now, his hands inside the tight-fitting basque, gentle on her breasts. "Perfect. Want to try on the other one, or do we go right to the payment?"

She gave him such an arch look that he burst out laughing. "All right! Let me help you into the next one."

The summery dress fit as beautifully as the dark one. "Oh, my," she breathed, looking in the mirror. "I've never had such a pretty gown." She stopped and turned to him. "How on *earth* did you find a dressmaker in Cheyenne? That can't have been part of your general wisdom."

"Certainly not." He looked all around the room, anywhere but at her. "Fifi and Claudine suggested her."

Susanna gasped, then put her hand over her mouth as the implication sank in. "If Claudine was still alive, that had to have been before you proposed!"

"It was." He began unbuttoning the dress, pulling it down from her shoulders and kissing them. "I guess I was just waiting for a romantic spot to propose, like a ward full of wounded men. Oh, Suzie."

He didn't say any more; he just held her.

Chapter Nineteen

They left in the ambulance early the next morning, sharing it this time with Major Townsend, who had also been part of the court-martial board. If Susanna thought she would feel uncomfortable around him—she had barely spoken to him since the Dunklins' house—it never happened.

The weather was a far cry from the bleak January when she'd made this same trip, sad, defeated and trying to start over. This time she sat close to her husband, deriving so much simple comfort from the pressure of his arm that she had no fear of the man who had commanded Fort Laramie.

And who would again, apparently. She listened as the two officers discussed the coming campaign, with Townsend's Ninth Infantry taking the field this time.

"That means you'll be losing Private Benedict," Townsend said.

"Anthony…Private Benedict and I have been planning a special day for our pupils and their parents. Would the quartermaster let us build a small stage in his warehouse?"

"Consider it done, Mrs. Randolph," Townsend said. "The fort's best carpenter is languishing in the guardhouse. He'll do it."

She hesitated, wanting to ask one more thing, but still not

sure of herself. Major Townsend's eyes were kindly, though, so she worked up her nerve.

"Sir, I know I was only contracted to teach through the middle of May, but I would like to continue teaching, even though it will be summer."

"Why?"

"It'll keep the children occupied and not thinking all the time about their fathers," she replied, her voice soft. "I know what it's like to dwell on someone absent."

The pressure on her arm increased and she silently thanked God for her husband.

Townsend considered the matter. "Why not? We have the funds for another term. Do it, but it can't be mandatory in the summer."

"Thank you!" she exclaimed, delighted, then remembered something she should have told him earlier, but was too shy to say. "I should also thank you for that extra ten dollars a month you have been giving me for teaching the women. They're ever so…"

She stopped, watched the significant glance that passed between the two men, and smelled a rat. "*What* has been going on?"

"Nothing," the majors said together.

"I don't believe either of you," she replied, suddenly aware of what her husband had been up to. "Not for a minute!"

"Blame your husband, not me."

She turned slightly, but not enough to escape the touch of his shoulder. "Well, let's see," she said, thoughtful. "Obviously, you've been paying that ten dollars from your own money, Major Randolph."

"Fooled you, though, didn't I?" he teased.

She turned her attention to Major Townsend. "And you, sir, probably have it written in stone somewhere that the army will pay for only *one* teacher for the enlisted men's children, no matter what the circumstances."

"I do," he said with a straight face.

Susanna looked at her husband, loving him with a fierceness that she could never have imagined in that bleak January, the worst of her life.

"You have been paying my twenty dollars a months, plus the additional ten," she said. She glanced at Townsend. "Should I take over the Randolph financial responsibilities?"

"Maybe you should." Townsend leaned forward. "There's a rumor that he has been buying expensive dresses in Cheyenne, too. Perhaps you should look into that, as well."

"Oh, I think not," she said immediately, which made both prevaricators laugh. "He has such good taste in women's wear."

Two days later, nothing felt better than to be home, even if the bed was lumpy, the kitchen woefully ill-equipped, and the sheets and towels threadbare. She looked around her new bedroom in the dining room, with the army blankets tacked up for blackout curtains, and called it good.

Her cup of plenty ran over when Emily came by for a hug, and was followed at intervals during the day by most of the officers' wives, some bringing food, and others towels and good sheets. Where these gifts came from, considering the shortage of such items in the post trader's store, she had no idea, but her thanks were sincere.

"Emily, why are they doing this?" she asked later in the afternoon, when they were alone.

"I organized a hen party last week. I suggested that we needed to atone for some real stupidity," her cousin, that most clueless of women, told her. "We were all wrong."

She helped Susanna remake the bed. "While you were in

Cheyenne, I received a letter from Mama and newspaper clippings, and I shared those with the ladies." Emily lowered her voice, as though all of Shippensburg crowded around her in the bedroom, "Susanna, Frederick left debts everywhere and seldom had a sober day."

If that jury of the good men of Shippensburg had believed me, I would still have my son, Susanna thought, unwilling to say it out loud, because Emily seemed sufficiently remorseful. "Imagine," she said instead, smoothing down the sheets that she knew would be quite rumpled before morning, if she and the post surgeon were of similar mind.

Emily sat down and smoothed out a pillow slip, remorse obvious in her eyes. "I also told them it was my idea to call you a Civil War widow. I never should have done that."

Susanna sat beside her cousin and hugged her. "You just tried to do the right thing. I know you did."

When Joe came home for supper that night, she told him about her day, and what Emily had said. He nodded, and there was no overlooking the admiration in his eyes.

"Why are you so pleased?" she asked, happy to sit on his lap when he tugged on her apron.

"It takes a strong person to apologize—I obviously underestimated your frivolous cousin—and it takes a stronger person to forgive. I've never underestimated you."

She kissed him, and decided that the odor of carbolic must be an aphrodisiac. "I wish General Crook were a strong person."

Joe kissed her back. "But then I would have to be a stronger person to forgive him."

"You could," she said simply.

"Did Mrs. Dunklin form part of today's officers wives' brigade?"

"No." Susanna rested her head against Joe's chest, her

face warm again as she remembered that horrible evening. "Just as well, because I'm not certain I can forgive her yet. Maybe later."

She watched time slip by in May, as more and more companies gathered at Fort Laramie. The flats by Suds Row bloomed with tents as the army took to canvas, in preparation for the coming roundup of Northern Roamers onto the Great Sioux Reservation. It became harder and harder to concentrate on school in the commissary storehouse, as more and more rations for the Big Horn Yellowstone Expedition piled into the building. And Private Benedict's teaching days became numbered.

Finally Susanna and Anthony declared classroom learning over, and spent the rest of the week fine-tuning the play *Our Century of Progress,* which Susanna had written about famous inventions of the nineteenth century, from telegraph key to Colt .45. All the boys clamored to demonstrate the latter. Joe was happy to loan an old stethoscope to the student portraying Arthur Leared.

Rehearsals began in earnest as soon as the prisoners from the guardhouse finished the stage, which Susanna knew was an engineering marvel. Two corporals' wives sewed a curtain from lightweight canvas, and Susanna assigned the student who simply couldn't memorize anything to open and close it, to the envy of his classmates.

Even in her classroom, the talk centered around the coming campaign. "I'm astounded what my students know about pincer movements and a three-pronged attack," she said to Joe early one morning when neither of them felt inclined to get up.

"What have they told you?" he asked.

"They tell me Colonel Gibbon has already started east from western Montana, General Terry is eventually going to move west from the Dakotas, and our own dear General Crook will head north from here and Fort Fetterman."

"Your students are already strategists." He kissed her breasts, which ended the discussion for a while. She made it to school on time, but Joe was late to the hospital.

Her own cherubs practiced their poems, with one little prodigy happy to learn Longfellow's lengthy *Hiawatha*. He came to class disgruntled, saying it made his father, an infantry sergeant, groan and assure him that Plains Indians bore no resemblance to anything created by the New England poet.

"Everyone is a critic," Susanna grumbled to her husband, trying to make him laugh.

He laughed a little, but she knew it was just to humor her. General Crook had arrived from Omaha to lead this expedition, and the general turned Joe silent. She made no comment, but made sure her husband had his favorite baked oatmeal for breakfast, and she took hot meals to the hospital on those evenings he was too busy to come home.

"Soldiers are everywhere," she remarked to Anthony Benedict on the morning of their school program.

"No one's bothering you, are they?" he asked as he handed a student the telegrapher's key. "There you are, Mr. Morse."

"No. In fact, as I crossed the parade ground, three soldiers rushed to help me carry baked goods and costumes! Of course, that meant I had to dip into the cookies in payment." Susanna took a deep breath. "Anthony, I'm going to miss you. Please be careful."

Private Benedict sent another student behind the canvas curtain. "I'll be careful, Mrs. Randolph." He took a piece of paper from his uniform pocket. "If anything happens, here's my special girl's address."

She didn't argue that nothing would happen, or put on dieaway airs. These weren't men to fool with silliness. "I'll take care of it, Anthony."

Private Benedict peered around the edge of the stage. "We have a full house, Mrs. Randolph. Think how they will exclaim over that McCormick Reaper that the guardhouse crew constructed. Good thing no one invented a flying machine in this century. We'd have needed a bigger stage!"

Thanks to Emily, Susanna had located a portable pianoforte on Officers Row, which Mrs. Burt obligingly played, Captain Andy Burt turning the pages for her. Susanna stood beside the stage, looking with pride at her students, their parents, all smiles, and a phalanx of officers along the back row, her husband among them. Her smile faded. There on the opposite end from Joe was General Crook himself. She resisted the urge to march to him and give him a generous helping of her mind. Instead, she took her seat in the front row next to Private Benedict.

She knew Maeve and Maddie had finished painting Fort Laramie on the curtain late last night, using the fort's endless supply of quartermaster red. The elegant scrollwork was a fitting testament to Maeve's confidence with letters and words. She was backstage with Mrs. Hanrahan, ushering each group of thespians forward for their part in the program. Susanna wasn't surprised that the star of the production was Samuel Morse and his telegraphic key, which tapped out the sentence "Fort Laramie will defeat the Northern Roamers." Children holding placards with each syllable came across the stage as though sprung from the key. True, "will defeat" was transposed by two children frozen with stage fright, but the sentiment received its due applause.

After a brief intermission, the students sat cross-legged on the floor and took their turns onstage for recitations. "The boy stood on the burning deck," as interpreted with true martial fervor by the son of an Arikara scout, drew such applause that he stared at Private Benedict in wide-eyed alarm, then ran to his mother.

Susanna took turns with Private Benedict, coaching where needed and nodding her encouragement when that was called for. She remembered other assemblies at the elegant girls' school where she'd taught, or the quality academy where Tommy had given his own rendition of that boy on the burning deck. Here she was in a commissary storehouse, the audience seated on planks and cracker boxes, with a stage built by convicts, and she felt nothing but contentment. *There is nowhere I would rather be,* she thought, as her last pupil, Eddie Hanrahan, whose father had been left behind on a cold battlefield, recited the Preamble to the Constitution, bowed and left the stage with all the aplomb of Daniel Webster himself.

As the applause went on, she thought through the past five months. In January, she wouldn't have thought such peace of mind possible. In May, she knew anything was possible. She turned to look at her husband, who was looking directly at her and applauding. "I love you," he mouthed, and her heart was full.

Major Townsend took the stage then and held up his hands until his audience was silent and seated again. It didn't take long in a military gathering. He looked down at the children.

"My dears, you amaze me." He looked at Susanna and Anthony next, with a slight inclination of his head. "Thank you, teachers. You've discharged your duties well." He smiled. "I *know* the army doesn't pay you enough!" He glanced at the back of the audience. "And in some cases, the army doesn't pay you at all."

Susanna laughed softly at that. "I'll tell you later, Anthony," she whispered, when her colleague looked at her, a question in his eyes.

"Mrs. Randolph informs me that she is a glutton for punishment. She has every intention of teaching a summer term, if any of you—and I include the officers' children—are inclined to more study." He looked at Anthony. "Private, is there anything else?"

"Only cake with actual icing and cookies with no raisins, over there in what we have dubbed the lobby, sir."

"Then let us adjourn. Dismissed!"

Susanna wanted to go to her husband, but there were students to congratulate and then parents to thank, and even a kiss on the cheek from Major Townsend. She walked toward Joe, who was talking to Mrs. Hanrahan. If there was a better doctor anywhere, Susanna couldn't imagine who it might be. *To think I share a bed with all that excellence,* she reminded herself, amused.

He saw her and motioned her closer. "Susanna, I've convinced Mrs. Hanrahan to come and work for my hospital steward. He's been complaining of overwork for years now, and I have enough discretionary funds to hire this kind lady. What do you think?"

Your discretionary fund comes right out of your salary, she thought. "It's a lovely idea. Mrs. Hanrahan, you are needed there."

"The surgeon said I can work when Eddie is in your school this summer. Maeve has already agreed that she and Maddie will watch my two little ones," Mrs. Hanrahan said, her eyes full of relief and gratitude.

"It was either that or heaven knows what, Suzie," he whispered after Mrs. Hanrahan left. "The army would send Corporal Hanrahan's dependents home, except that home is County Wicklow. Her pension alone is too small to live on. Ted Brown will need more assistance this summer."

Susanna kissed his cheek. "When did I last tell you how magnificent you are?"

"I think it was about three this morning," he teased, his eyes lively. "See you for supper, Mrs. Randolph. Bring along any leftover cake, if there is any. If not, you are dessert."

In a few minutes the bugler that regulated their lives blew recall from fatigue, and the storehouse cleared out, except for the older students who had agreed to help Private Benedict store the props and remove the curtain. Susanna went back to her corner of the classroom to tidy her desk. She glanced up after a few minutes, surprised to see General Crook standing there.

I can smile and say nothing, she thought. *He doesn't know me from Adam.*

"General?"

"I enjoyed the program, Mrs. Randolph."

He does know who I am; he must. "Thank you, sir."

He stood there and she didn't know why. Probably nothing she could say would make matters better, but she wasn't the same cowed woman now, the one with no hope and no future and too much past to ever forget.

"Would you sit down for a moment, General?" she said, her voice soft. She sat next to him. "Sir, you know who I am."

"I do."

"First, let me wish you all success on your travel north."

"We'll do our best."

"I don't doubt that for a minute. Sir, I'm in no position to tell you what to think or do, but I love my husband."

He smiled at that, and looked away.

"Sir, the only mistake he made in that aide station at South Mountain was to practice good medicine. He turned away from a dying man to a man he could save, if he worked fast."

Crook was on his feet now, headed for the door.

"I'm not through yet," Susanna said, putting all her conviction behind her words. "You have to understand—doctors don't look at uniforms. They look at injuries."

He turned back to her, and she saw the anger in his eyes. In January, his expression would have terrified her into silence. In May, it didn't. No matter what happened in the next few moments, she knew she would be going home to cook dinner for a wonderful man who loved her; so simple, but so profound to her heart. What General Crook thought of her didn't matter. She could live with that.

"It happened almost fourteen years ago. I wish you would let it go now. That's all." She said it to his back, because he had turned away.

She turned her attention to the papers on her desk. She knew he stood there a few more moments, then she heard his footsteps going through the warehouse. She finished gathering together her end-of-term papers, stacked them neatly on the desk and left the warehouse.

The sun was angling lower now, but the retreat gun hadn't sounded yet. Holding the rest of the cake, Susanna stood for a long moment on the edge of the parade ground. The new guardhouse was almost completed. Major Townsend must have put more soldiers at work on the building, now that most of the regiment had assembled for the upcoming campaign, and he had more men to work with. Other men policed the grounds, and still others moved more supplies into the other quartermaster and commissary storehouses. There was a fair amount of cussing coming from the direction of the quartermaster's corrals as mules were introduced to new wagons. She smiled to herself, thinking of the little boys watching on the other side of the fence, who were probably going to dismay their mothers with an appalling increase in their vocabulary. At least her nephew, Stanley, wasn't there, and Emily was willing now to admit where *his* bad language had come from.

On the parade ground itself, sergeants were taking their companies through the manual of arms, each company trying to outdo the other. She waved to Sergeant Rattigan, and he gave her a smart salute, which made her pink up. "Maddie, you are a lucky girl to have such a father," she murmured. "He'll make your beaux toe the mark someday."

She shook her head over the shabby red buildings. Too much quartermaster red, too many raisins, liniment by the barrel, but not enough wool socks. Next year the shortage might be tenpenny nails and India ink, and the surplus pickles. "It's the army way, Suzie," Joe was fond of telling her as he coped with his own shortages and taught one of the blacksmiths how to make forceps.

Joe's timing was exquisite. He came through the front door calling, *"Bonsoir, mon petit chou"* at the same time she took the roast out of the oven and put in the pan of rolls. Stewed tomatoes, humble indeed, made up the rest of dinner. She resolved again to plant a garden in her backyard, almost tasting tender lettuce and a radish or two already, provided the deer weren't oversolicitous.

She could tell by his squint that he had a headache, so she made small talk about that afternoon's school program. By the time they reached the leftover cake, the squint was gone, and she knew she should confess.

"I may have done a bad thing, dearest," she said after he had eaten two bites of cake.

"What could that possibly be?"

She told him about General Crook's visit. Joe just continued to eat the cake, saving the icing for last, because he liked it so well.

"I told him it had been fourteen years, and he should just let it go."

"What did he say?"

"Nothing. I don't know why he came to my classroom. Do you?"

"Not a clue," Joe replied. He put down the fork and took her hand, kissing it and leaving little sugary crystals behind. "You're going to fight my battles for me?"

"You fight mine."

"Of course. You're my wife." He picked up the fork again and finished the piece of cake, then eyed hers. She snatched it away and he laughed.

"Funny thing," he told her later, when they were both crowded into his armchair. "General Crook came to the hospital, probably after he left you."

"Goodness. What did you do?"

He shrugged. "I was busy, of course, so I just saluted with a pair of scissors in my hand—so military—and said hello." Joe tugged her back to rest against his chest, his hand on her hair. "It was funny, but I didn't feel tense, or defensive, or… or anything, really. I just said hello, and went back to work."

"Did he say anything?"

"Not a word. He just stood there a little longer, then left." Joe kissed her cheek. "I wonder…maybe it's too hard for some people to apologize, if that's what he was trying to do."

They sat close together in silence, until Susanna closed her eyes and slept, content in her husband's arms.

Chapter Twenty

All the regiments except Jim O'Leary's troop left Fort Laramie four days later, leaving behind a scattering of infantry borrowed from other posts. The infantry marched out first, and the cavalry later that afternoon, heading to Fort Fetterman to rendezvous with other regiments. Susanna felt tears in her eyes as she watched Private Benedict march away with his company, and Sergeant Rattigan with his. And there were the other fathers of her students; it was really too much, and she told her husband so that night in bed.

"I envision a long campaign," he said. "I sent Al with everything we could spare from the hospital."

"Emily is crying in her quarters, and even Katie looks grim, although Jim and his troop are still here."

"Katie's a veteran campaigner. She knows how busy he will be, patrolling between here and the Black Hills. She'll barely see him, and when she does, he'll be so worn down that it will break her heart every time."

Susanna thought about that, as her husband pulled her closer. "You're saying maybe it's better the ladies don't know how their husbands will look by the time this is done?"

"I probably am."

She raised herself up on her elbow for a good look at her

man. He was tired, too, but she didn't state the obvious, beyond asking if he was going to get any extra help.

"A contract surgeon is coming, Suzie," he told her. "The wounded who survive the transport back here will come to us. We'll be busy."

She stayed in their quarters the next morning, watching the under-strength garrison carry on guard mount with a ghost crew. There was constant activity at the Rustic Hotel as more miners headed for the gold fields. The post felt deserted, which gave her no peace of mind, considering all the local Indian activity recently. The Indians who hadn't fled the reservations to join the Northern Roamers considered it their duty to disrupt life elsewhere.

She spent the afternoon with Emily, soothing her dear cousin, who cried and worried like every other woman on Officers Row. Then Susanna played jackstraws with Stanley. A welcome walk took her to Maeve Rattigan's quarters, where Maeve and Maddie tended Mrs. Hanrahan's children.

"Your husband has even hired Eddie to sweep floors for him," Maeve said. "He says he has a discretionary fund."

Susanna smiled at that. *He does, indeed,* she thought as she took a crying baby from Maeve. *He'll be in the poorhouse someday and no man will be happier.*

She looked at Maeve, healthy and smiling, color in her cheeks again, where last winter she had been ghost-pale.

"You're looking ever so good, Maeve. I know Maddie agrees with you."

She nodded. "It's more than that, Susanna. Ask your husband."

Susanna asked Joe that night over supper. "Is she anticipating, and just too shy to tell me?"

He reached for the last roll. "No. The blessing is that she's not. I sometimes get to experiment, and Maeve's the beneficiary."

Susanna listened, fascinated, as he told her of the article
by George Drysdale, and his theories about fertility at certain
times of the month. "If the Rattigans could time their love-
making to *keep* her from getting pregnant, she might have
time to heal, grow less anemic, and stay alive. I doubt she
will ever carry a child to term—some women can't—but at
least she won't suffer from miscarriage after miscarriage. It
was killing her, Suzie, in her mind and in her body."

She thought about that all evening, after Joe returned to
the hospital, then thought about Louis Pasteur and his Paris
lycée. If ever a physician was suited for scholarship, it was Joseph Randolph. Too bad they had heard nothing from France.

There was a letter for them the next day, delivered in person by Captain O'Leary, back from patrol, standing on their
porch and practically swaying with exhaustion. She thanked
him, looked at the return address—Pinkerton National Detective Agency—and hurried to the hospital.

She stood in the entrance to the ward a moment, catching
her breath. Wordless, she held out the letter to Joe.

"It's addressed to you, but I couldn't have opened it anyway."

He certainly knew his hospital steward. All it took was a
look in Ted Brown's direction for the man to take over. His
arm around her waist, Joe headed her toward his office, closing the door behind them. He opened the envelope and offered
the letter to her. He took it back when she shook her head.

"Calm down, Suzie," he admonished, then sat with her on
his lap. "This better?"

"Just read it, then tell me."

She closed her eyes and rested her head against his chest
while he read the letter.

"This is the damnedest thing. No, it's not bad news. I'm
not sure what it is. Go ahead. It won't bite."

She took the letter from him and read. When she'd finished, she just looked at him. "He thinks he saw a tall man and a blond boy around Omaha, and they gave him the slip?" she asked, hardly believing it.

Joe was silent a moment. "We've been underestimating Nick Martin," he said finally. "If I'm reading this right, Nick knows he's being tailed, but he doesn't know by whom! Do you think I should call off the Pinkertons and just trust Nick to get Tommy to us?"

After some consideration, Susanna nodded. "I think you'd better, else Nick might go to ground and we'll never find Tommy." She started to cry.

Her husband's arms were around her then, holding her close. "I'll send a telegram today."

"Pray Nick won't try to get here on foot!" she said, wiping her eyes. "There are so many Indians between here and Omaha."

"We have to trust him." Joe kissed her hair. "This is another moment when you're going to have to be brave a little longer."

"It's so hard," she whispered.

"Good thing you're equal to it."

"Not at this moment."

"No shame in that. See my cot over there? Curl up, take a nap, and I'll walk my best girl home for supper."

The contract surgeon arrived, fresh out of school and greener than grass, which meant more supervision rather than less. Joe tried to make light of it, making her smile with his description of the new doctor, who went through four methods to determine death, where one would do.

"I swear his eyes turned into saucers when I leaned over, put two fingers against the patient's neck and covered his face with his sheet." Joe shook his head at his colleague's afternoon antics. "Shame on me, but I peeked back in the ward later, and there was Dr. Petteys, making really sure that the dead man I'd pronounced dead really *was* dead." He gave Susanna his tired smile when she massaged his back. "Maybe I used to do that, too."

The nights were long. She feigned sleep after they made love, just so Joe would sleep, too, and not stay awake worrying about her. The sick, and those wounded by carelessness or other accident on the march north, came dribbling back to the fort to be evaluated, cured or buried. Joe looked almost as tired as the men of Company K, riding their ceaseless patrols.

Susanna lay awake long into the night, wondering where Tommy was, and if Nick Martin had the slightest idea what he was doing. She was awake when someone banged on the door in the middle of the night. She leaped from bed, tugging at her nightgown, even before Joe had raised his head from the pillow.

Bobby Dunklin stood there, his eyes wide with fright. Susanna grabbed him to her and pulled him inside, kneeling by him, her hands around his face as he began to cry. "It's my mother," he said.

Susanna sat him down in the parlor and ran to shake her husband awake. "It's Mrs. Dunklin. Bobby's here."

Joe was dressed in a moment and hurrying into his home office for his medical bag. "Keep Bobby here," he ordered as he ran outside, his suspenders down around his hips, and wearing his moccasins with no stockings.

She took Bobby into the kitchen, talking with him about summer, and the pony she knew he loved to ride, and the games of catch he and his friends played near the stables. She dried his tears, made him blow his nose, then held him on her lap with no protest as he ate the cinnamon rolls she had promised Joe for breakfast.

"Bobby, what happened?"

"I don't know. Mama called me from her bed and told me to get the post surgeon."

He clung to her and Susanna held him close, forgetting every slight, every humiliation that still made her turn her face away when she passed the Dunklin quarters.

"She won't die, will she?" he asked finally.

Two months ago Susanna might have wondered that any boy could love the vindictive woman she remembered from that awful night. She didn't wonder now. "Bobby, she has the most wonderful post surgeon in the army looking after her," she murmured into his tangled hair. "She couldn't be in better hands." *Please, Joe,* she thought, *do your best.*

When Bobby Dunklin slept, she carried him into the parlor and made him comfortable on the packing crate settee. Quietly she pulled a chair from the kitchen and sat there as another hour passed.

She was about to doze off when she heard the door handle turn quietly. She was up in an instant, tiptoeing across the room to open the door and step outside into the warm June night.

"He's sleeping on the settee," she whispered, her lips close to Joe's ear. She kissed him for good measure.

Joe shook his head and sat on the bench by the front door, tugging her down beside him. "A miscarriage. I hate those! She lost a lot of blood and she's weak. No telling how long she called for Bobby before he woke up."

"What should I do?"

"I cleaned up what I could, but can I ask…"

"You know I will."

"I thought so. I'll wake up Katie and take Bobby there after I talk to him."

Susanna opened the door quietly and looked back at her husband. "I don't even know her first name."

"Lavinia."

He had sent for Mrs. Hanrahan, who waited by the Dunklins' door. They completed the work Joe had begun, washing Lavinia Dunklin, her face a mask of sorrow, and easing her into a clean nightgown. Mary Hanrahan made up the bed with clean sheets, carefully rolling Mrs. Dunklin from side to side while Susanna held her steady. When they finished, Mary went downstairs and came back soon enough with a cup of tea.

"Works wonders," she whispered, and set it by the bedside. She touched Susanna's shoulder and left the house as quietly as she had entered it.

Mrs. Dunklin slept and Susanna kept watch over the woman she should have hated, in a house full of terrible memories. She remembered what she had told General George Crook's back as he had walked away: *Just let it go.* As the sun rose and the bugler attempted to play reveille—the good buglers had gone with Crook—Susanna Randolph let it go.

Like most boys, young Joe Randolph had had his heroes. From Washington to John Marshall to James Madison, most were Virginians, as he was. He had admired Robert E. Lee for years, until his own adult leanings kept him in the Union army when Lee followed the South. General George Thomas, another Virginian and Union exile like him, became his hero then, being all that an officer should be.

Joe had a heroine now, his wife. Until Lavinia Dunklin was safely out of the medical woods, Suzie had sat by her bed, holding her hand, cleaning her, feeding her, crying with her. She did it without complaint or much comment, keeping her own counsel even at night in bed, when other officers' wives took over night duty, and Suzie was released to sleep beside him.

She curled up beside him as always. He used to think he wouldn't care for that much closeness during summer, when it was hot and two people could get sticky being together; he was so wrong. Suzie just naturally went into his arms when the light was out. So what if they sweat? He didn't want her any farther away than his fingertips.

He knew how tired she was, but she hesitated not a second when he wanted her, loving him and letting him know with a gentle sigh—as if he needed a prompt—just how deep her own pleasure was. He had never met anyone remotely like Susanna Randolph. If word ever got out what a lover she was, what a friend, he'd have been stabbed and dumped in a borrow pit.

She continued to amaze him. He asked her if Lavinia Dunklin had apologized for her reprehensible behavior.

"No. I think it's too hard for her. I let it go" was Suzie's serene reply.

He also knew she cried as quietly as she could as the sun rose, mourning a beloved son she feared she would never see again, no matter how cheerful her face throughout the day. Joe allowed her those private moments of sorrow, because to interfere with them would have been unkind. After his own sorrow with Melissa's death, he knew better than to mess with someone else's grief.

He lay awake worrying sometimes at night after she slept, wondering where Tommy was, wondering if he should have sent Nick Martin to an asylum, as Al Hartsuff had advised. Maybe Joe was wrong to trust a man three-quarters insane.

His happiest moment came when Suzie met him at the door nearly jumping up and down in her excitement. "You won the poker jackpot at the Rustic Hotel today?" he teased, and laughed when she thumped him.

"Even better, my love," she said, sitting with him on the front porch, her hand in his. "Today, all the officers' wives with children, Lavinia Dunklin excepted, brought them to my summer school." She mentioned a stickler who had held out longer than some of the others in forgiving Susanna for being human. "Joe, she told me I was the best thing that had ever happened to education at Fort Laramie."

"I could have told her that," he said, his lips against her cheek now.

"She invited us to play cards tonight."

"You know I hate cards," he said.

"But you love me, and you'll go."

Something in the words smacked of enormous confidence. As a doctor he could not have diagnosed what had happened to his wife. As a husband, he knew she was whole again.

As June passed the halfway mark, disquieting rumor made its way to Fort Laramie. It came as it always did, a thief in the night, carried by Indians, or Black Hills gold seekers. News of battle began to flicker like heat lightning. Joe never talked about it, knowing that a row of officers' wives and a small community of enlisted men's wives worried enough, without borrowing rumor. But there it was, and the feeling only grew stronger.

He didn't say anything to Dr. Petteys, but he didn't need to. When he sent Petteys south to Fort Russell for more medical supplies to bolster their depleted stores, the contract surgeon had made no comment beyond, "I'll be back as soon as possible, Major." It was as if talking about the possibility of high casualties was better not voiced, or it would be worse. Joe never had time to hang around the telegrapher's shack, but he noticed others doing that.

Suzie didn't know the rules of rumor-laden warfare and asked him at breakfast, "There's been a battle, hasn't there?"

He was a little short with her, but she knew him too well to take offense at such childishness. She gave him that level stare that reminded him of Melissa. Maybe it was a woman thing.

He nodded, reluctant to voice his concerns. Susanna

stopped moving between the stove and the table to sit beside him, take his hand and hold it to her breasts.

"Whatever I can do to help," was all she said, and then got about her business again, which meant her little classroom in the commissary warehouse.

He was grateful for the school, and not because he thought any great learning was going to take place during a Fort Laramie summer. He appreciated that it kept Susanna busy and took her mind off Tommy, if only briefly. He came to love her animated description of the day's events in her school, which were always more interesting than his stories of pus, diarrhea and dry cough.

When the news came, it hit hard. There was no school on Saturday, and Petteys was on duty, two reasons for Joe to lie in bed and explore his wife's body thoroughly. He had taken his leisurely time providing sufficient foreplay to earn a final objection from Suzie, in her own eagerness, who was ready and getting impatient. She typically climaxed twice, so the third time came as a testimony to the rare leisure of Saturday, leaving them both calm and content.

At least they would have been if the bugler hadn't blown officers call. In a fort so understaffed, it was a summons closely akin to a fire bell in the night. Joe got up quickly, doing a quick wash while Suzie watched him, her blond hair so pretty and disheveled around her face, and her eyes drooping, tribute to his amazing prowess.

"What's that call?" she asked. "I can't remember."

"It's trouble, Suzie."

"Comb your hair," she called after him as he ran down the stairs, his mind already off Venus and centered on Mars.

He ran his fingers through his hair and hurried to the admin building, joining the small cadre of officers still at Fort Laramie. No one looked too soldierly, so no one commented on his own dishevelment at an hour when proper gentlemen were more sedately clothed.

Major Townsend, his eyes two coals in his head, cleared his throat. "Bad news, gentlemen. General Crook suffered a defeat at Rosebud Creek last Saturday and has withdrawn to the Big Horns. The wounded are at Fetterman now and headed our way."

No one said anything; they had been expecting battle. But defeat? Good God, Crook had twenty companies in his part of the pincer movement. Joe looked around, and knew every man there was thinking the same thing.

Training took over. Townsend told the cavalry lieutenant on loan from his Nebraska post to saddle up two fast riders and locate Jim O'Leary and K Company. "If they're near enough, tell them to ride to Fetterman and offer support," Townsend ordered. The lieutenant left on the run, not bothering to salute.

Townsend issued orders that sent everyone moving, then looked at Joe, the only officer remaining. "Do what you do, Joe," he said, sounding infinitely weary. "They'll be here Monday. Expect the worst and be ready to transport."

Monday turned into the blur he remembered from the Civil War, with his ward full of dirty men and dirty wounds. He dismissed ambulatory patients to make room for hard cases. His hardest case was a captain of the Third Cavalry, shot through the face, maybe blind and with teeth missing. Joe tended him in Ted Brown's quarters behind the hospital, desperate to keep the man nearby, but in a quiet place.

Without asking, Suzie and Mary Hanrahan took over his ward, washing the men and sitting with them. Joe steeled himself for Suzie's gasp when she saw Private Benedict, his leg ruined and full of gangrene. She was a novice around that kind of gross wound, but he still had to pry her away so he could remove Anthony's leg below the knee.

He and Petteys, a veteran overnight, doctored for two days straight, taking turns sleeping on his cot. Suzie brought food for both of them, then sat with Anthony Benedict, just holding his hand. Joe watched her droop and knew it was too much, but he needed her.

Other wives came, too, unable to stay away, some more useful than others, but all a cheerful presence. He spent more time in his hospital steward's quarters, watching the captain suffer in silence, his iron will evident.

Finally the ward was quiet, filled with clean, well-fed men who lay half awake, half asleep, in that curious somnolence of the wounded. The ward was just the way he wanted it, so the steward could watch tonight. Joe went to Anthony Benedict's bedside and tapped Suzie's shoulder.

She looked up, pleased to see him.

"Private, I'm taking my wife home. Go to sleep, and that's an order."

To his amusement, Anthony snapped his eyes shut.

"You're a faker," Suzie told the private, but she let Joe lift her to her feet.

They strolled down the hill hand in hand, silent. Inside their quarters, he took her in his arms.

"You know, Suzie, after two days of the three *D*s—death, dirt and dismemberment—all I want to do is make a baby."

She understood exactly what he was trying to say. Her clothes came off at the bedroom door, and she helped him out of his.

"You could use a bath, but I don't care," was all she said as she took care of his needs, her own, and proved to him how competent was woman—specifically, his woman.

Chapter Twenty-One

"I'd like to think we made a baby," his charming wife whispered in his ear as she sent him off to Fort Russell with an ambulance and three wounded soldiers. "It's our turn to get lucky."

When the ambulance stopped that night near Hat Creek, the courier riding the mail from Fort Russell to Fort Laramie recognized Joe and handed him a letter postmarked Omaha. After tending to his patients, Joe leaned against an ambulance wheel and opened it.

It was from Will Pinkerton. "I thought we asked you to stop," he murmured as he scanned the lines, then reread them, impressed with the equally clever son of the detective he remembered from the war. He read the part again about Will preparing to leave for Chicago, and coming upon what he thought was Nick Martin in the army wagon yard.

"He led me a merry chase," Joe read. *"It was as though Nick was drawing me away from the wagon yard, like a mother bird from her chicks. I finally lost him, but resolved to search the yards in the morning, when I could see better. When I did, the wagons had already pulled out, heading for Fort Russell. I was advised not to follow, because of Indi-*

ans. Major, keep your eyes open. Tommy's heading right to you, I think."

Joe closed his eyes in relief, then opened them, to look in the envelope. He sighed with gratitude. Will had included the photograph of Susanna's son. "I'm going to find you," he murmured.

His patients were silent for the most part, as contemplative as Trappist monks, except when the ambulance hit a particularly bad spot. Then they sucked in their breath, hissing in pain. He knew the sound from years of experience, but it always unnerved him.

By the time they arrived at Fort Russell, the captain's wife, alerted by telegraph, waited by the hospital entrance. Joe held her as she sagged against him, aghast at her husband's wounds, then straightened and followed the stretcher into the hospital, her tread firm. Joe could only admire that much resolution, even though he knew Susanna was her equal. For some reason, he thought of foolish, faulty Emily Reese and her own devotion to her captain, and then Maeve, so loving, and now adored by a daughter as well as her sergeant. Perhaps it was just as well that Louis Pasteur had not answered his letter. He belonged with these intrepid souls.

It was a bracing thought that kept him awake long enough to hand over his patients and their charts, and find a bed in Russell's orphanage, the army nickname for temporary quarters for those officers casually at post. Joe soaked in a cramped tin tub, then crawled between sheets that lacked one key ingredient in his life—his wife.

He went to breakfast, pleased to see Jim O'Leary and his men in the mess hall. He sat with them, listening to Jim's stories of patrol and rumor.

"Gossip says Crook is holed up at Goose Creek, fly-fishing and determined not to move forward without ample reinforcements," Jim told him in disgust.

Joe listened, wondering again why Crook had come to his hospital to stand there in silence. He was about to say something when someone dropped a pan and all the men at breakfast whipped around to look, some with their hands on their sidearms.

"We're on edge," Jim commented.

Joe looked beyond the mess tables toward the source of the noise, where a boy was picking up the pan. "Army's getting younger every year, or I'm getting older," he said.

"You're getting older, Major dear," O'Leary said, familiar in his Irish way. "The cook told me he's so shorthanded, with all soldiers in the field, that he's practically snatching civilians and throwing them in the kitchen."

Joe looked at the boy, on his hands and knees now, wiping up porridge. He looked again. He felt his face drain of color, then shook his head to clear it. The boy was tall and thin. His hair might have been blond, but it was dirty. *Look at me, lad,* he thought, suddenly alert. *Just look at me.*

He got up slowly, his attention focused on the child, who was mopping up the mess he had caused, while the cook scolded him. *Just look at me.*

The boy did. His eyes were brown and he looked very much like Susanna Randolph, with her heart-shaped face. Joe held his breath to observe the mole under the boy's eye.

The cook swore and the boy looked in his tormenter's direction. Joe let his breath out in a whoosh. The boy had a patch of much darker hair by his temple. This was the boy in the photograph that Susanna had treasured, and surrendered so reluctantly. Will Pinkerton was right; Tommy had been making his way west, set on this path by Nick Martin.

"Tommy," Joe said, tentative and still unsure.

No reaction. *I'm a fool,* Joe thought, and turned away. He turned back. The cook had set up a scold so shrill that Joe could barely hear himself. He walked closer, giving the cook such a glare that the man went silent.

"Tommy Hopkins," Joe said, distinctly this time.

The boy looked up, startled, poised for flight. He balled up the rag in his hand, which dripped porridge, ready to throw it if Joe took one step closer.

Joe stopped. He took a deep breath and spoke softly. "Tommy Hopkins, your mother's been missing you."

The hard eyes of a boy too soon old softened as he turned into the child he was. Slowly he lowered the rag to his side, then dropped it, which made the cook raise his big spoon.

"Don't!" Joe ordered.

If the boy had any doubts, that ended them. With a sob, he stepped over the mess he had made on the floor. Joe knelt and held open his arms as the lad came closer, hesitated, then threw himself into the embrace of a man he had never seen before.

"Tommy, we've been looking for you," Joe murmured as the boy wept in his arms. "Your mama's at Fort Laramie and that's where I'm going."

"He *told* me Mama was alive. I hoped, but it's been so long," Tommy Hopkins said when he could speak.

Joe took his hand and led him back to the bench where Jim O'Leary sat, his eyes big.

"This is Susanna's *son?*" he asked. "Have a seat, lad. Have some porridge." The captain pushed Joe's barely eaten porridge closer.

"I'm not supposed to eat until I finish cleaning pans," Tommy said, his eyes on the cook, who still glowered by the kitchen door.

"You're through cleaning pans," Joe said.

The other troopers from K Company gathered around their commander, their expressions of amazement mirroring their captain's. "When are you heading for Fort Laramie?" Joe asked O'Leary.

"In an hour or two."

Tommy was eating Joe's porridge now, his economy of motion telling Joe worlds about how rough he had been living lately. Joe sprinkled more sugar in the bowl and got a fleeting smile for his thanks.

"Take us with you, Jim. I'm supposed to collect more supplies here, but they can come in the ambulance with the escort heading north tomorrow."

"I can do it," Jim told him. "Lad, can you ride?"

The fleeting smile returned to stay. "That's what we've been doing, all across the country."

"You're probably a better horseman than I am by now," Joe said. "I'm a post surgeon."

The smile grew larger, reminding Joe forcefully of Tommy's mother at her most impish. "Then I *know* I'm a better horseman than you are!" His voice became more confidential. "Aaron told me you weren't too handy in the saddle."

"Who?"

"Aaron Belknap."

"Not Nick Martin?"

"Who's that?"

Joe sat back. "No one, I guess." He looked at O'Leary, who seemed to be enjoying the whole exchange hugely. "Jim, *you* have a son. Take a good look at this lad. Will you go to the stores and get him a pair of trousers and a shirt?" He looked at Tommy's broken shoes. "Maybe some shoes? Bring them to us at the orphanage, and we'll ride with you."

He looked at Tommy again, seeing relief in his eyes now. "Do you trust me to get you to your mother?"

The boy nodded. "Aaron told me someone would come," he said simply. "I believed him."

* * *

Tommy had no objection to a bath. Joe scrubbed him from hair to heels while he sat silent, a dazed expression on his suntanned face. By the time Joe finished, O'Leary showed up with clothes. Everything was too big, but a belt with new holes helped.

"My word, he *is* blond," the captain said. "How on earth did you know?"

"Don't even ask, because I couldn't explain," Joe replied. "There was something about the set of his shoulders. And when I saw his eyes…Susanna all over. The mole and blaze clinched it."

Tommy was suitably impressed with Captain O'Leary's K Company, which boasted the only matched grays in the regiment. He needed a boost into the army saddle, but then sat with the ease of an intuitive horseman. Joe shortened the boy's stirrups, then swung onto his own horse.

When they were clear of Fort Russell and riding with that steady lope that O'Leary's grays were famous for, Captain O'Leary motioned them forward.

"Tommy, you ride between me and Major Randolph," he instructed. "I'm going to pop if I don't hear this story, too. How on earth did Nick Ma— Aaron Belknap find you?"

Before he could begin, Joe put up his hand. "Let me start with our end. Tommy, we called him Nick Martin because he never told us his real name. He just disappeared one night, taking some money and a handful of letters your mother had written to you. She used to give them to Ni…to Aaron to mail for her."

"I wondered. He never said how he came to Carlisle." Tommy shrugged. "He never said much of anything."

Joe looked over Tommy's head to Captain O'Leary. "That's our Nick." He looked at the boy, who rode with such ease. "Did he just show up?"

"I guess," Tommy said, unsure. "He's kind of secretive, but you might know that."

"Do I ever."

Tommy laughed, and the sound punched Joe hard. It sounded just like his mother's full-throated laugh. "He said you talked funny. Where are you from?"

"Virginia, lad, and *you're* the one who talks funny."

Both the captain and the boy smiled at each other, humoring him, obviously.

"I was walking to school one morning and noticed a bit of paper in the low branch of a tree. I stopped to look at it." Tommy's eyes filled with tears, and he expertly moved his horse out of the line.

Captain O'Leary halted the troop and called dismount and walk. They all dismounted and Joe walked beside Tommy, his arm on his shoulder now.

"It was from Mama," the boy said, tears on his face. "I read it, and then read it again, and hid it in my books."

"She wrote you every week, son." Joe hadn't meant that to slip out, but Tommy didn't seem to mind. He leaned closer. "Every week, without fail." Then it was Joe's turn to falter. "She...she still does." He glanced at O'Leary and noticed the captain having his own struggle.

"There was another letter the next morning, a little farther on, and then another farther on. By the end of the week, I was out of sight of my house and my father. Aaron stepped out from behind a shed then."

"He's quite a hulking presence. Did he frighten you?" Joe asked.

"A little," Tommy admitted, "but he had another letter in his hand, and I wanted it." He spoke to Captain O'Leary. "We can ride now, sir. I don't mean to slow you down."

They mounted and rode steadily on. Tommy was silent then, and Joe respected his silence. When they stopped briefly at noon, the boy sat cross-legged and close to Joe, eating his hardtack and cheese.

"After that, Aaron walked me to school every morning, once we were out of sight of the house. He told me I wasn't to say anything to anyone, and I didn't. He also said he'd take me to Mama when the time was right."

Joe nodded, the time right for something else. "Lad, I married your mother in April."

He decided that Tommy was probably going to amaze him as much as Suzie did. "Aaron thought you might do that if…" He stopped.

"If what, lad?"

"If you worked up your nerve. Sorry, sir, but that's what he said."

Captain O'Leary shouted with laughter and flopped back on the grass. "Jesus, Mary and Joseph! Major, Nick Martin had your number, same as the rest of us!"

"Was I that obvious?" Joe exclaimed.

"Aye, even to a crazy man."

Tommy grinned and looked away. When he turned back, his face was serious, the grown man painfully evident in the child's face. "You'll treat her kindly," he said, and it was no question.

"Cross my heart, Tommy. I can do no less."

With a sigh, the boy leaned against Joe, and the post surgeon felt the last callus drop away from his own hesitant heart.

They rode into the afternoon, Tommy having no trouble with the steady but rapid pace. In midafternoon, a small party of Cheyenne decided to get surly, which meant dismounting and hunkering down while the troopers fired back, not wasting a single bullet. Joe wrapped himself around Tommy, who clung to him, frightened but determined not to show it.

When a sadder but wiser war party rode off, Joe enlisted Tommy to hold a trooper's hand while he slit the man's pant leg and doctored a flesh wound. Tommy turned pale as Joe worked, but hung on.

"We're a little hard on you," Joe apologized, wiping his hands on the grass when he finished. He signaled for the trooper's bunkies to help their comrade back into his saddle.

Tommy's eyes were wide. He let out a breath he must have been holding since the fight began. "This is a whole lot more exciting than Carlisle, Pennsylvania," he declared, which made Joe smile.

They camped that night at Hunton's roadhouse, so empty without its owner, dead in an Indian raid, even though his employees still carried on. When Tommy was comfortable by the campfire, he continued his story, the part that had been nagging Joe since Nick Martin disappeared.

"How did your father die, Tommy? Can you tell me?"

He nodded, but still took his time. "It was a month after Aaron started walking me to school. He said he did odd jobs around town, and that he watched my house, but I never saw him." The boy looked at Joe. "Sir, for all his size, he's hard to spot."

"He was looking out for you."

"I think so. That night...that night..." He swallowed, and Joe's arm went around him. "I was studying at the dining room table and Papa was drinking. He always did that. I can't remember what I said to him—it never took much—but he started to shout. When he swung his hand out, I ducked and he knocked over a lamp. It fell against the wall and set the curtains on fire."

He sobbed now, reliving the moment, holding out his arms. Joe grabbed him and held him close as he cried. Tommy made no move to leave Joe's lap when his tears subsided.

Captain O'Leary had been toasting cheese. Silently he pulled the cheese off the stick with two pieces of hardtack and handed it to Tommy. The boy accepted it with the ghost of a smile and leaned back against Joe as he ate.

"Will you tell me exactly what happened then?" Joe asked quietly. *I have to know what Nick did,* he thought. *I just have to.* "Close your eyes and think. I promise I will never ask again."

Tommy obediently closed his eyes, relaxing in Joe's arms. When he spoke, his voice was calm. "Papa grabbed his shoulder and rubbed it, and then he grabbed his chest and fell to his knees. The room was on fire."

"He had a heart attack," Joe said, more to himself than to the boy in his arms. Nick Martin didn't murder Frederick Hopkins to save Suzie's son. He was there to watch, a guardian.

Tommy turned slightly to look at him. "A heart attack? I tried to pull Papa away from the flames, but I couldn't. I…I thought maybe he would live if I pulled him out."

"He was probably dead before he hit the floor. It happens. There wasn't anything you could have done."

Tommy sobbed and turned his face into Joe's chest. Joe just held him until he was calm again.

"Did Aaron get you out?"

Tommy nodded. "I heard a window break, and he was there. He picked me up and didn't stop running until we were out of Carlisle."

"Did you start working your way west then?" Captain O'Leary asked, to fill in the silence. Joe noticed that all the troopers were seated near the fire now, listening.

"We'd walk, and stop and work, and then maybe hitch a ride, and work some more."

"What kind of work did you do?" Joe asked, interested.

Tommy grinned. "You name it, we did it! Washed dishes, wrangled horses—I liked that best—painted a church, shined shoes, mucked out a stable or two, slaughtered hogs." He made a face. "Aaron dug graves once. I got paid to be a mourner at a funeral. One whole dollar." That must have been a good memory because he looked satisfied. "It was supposed to be fifty cents, but I sang 'Rock of Ages' and the old ladies cried."

"You're pretty resourceful," Joe told him. "Your mother will be impressed."

Tommy chuckled. "Promise me you won't tell her that I stole a pie once."

"Cross my heart. Good pie?"

"The best. Aaron was a bit strange. He told me we were visiting the seven churches of Asia. When we passed through Smyrna, Indiana, he wanted to preach there. I talked him out of it. Kind of hurt his feelings. He said I reminded him of unfruitful missionary companions. I don't know what he meant."

"I'll explain it to you someday, son."

Tommy grew serious then. "Things changed in Omaha, because Aaron was sure we were being followed."

"You were. Your mother and I hired a detective from the Pinkerton National Detective Agency to find you."

Tommy stared at him, his eyes wide, very much a little boy again. "Pinkerton? *Really?*"

"Cross my heart again. I got a letter from William Pinkerton himself, telling me that you and Aaron gave him the slip."

Tommy's mouth was a perfect O. "We fooled *William Pinkerton?*"

"You did. He lost your trail." He looked at Tommy's expressive face, so like his mother's. "What else happened in Omaha? Aaron didn't come with you to Cheyenne, did he?"

"No. We spent three weeks in Omaha with the army, taking care of mules and wagons. Did you know the army is planning a big expedition against the Indians?"

"We've heard rumors," Joe said mildly as the troopers in the background chuckled. "Did you stow away in a wagon?"

Tommy nodded. "Aaron told me to. He boosted me into a

wagon full of rations. Told me he was staying behind to make sure that man on our trail was confused."

"We received a letter from Mr. Pinkerton, describing someone that had to be Nick Martin. Will thought he might have seen you, which made me pretty sure you were on your way here." Joe nudged Tommy's shoulder. "Did you actually make it all the way to Fort Russell without discovery?"

His face fell. "A teamster found me around Grand Island, but let me stay, since I'm good with mules." He leaned closer. "I learned a lot of words that I'm never going to tell Mama."

"Wise of you. How long were you at Fort Russell?"

Tommy's eyes started to close. "Maybe two weeks. I lived in the stables and worked for the cook." He settled himself more comfortably in Joe's lap. "Aaron told me—" he yawned "—told me that I was to wait there for a tall man with a funny accent. He couldn't remember your name. You know he's a bit slow."

"Not where it matters," Joe said.

Tommy closed his eyes. "He said you'd figure it out." He chuckled, his eyes closed. "He told me that if you didn't, I was to figure out how to get to Fort Laramie." He settled in on Joe's lap. "He said he knew I could."

"I know you would have, son," Joe said, and kissed Tommy's head.

Tommy slept. Joe held him all night. Once he thought he heard a noise in the brush, just beyond the light from the campfire. He wondered if Nick Martin would always be just out of his vision, a step behind or a step ahead, guarding his dear ones.

Chapter Twenty-Two

Tommy rode without complaint to Fort Laramie, taking his turn caring for the horses, and even holding four of them rock-still when Lakota attacked and even Joe joined the troopers on the firing line. Maybe it was good for his image, for Tommy looked at him with real respect when the Indians rode away. Obviously firearms trumped field surgery.

"Your mama's going to be angry with me for exposing you to danger," Joe said, and sewed a flap of skin back onto a trooper's forearm.

Tommy just shrugged. "I'd like to know how we were supposed to get to Fort Laramie without trouble."

"I'll sign him on any day," Captain O'Leary said as the boy walked back to his horse and calmed the still-skittish animal with a few words spoken nose-to-nose.

"He's only twelve!" Joe protested. "I believe his mother will have different ideas. I will, too."

Hard riding brought them to Fort Laramie as the shadows of early evening gathered on the parade ground. Tommy had gone completely silent, straining forward as he rode, as though he could urge his tired mount to go faster.

They came first to the cavalry stables, where K Company peeled off, with a salute from Captain O'Leary.

"We must go to the hospital first," Joe said as he took the reins from the soldier with the wound in his leg. "Private, you will spend the night in the hospital so I can look at your leg in the morning. End of the trail, Tommy."

The boy did as he was asked without question, dismounting and handing the reins of his horse to the bunkie, who saluted Joe and headed back to the stable with the horses. It took only a few minutes to sit the private down on a cot and turn him over to the hospital steward. A few words with Dr. Petteys relieved Joe of night duty.

"Your mother has been waiting for you for months," Joe said, his hand on Tommy's thin shoulder.

"Longer, sir," the boy said. "I haven't laid eyes on her since…since that night she ran away. It's been a year and more." His expression turned wistful, and Joe had an inkling what the time had cost Thomas Hopkins. "I was barely eleven and now I am twelve." He frowned. "I know I have changed. Has she?"

"Probably, but let me assure you she is wonderful."

"Then she hasn't changed."

They walked slowly down the hill toward the parade ground and Officers Row. More tents had sprouted on the ground between the storehouses and infantry barracks, probably reinforcements for General Crook. Tomorrow was the Fourth of July. Joe knew there was to be a picnic at nearby Deer Creek. He hoped Suzie hadn't committed herself to anything beyond preparing some food that someone else could take.

It was too much to hope that his dear wife, the keeper of his heart, would be outside, but she was, walking from Emily Reese's quarters to their own home.

"Your mother, lad," he whispered to Tommy, and gave him a little push.

Tommy stood still, suddenly shy. "Let's go together," he whispered back, which touched Joe to his very core.

"With pleasure."

They were still not close, walking past the post trader's store now, and he knew Suzie's left eye saw only blurry images. Still, she stopped walking and stared. She slowly put her hands to her mouth, then brought them down to pick up her skirts and run. The wind caught her dress and showed off a fine pair of ankles but her arms were open wide now, her hairpins probably escaping with every step. Joe knew her.

"She's going to grab us both," Tommy said.

"I believe she is, son."

Suzie stopped only steps from them, her eyes on her son, adoring him, then on Joe, with an expression so happy that it stunned him. He and Tommy took the last few steps into her arms, both of them holding her close as she cried, her hands first in Tommy's hair, and then his. She gave Joe as fierce a kiss as any woman had ever given a man, then knelt beside her son, just running her hands from his head to his face to his shoulders and arms, saying his name over and over.

Joe knelt, too, because she was suddenly too far away, this wife who had become everything to him. They stayed that way, arms around each other, Tommy between them, until she looked up at his face. She didn't say a thing, but her expression burned itself into his soul and heart.

Neighbors came and went all evening, bringing food, heaven knows why. Mrs. Burt visited briefly, left, and returned with two pairs of trousers. "My son outgrew these. I knew I was keeping them for some reason," she said, pressing them into Suzie's hands.

The biggest surprise was Lavinia Dunklin, still pale from her recent medical ordeal. She had three shirts over her arm, which she handed to Suzie, and left without saying a word.

The news traveled almost as rapidly across the footbridge to Suds Row, which meant Maeve and Maddie, then Mrs. Hanrahan came by to hug Tommy and kiss Suzie, who was starting to resemble a woman on her last legs.

In the kindest way he knew how—it took all his Southern diplomacy—Joe finally closed the door on well-wishers. With a doctor's eye, he looked at the two patients in his care and sat them both down on the settee.

"We've had enough visitors," he said. "Tomorrow, my prescription is that the only person who leaves this house is me." Suzie nodded, her eyes never straying far from her son.

He looked at Suzie's son, the boy he already considered his, and saw exhaustion writ large.

"You will sleep here tonight," he said. "Tomorrow I will procure a cot from the quartermaster's clerk and you'll have a bedroom upstairs."

"I haven't had a bedroom in a long time," Tommy said. He leaned against Suzie's shoulder, not too tired for the impish humor Joe had come to know on the ride from Fort Russell. "Mama, I've been living rough and traveling with Saint Paul."

Suzie laughed. "*This* missionary journey is over! I believe I can prevail upon my husband to round me up some sorry cases from the guardhouse to move our bedroom upstairs, too, where it belongs. It's time we turned the dining room into a dining room, now that we're..." She stopped as her eyes filled with tears. "Now that we're a family. Oh, Tommy, how I yearned for you."

"I know, Mama. Joe told me about the letters," her son said. He yawned. "I'm so tired." He looked at Joe seriously, man to man. "You can tell her."

Joe found a nightshirt of his own and cut off a foot of it using his surgical scissors, while Suzie pointed her son toward the privy. She handed him a candle and stood at the back door, not letting him out of her sight. When he came back in, he went to her and put his arms around her. She held him close as he started to sob. She picked him up and sat with him on the settee, crooning to him like a baby.

Joe watched the boy who had been through so much, and the woman who had suffered so long.

Through his tears, Tommy pleaded with her to understand what had happened. "Mama, I couldn't save him!" he sobbed.

God bless his wife. She dried her son's tears with her apron, and put her hands on each side of his head, capturing his attention in her gentle way. "Tommy, I have learned something you need to know. It's very important, so heed me. Sometimes the only person you can save is yourself. This was one of those times."

She hugged him, soothed him, sang him to sleep and tucked the covers around him as Joe marveled at the strength of women and the resiliency of children.

When Tommy was asleep, Joe took his wife by the hand and led her to bed. He stretched out and pulled her close, as he always did. It took him an hour, but he told her everything Tommy had told him. "Do you think we will ever see Aaron Belknap again?" she asked, her voice drowsy.

"Nothing would surprise me." Joe kissed the top of her head.

"We should look for him," she insisted, then seemed to reconsider. "If Pinkerton couldn't find him..."

"Nothing would make me happier than to see Nick—Aaron—again. I'd happily employ him in any hospital where the army sends me." He chuckled. "I have this discretionary fund."

His sweet wife thumped him where it hurt. "You do not!" She softened the blow by kissing his shoulder. "I think you're telling me that we'll only see Aaron again if it suits him."

"I think I am, dear heart. I do know we'll never be out of his debt."

Their talk turned to mundane matters then as she assured him she could find someone else to take her batch of rolls to the picnic tomorrow. He said he was on duty at the hospital, but would come home as soon as he could.

"Go to sleep, Suzie," he whispered in her ear finally. "You're starting to mumble."

"No, I'm not! There *is* something you should know. There's a letter for you from France."

"My God. What does it say?"

"You know I don't read your mail! Something else—there's a funny feeling around here. Major Townsend thinks there's been another battle."

"Wouldn't surprise me. I wonder if Custer or Gibbon got hit. We know Crook is fly-fishing in the Big Horns. Custer's tough, though. He'll pull through."

"One more thing. I've been feeling off this past week. We need to discuss the matter."

He smiled in the dark; he'd had his suspicions. "It'll keep, wife. Go to sleep."

She did, breathing so softly against his chest that he felt himself relax all over and close his eyes, too.

When he woke, he knew Suzie wouldn't be lying beside him. He walked into the parlor to see her curled up in his armchair, just watching Tommy sleep. He gestured and she stood up, then sat on his lap when he settled in the chair, their arms around each other. They both watched their son until the inexpert bugler played his version of reveille, which woke the boy.

Tommy rubbed his eyes, sat up, then joined them in the chair, which was big enough for them all. Joe thought about the letter from Paris. If it was *non,* it was just as well. He knew he was too busy to leave Fort Laramie, especially if more trouble was coming. If it was *oui,* he knew he didn't want Suzie traveling this year. Pasteur could wait. Besides, Joe had already promised Tommy a horse, and he needed the West to ride it in.

* * * * *

COMING NEXT MONTH from Harlequin® Historical
AVAILABLE MAY 21, 2013

THE HONOR-BOUND GAMBLER
Lisa Plumley

Plain preacher's daughter Violet Benson is always the wallflower—until charismatic gambler Cade Foster takes her under his wing. Suddenly the men of Morrow Creek start looking at her with new eyes—and the women with envy—but Violet is only interested in one man: Cade.
(Western)

REFORMING THE VISCOUNT
Annie Burrows

Viscount Rothersthorpe can't tear his eyes from Lydia Morgan any more than he can calm the raging fury coursing through his veins. Is there no end to the irony? Come to town to find a wife, only to be taunted by the past? Furtive glances across the ballroom are not helping to ease Lydia's state of shock—the man who once uttered a marriage proposal as one might remark upon the weather has returned!
(Regency)

A REPUTATION FOR NOTORIETY
The Masquerade Club
Diane Gaston

As the unacknowledged son of the lecherous Lord Westleigh, John "Rhys" Rhysdale was forced to earn a crust gambling on the streets. Now he owns the most thrilling new gaming establishment in London. Witnessing polite society's debauchery and excess every night, Rhys prefers to live on its fringes, but a mysterious masked lady tempts him into the throng....
(Regency)

THE SWORD DANCER
Jeannie Lin

Sword dancer Li Feng is used to living life on the edge of the law—a woman alone in the dangerous world of the Tang Dynasty has only her whirlwind reflexes to trust. She *will* discover the truth about her past, even if that means outwitting the most feared thief-catcher of them all....
(Chinese Tang Dynasty)

HHCNM0513

REQUEST YOUR
FREE BOOKS!

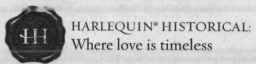

HARLEQUIN® HISTORICAL:
Where love is timeless

2 FREE NOVELS PLUS 2 **FREE GIFTS!**

YES! Please send me 2 FREE Harlequin® Historical novels and my 2 FREE gifts (gifts are worth about $10). After receiving them, if I don't wish to receive any more books, I can return the shipping statement marked "cancel." If I don't cancel, I will receive 6 brand-new novels every month and be billed just $5.44 per book in the U.S. or $5.74 per book in Canada. That's a savings of at least 16% off the cover price! It's quite a bargain! Shipping and handling is just 50¢ per book in the U.S. and 75¢ per book in Canada.* I understand that accepting the 2 free books and gifts places me under no obligation to buy anything. I can always return a shipment and cancel at any time. Even if I never buy another book, the two free books and gifts are mine to keep forever.

246/349 HDN F4ZY

Name   (PLEASE PRINT)

Address   Apt. #

City   State/Prov.   Zip/Postal Code

Signature (if under 18, a parent or guardian must sign)

Mail to the **Harlequin® Reader Service:**
IN U.S.A.: P.O. Box 1867, Buffalo, NY 14240-1867
IN CANADA: P.O. Box 609, Fort Erie, Ontario L2A 5X3
Want to try two free books from another line?
Call 1-800-873-8635 or visit www.ReaderService.com.

* Terms and prices subject to change without notice. Prices do not include applicable taxes. Sales tax applicable in N.Y. Canadian residents will be charged applicable taxes. Offer not valid in Quebec. This offer is limited to one order per household. Not valid for current subscribers to Harlequin Historical books. All orders subject to credit approval. Credit or debit balances in a customer's account(s) may be offset by any other outstanding balance owed by or to the customer. Please allow 4 to 6 weeks for delivery. Offer available while quantities last.

Your Privacy—The Harlequin® Reader Service is committed to protecting your privacy. Our Privacy Policy is available online at www.ReaderService.com or upon request from the Harlequin Reader Service.

We make a portion of our mailing list available to reputable third parties that offer products we believe may interest you. If you prefer that we not exchange your name with third parties, or if you wish to clarify or modify your communication preferences, please visit us at www.ReaderService.com/consumerschoice or write to us at Harlequin Reader Service Preference Service, P.O. Box 9062, Buffalo, NY 14269. Include your complete name and address.

HH13R

*Jeannie Lin takes you on a journey of
discovery, temptation and passion in her brilliant
new title THE SWORD DANCER.
The thrill of the chase! How far would you go for love?*

"A private bath, thief-catcher?" she remarked lightly.

His eyes snapped open and he started, sending a cascade of water splashing onto the floorboards.

"Wen Li Feng," he choked out. His hand gripped the edge of the tub and his muscles tensed all up his arm and throughout his body.

There was something both vulnerable yet undeniably virile about the sight of Han naked. Her tongue cleaved to the roof of her mouth. She attributed the warmth creeping up the back of her neck to the steam that surrounded her, dampening her skin. Needless to say, she was no longer thinking about battle scars.

She worked to keep her gaze on his face. "Your work must be quite profitable."

His breathing had quickened and he fought to regain his composure. "You should be careful of your reputation, Miss Wen. Everyone will assume you are here to provide me with an intimate service."

Men's bodies weren't unknown to her. Li Feng had lived in close quarters with other performers. Before that, she'd been isolated on a mountain sparsely inhabited by monks. She may have lost her first kiss along with her virginity recently, but even before that she'd simply never learned to be shy. Despite having had a lover in the past, it was still a shock to see thief-catcher Han's naked form.

The two of them had wrestled, fought and had so much physical contact that now the sight of him unclothed completed the picture. Her knowledge of his body was nearly as intimate as a lover's.

She moved to stand over him. All that shielded him from her

view was a layer of bathwater and the haze of steam. Neither the water nor the steam was clouded enough.

An unwelcome heat flooded her cheeks. She hoped it wasn't accompanied by a blush that Han could see. Li Feng had chosen this particular location to confront him so she could finally have the thief-catcher at a disadvantage, and she hated the thought of losing her edge.

"You should know that I can track you as easily as you can track me."

Han made no effort to curl up his knees to hide that part of himself. "You are relying on my sense of modesty to prevent me from capturing you right now," he said as he started to rise.

With a flick of her hand, she unsheathed the short sword hidden beneath her sleeve and pressed the tip to his chest. "I'm relying on this blade."

His gaze remained on her, unflinching, but he did sink back into the tub. "Have you ever killed anyone, Miss Wen?"

She cocked her head. "You can be my first," she said with a smile.

His eyes darkened at that and the air thickened between them. She suddenly wished she had brought a longer blade. The length of the sleeve sword kept her too close to him. The point of it remained over his heart, pressing firmly against flesh without breaking skin. He seemed unafraid. She, by contrast, was suddenly very afraid. Not of him, but rather the skip of her pulse.

Relentless thief-catcher Han sees life—and love—as black-and-white. But when he finally captures the spirited Li Feng, she makes him question everything he thought he knew about right and wrong. Will Han betray the elusive sword dancer he is learning to love, or trust his long-disregarded heart and follow her to dangerous, tempting rebellion?

Look for Jeannie Lin's THE SWORD DANCER. Available in Harlequin® Historical June 2013.

HARLEQUIN® HISTORICAL:
Where love is timeless

TEMPTING THE PREACHER'S DAUGHTER

Plain preacher's daughter Violet Benson is always the wallflower—until charismatic gambler Cade Foster takes her under his wing. Suddenly the men of Morrow Creek start looking at her with new eyes—and the women with envy—but Violet is only interested in one man: Cade.

Agreeing to be his "lucky charm," Violet becomes embroiled in the gambler's thrilling world. With her newfound confidence, she is determined to uncover the secret sorrow behind the eyes that smolder beneath his Stetson, and prove to this fascinating man that he can take the biggest gamble of all…with his heart.

Look for

The Honor-Bound Gambler

by Lisa Plumley in June 2013.

Available wherever books are sold.

HARLEQUIN® HISTORICAL:
Where love is timeless

RAISING THE STAKES...

As the unacknowledged son of the lecherous Lord Westleigh, John "Rhys" Rhysdale was forced to earn a crust gambling on the streets. Now he owns the most thrilling new gaming establishment in London.

Witnessing polite society's debauchery and excess every night, Rhys prefers to live on its fringes, but a mysterious masked lady tempts him into the throng.

Lady Celia Gale, known only as Madame Fortune, matches Rhys card for card and kiss for stolen kiss. But the stakes are raised when Rhys discovers she's from the very world he despises...

Book One in The Masquerade Club
Identities concealed, desires revealed...

Look for

A Reputation For Notoriety

by Diane Gaston in June 2013.

Available wherever books are sold.

HARLEQUIN® HISTORICAL:
Where love is timeless

COMING IN JUNE 2013

Reforming The Viscount

BY FAN-FAVORITE AUTHOR

ANNIE BURROWS

TO REFUSE HIM ONCE WAS A MISTAKE—TO REFUSE HIM TWICE WOULD BE MADNESS!

Viscount Rothersthorpe can't tear his eyes from Lydia Morgan any more than he can calm the raging fury coursing through his veins. Is there no end to the irony? Come to town to find a wife, only to be taunted by the past?

Furtive glances across the ballroom are not helping to ease Lydia's state of shock—the man who once uttered a marriage proposal as one might remark upon the weather has returned. But when he stuns her with a second outrageous—but now wickedly delicious—proposal, it is clear that, despite the rumours, the rake from her past has not reformed!

Available wherever books are sold.